Murder in Fifth Position

Murder in Fifth Position

An On Pointe Mystery

Lori Robbins

To Glenn

Praise for Murder in Fifth Position

"Lori Robbins's newest entry in her delightful On Pointe mystery series finds ballerina Leah Siderova grappling with threats to her career, her heart, and her life. Leah is delicate as fine-gauge wire but tough as iron rebar; when a wealthy arts patron is murdered, Leah uses her insider knowledge of the closed world of ballet to draw back the curtain on the crime. The classical dance scene, with its obscure rules, vicious jealousies, and eccentric personalities, makes a swoon-worthy setting for this dazzling mystery."—Delia Pitts, author of the Shamus award-winning *Trouble In Queenstown*, book one in the Vandy Myrick mystery series.

"A resounding standing ovation for Lori Robbins and her brilliant ballerina sleuth Leah Siderova! *Murder in Fifth Position* takes readers deep inside two close-knit and cutthroat little worlds—ballet and the super-rich—for a tightly-plotted, twisty, and dangerous adventure. With a sharply-drawn crew of amateur and professional sleuths to love and root for, and a wonderfully wicked lineup of potential villains, it's a marvelous, and murderous, ride. The first books in the series aren't a prerequisite to enjoy this one...but readers will want to go back and grab them. Lori Robbins puts on a devious and delicious show—more On Pointe mysteries, please!"—Kathleen Marple Kalb, author of the Old Stuff and Ella Shane Mysteries

"In *Murder in Fifth Position*, celebrity ballerina Leah Siderova, newly nominated for a prestigious choreography prize, finds herself center stage in a real-life drama when the wealthy benefactor behind the award is murdered. At the widow's request, Leah is drawn into a high-stakes investigation that exposes the rivalries, jealousies, and ruthless ambition of the ballet world. With high suspense and elegant plotting, author Lori Robbins keeps readers guessing until the final curtain. Fans of the series will enjoy Leah's continued evolution, while newcomers will be hooked by the novel's crisp prose, sly humor, and unrelenting tension. It's a must-read. I highly recommend it!"—Lori Duffy Foster, author of the Agatha-nominated Lisa Jamison mysteries

"In award-winning author Lori Robbins' *Murder in Fifth Position*, the latest installment of her On Pointe Mysteries, Leah Siderova is once again tracking down a murderer, maybe more than one, while she navigates the ongoing crises, jealousies, and rivalries that inhabit the backstage world of ballet. Rumors swirl, accusations multiply, and Leah is swept into the investigation in this engaging, at times laugh-out-loud page-turner full of suspense and nail-biting tension. Ms. Robbins does a wonderful job of creating the dance world and its behind-the-scenes practices and pettiness, both competitive and supportive, and meshing it with the specifics of detection. Events crash, one into another, until Leah must follow her instincts and confront the killer, jeopardizing her life and her career. *Murder in Fifth Position* is witty, fast-paced, and unputdownable, and will keep you guessing and weighing the guilt or innocence of multiple suspects until the end. Five stars!"—Suzanne Trauth, award-winning author of *What Remains of Love* and the Dodie O'Dell mysteries.

Praise for the On Pointe Mystery Series

"Robbins, a former ballerina, steeps the novel in the glamorous grunge of the dance world…The result is a suspenseful romp with loads of atmosphere. A highly entertaining whodunit with a twisty plot and plenty of biting ballet intrigue."—*Kirkus Review* [starred review]

"Robbins does an outstanding job of juxtaposing the ballet world with the investigative process that challenges Leah's set roles, forcing her to new heights of realization about the world of dance, her colleagues, and her own ambitions. This makes for compelling reading... the tension is finely drawn and the movements between dance and death assume their own form of masterful entwining that keeps readers involved in a realistic character's moves. Exquisitely complex, nicely steeped in both drama and the competitive atmosphere of the dance world."—D. Donovan, Sr. Reviewer, *Midwest Book Review*

Chapter One

Sometimes, it's a good idea to ask yourself why you're here.
—Rosemary Sabovitch Blech

I was on the roof of the Vanderhof Building when the first victim died. Two hundred dressed-to-kill guests besides me attended Leland's birthday party, but only one of them knew for sure our host's death was neither an accident nor a suicide.

If I'd known earlier about threats against the powerful head of the Vanderhof Foundation, was there anything I could have done to save him? The warning signs were well hidden, but that didn't stop me from obsessively, bitterly, guiltily revisiting all that I'd missed. As a practical matter, though, as the clock ticked closer to midnight, only Superman could have rescued Leland Vanderhof from his sixteen-story plunge.

Although I'm a small ballerina and not a muscle-bound superhero, I do share some similarities with the Man of Steel. We both wear tights, perform for a fickle crowd, and worry about the state of the world. Unfortunately, the traits we had in common ended with that slender list, unless you include the part about complicated family relationships. My earthbound parents hail from the Upper West Side of Manhattan, which is about as far from Krypton as you can get. On the other hand, there were times when the Siderova family's quirkiness crossed the line into alien territory.

There was, of course, one additional characteristic Superman and I shared, not only with each other, but also with the victim. Despite good intentions, all three of us had made powerful enemies. Leland survived his for nearly eighty years. I hoped to do the same, minus that abrupt ending.

* * *

The elevated setting of what later became a crime scene matched the star-studded guest list. Three people had attained such glittery heights of fame, they were known only by their first names. Most of the rest were less recognizable, but they were rich or accomplished enough to score an invitation. A sizable donation to the Vanderhof Foundation was the more explicit price of admission.

I wasn't a member of this elite group and attended Leland's birthday celebration as a paid entertainer and not a paying guest. Arabella Vanderhof, Leland's wife, had hired a group of American Ballet Company dancers to perform for the crowd. My role onstage kept me at an emotional and physical distance from the audience below.

No premonition of coming violence disturbed me, possibly because stage fright, my longtime frenemy, had the upper hand as I went through all the pre-performance rituals designed to propitiate the dance gods. In the last seconds before my entrance, I exchanged a whispered *merde* with Olivia Blackwell, my closest friend in the company. For obvious reasons, dancers don't tell each other to break a leg, not even to our fiercest rivals.

The ballet was a brutal test of endurance for me and Joaquin Texeira, better known as Tex. He was on fire that night, and he inspired me to technical feats beyond what I thought I could still do. As the music rose to its triumphant conclusion, Tex lifted me high above his head with one hand. It was a dramatic finale, made more so by the sudden flash of sparklers that hissed streams of light along the perimeter of a makeshift stage. Tex carried me off to gasps, cheers, and applause.

When we returned for our bows, Leland ascended the steps of the stage to join us. In that last hour of his life, he looked pale and frail, and I remember thinking that the glare from the fizzy sparklers might have been disorienting for him.

He skipped his prepared speech and presented me with an extravagant bouquet of red roses. "Lee, you've done our name proud."

My name is Leah, not Lee, but it pleased Leland to pretend we shared a nickname. I smiled and plucked one pre-loosened blossom to present to him, and a second that I gave to Tex. It was a cheesy bit of stagecraft that audiences have come to expect, but on that night, the gesture had real meaning. There were many times when I'd danced with a partner who deserved, not a flower and a curtsey, but a kick in the shins. The same went for heads of charitable foundations, but my gratitude to both men was unfeigned.

Leland kissed my hand with a courtly, old-world gesture, keeping a prudent distance from my sweat-soaked body. He reminded me of the promise I'd made earlier, "If you're not too tired, you must save me a dance." With a playful wink that didn't match his labored breathing, he said, "Better make it a slow one."

Tex helped him down the stairs, where his wife and the director of American Ballet Company were waiting. I was still in costume and still in performance mode, and those were the only faces that stood out from the rest. Antoine Moreau, the documentary filmmaker who'd recorded our performance, followed them down the aisle.

Some of my visual confusion was a consequence of the sputtering sparklers, the narrow view, and the unfamiliar surroundings. I assumed all of the dancers were with Tex and me when we entered the Vanderhof apartment to change out of our costumes, but as I later told the police, I couldn't swear to it.

Unlike at public performance venues, where the use of cell phones was prohibited, the Vanderhofs encouraged the audience to take photos. I averted my eyes from the pops of light, wishing they hadn't insisted on this added opportunity to publicize their Foundation.

It was the last time I saw Leland. The mangled shell of his slight body, spread across a concrete patio in the back of his Park Avenue apartment building, didn't count.

Chapter Two

...music begins to atrophy when it departs too far from the dance.
—Ezra Pound

Arabella Vanderhof's assistant escorted the dancers from the stage and down a path lined with waist-high stone planters. We waited as he unlocked the door to the penthouse and followed him past a living room that could have accommodated an Olympic-sized pool. I was surprised and pleased to see my mother's novels on a sharp-edged glass bookshelf, next to a complete set of Agatha Christie.

I snapped a picture and sent it to Barbara. She texted back a double exclamation point and a single command: **Introduce me.** I responded with a thumbs up, but didn't commit to any action. My job that night was to promote the Vanderhof Foundation and not my mother's books.

The costume mistress stalked out of the dressing area and hurried me along. Never pleasant, she was in a particularly foul mood that night, perhaps because, unlike the dancers, she hadn't been invited to the party. No one talked much until she left.

When the door closed behind her, the atmosphere lightened. I sat next to Olivia, pushed my swollen feet into a pair of unforgiving high-heeled shoes, and said, "The hard part is yet to come. I'd rather dance on a broken toe than hang out at another fundraising extravaganza, where I'm part of a PR pitch to separate rich people from large sums of cash. I'm not even very good at it."

Olivia drew a brush through long dark hair, which was so much like mine people sometimes mistook us for sisters. "That's the price of being a star. Nobodies like me are free to eat, drink, and take the leftover food home."

When we finished primping, which took the fastidious Olivia longer than it did me, Arabella's assistant escorted us back outdoors. Whether he was there to guide us or to make sure we didn't swipe the silver was unclear.

We were greeted by the sounds of a big band serenading a big crowd. Remembering Leland's request, I circled the dance floor searching for him. He wasn't there, but his absence didn't worry me. I figured he was tapping prospective donors for his latest project, the Poppy Vanderhof Prize for Choreography.

Two weeks earlier, when the judges revealed the names of three finalists for the prize, no one was surprised to learn that up-and-coming Sierra Younger and indie-fave Hollis Mark made the cut. Everyone in the dance world, including me, was shocked that my name appeared alongside the other two. With that very public announcement, my dream of someday choreographing a ballet got a whole lot more real, a whole lot more quickly, than I ever imagined it could.

The eleven-page contract I signed with the Vanderhof Foundation required me to donate a personal item for the evening's silent auction. My contribution was an autographed pair of pointe shoes, which I hoped would inspire a storm of competitive bidding. And yes, it was all for a good cause, and selfish concerns were inappropriate, but my rivals for the Poppy Vanderhof Prize had teamed up against me with a spate of backhanded social media posts, and I longed to notch a minor victory over them. A more high-minded woman would have been above such petty jealousies, but my fractious relationship with the other two made me feel as if I had to prove my worth.

Olivia blocked me from view while I moved my pointe shoes to a more advantageous position. Though I wouldn't have told most people, I didn't mind admitting my fears to her. "This is my least favorite part of the night. I'm always nervous no one will bid on my donation, and I'll feel like the last kid picked for the soccer team."

The comparison wasn't metaphoric. I was the last person picked for every sports team, until my parents gave up trying to make me a well-rounded child. In the spirit of those cutthroat early years, I checked out my rivals' offerings. Compared to Sierra's orange sneakers that she'd printed clever sayings on, or Hollis's embroidered boxers, my contribution lacked originality.

Olivia examined the pointe shoes, which someone, probably Ms. Vanderhof's assistant, had placed in a box lined with black velvet. With an irony that wasn't evident until later, she said, "The shoes look like they're in a coffin."

I eased the straps on my stilettos. "An apt symbol for my half-dead feet."

Most items on the auction table were traditional prizes, like opening night tickets to the Metropolitan Opera and a handbag from haute couture designer Terrence Benson. I inspected each with great interest, but my friend had more practical matters in mind.

"We're not bidding, so what's the point? I'm beyond hungry and am now hangry." She pulled me away from a pair of diamond and sapphire earrings I was sure I'd seen before.

A black-clad server who looked like an aspiring model or actor approached. He revealed perfect teeth in a friendly smile and said, "That was a fabulous performance, Ms. Siderova." With an apologetic look, he turned to Olivia. "And you too, Ms., er, and you too. You both must be starving."

If Olivia was upset at playing so forgettable a role, it didn't dent her appetite. She chose several tempting morsels, which were wrapped in layers of puff pastry that were the dietary equivalent of a one-night stand. Briefly delicious, but not worth the morning-after regrets.

I peeked at the server's nametag and said, "Thanks, Morgan, but I'm going to hold off for now."

My bone-thin friend reached past me and said, "I'm her understudy, so I'll take hers."

Too dehydrated for wine, Olivia and I were chugging water when Sierra, whose orange and red hair matched her artistically inked sneakers, stepped out from the shadows. "Apparently, your pointe shoes are a hot ticket. I wish I had friends in high places to bid up my stuff."

It's never pleasant to have someone you don't like express the type of competitive feelings you wished you didn't have. Into an awkward pause that should have been filled with a witty or pointed answer from me, Olivia leaped to my defense. "Leah's a star. She's got a million fans."

Hollis Mark joined us to even the odds. He and Sierra were modern dance choreographers with their own companies. They thought my fame, and not my talent, persuaded the judges to include me in the final round of the competition. It's possible they were correct.

For most of my career, only diehard balletomanes knew who I was. That comfortable state of affairs changed after I starred in the Broadway musical *Mad Music*. The show shattered box office records, partly because it was a great piece of theater and partly because of explosive backstage episodes that enlivened an otherwise slow news cycle. My role in unraveling those events made me famous in a way I'd never experienced before.

Hollis waved at the elegantly dressed throng before training his round blue eyes on me. "This crowd knows nothing of art. You gave them circus tricks. We made them think."

Those circus tricks had taken me a lifetime of practice to master. I'd heard it all before but wasn't interested in escalating tensions between us.

Sierra was. She linked her arm in his. "We all know why Leland chose Leah for the prize, and it wasn't her creative talent that persuaded him."

Unpleasant gossip about Leland's affection for me had made the rounds in our claustrophobic and jealous world after news of the Vanderhof Prize finalists hit social media. The hashtag *#dancingfordollars* got a lot of mileage, as did *#vanderslut*. Any attempt to defend myself would have added fuel to that catty fire, as I knew from the last time I'd gotten slammed. I suspected Hollis and Sierra started the rumors, but having been snubbed in multiple languages by legendary ballerinas, their barbs didn't move me.

The jealousy between us, however, cut both ways. Sierra and Hollis went to college and became cutting-edge choreographers. People took them seriously, as thinkers and creators. No one wanted my opinion on anything weightier than the type of pointe shoes I favored.

I joined American Ballet Company straight out of high school, to my highly educated parents' eternal grief. And that wasn't the worst of it. Although my father insisted his heart attack had nothing to do with my decision to forego higher education, I still felt guilty about disappointing him.

The wail of many sirens put an end to these troubling memories and to my conversation with Sierra and Hollis, who left to join a growing crowd on the Park Avenue side of the terrace. With no sense of urgency, Olivia and I grabbed glasses of champagne and celebrated the bonus paycheck we'd earned for the night's performance.

Chapter Three

No art is possible without a dance with death.
—Kurt Vonnegut

There was a pleased buzz of excitement when circling lights flashed on the street below. Dozens of elegantly dressed guests looked over the railing and speculated about why the police had blocked off the street. The partygoers acted as if the NYPD had staged a second performance for their amusement.

Olivia and I didn't yet know what brought so heavy a police presence to the entrance of the Vanderhof Building and were more interested in eating than gawking. She took three mini lobster rolls from a waiter's abandoned tray and said, "This food is incredible. I wish I'd brought a bigger bag."

I picked shrimp out of a puff pastry shell and doused a few carrot sticks in caviar dip. "It's very difficult being friends with someone who can eat whatever she wants, so don't push it."

She laughed and stuffed a napkin filled with cookies into her purse. I checked my phone for the tenth time, hoping my extremely significant other would finish work in time to meet me at the party, but the screen remained blank. As the mood around us changed from excited to sober, it became clear that something unusual was underway. Balancing full plates, we joined the growing crowd of onlookers.

When I saw the entire street was lined with cop cars flanking an ambulance, and that no rock legend or Hollywood star was making their way toward the building, I was as anxious as my companions to learn what catastrophic event had occurred. Fear of heights, however, proved stronger than curiosity. My dance partner's over-the-head lift was the limit of my comfort zone, and I stepped back from the edge. Shunning the bird's-eye view in favor of a closer look, I left the gawking mob and headed for the elevator. Any excuse to leave a party with high-calorie food and ballerina-stomping rivals was fine with me.

When I arrived at the gilt and marble lobby, a six-foot-tall police officer stopped me. Francie Morelli sighed without pleasure. "Leah Siderova. Why am I not surprised to see you?"

I placed a hand on my heart as if wounded by her words. "How soon they forget. Don't hold out on me. What's going on?"

The police officer's pinched mouth and hunched shoulders belied the casual greeting. She pulled me aside as crime scene techs crashed through the doors and said, "We got a jumper. It's—" With a sharp intake of breath, she stopped short before continuing in a gentler tone. "I-I'm sorry, Leah. I just realized you must know him. It's Leland Vanderhof."

My knees buckled. "*No.* Not Leland. There must be some mistake. He's—I saw him an hour ago. He was—he looked fine."

She took my elbow and dragged me to a sofa that looked as if no one had ever sat on it. "I wish you didn't have to hear about it like this, but there's no mistake. When you've been on the job as long as I have, nothing surprises you. Who knows what drove the guy to off himself?"

I fought the tremors that coursed through me. "That's not what happened. Leland didn't commit suicide. Not one hour ago, he asked me to dance with him. There's no way he'd kill himself. Not at his own birthday party. Not under any circumstances."

I reached for my phone to call my date. He'd know what to do.

I listened to his voicemail without leaving a message, because when the doors reopened, two familiar figures entered. Detective Henry Farrow wore a shabby suit and a scowl, the same as the last time I saw him. Detective Jonah Sobol wore a tuxedo and a far more inscrutable expression. The last time I saw him, his clothes were on the floor of my bedroom, and his lips were on my mouth.

Jonah took in my party dress and sparkly shoes and said, "Sorry to be late."

***

Three uniformed cops stopped me from following the detectives to the rear of the building. Over my protests, Francie escorted me back to the rooftop. News of Leland's shocking death traveled faster than the elevator, and the doors opened to a very different scene from the one I'd left. The band was silent and the dance floor deserted.

When I'm sad, or scared, or overwhelmed, I leave my real self behind and take on the persona of a favorite ballet heroine. Swan queens and firebirds were the most reliable alter egos, but this time felt different. I rejected those mythical creatures and instead became The Girl in *The Afternoon of a Faun*. She's completely detached and views herself and her surroundings through the filter of a mirror. I needed that distance.

With more coolness than I could have managed without inspiration from The Girl, I turned to Francie and said, "You have to believe me when I say this wasn't a suicide. Were there any witnesses?"

The police officer took off her hat and wiped her forehead with her sleeve. "You know I can't tell you anything."

Her fierce expression didn't deter me. "Any minute, you or one of your fellow officers will be questioning me. We might as well get it over with now."

Underneath Francie's hardened exterior, she was a cupcake, but a cupcake with strict standards of professional conduct. "Exactly right, Ms. Siderova. I will be questioning you. Not the other way around. You'll have to go elsewhere to satisfy your curiosity."

She was being diplomatic. Francie knew about my relationship with homicide detective Jonah Sobol, but she would treat me the same as everyone else.

Hours would pass before Jonah and I were alone, and I sought a way around her scruples. "I've worked with the department in the past, and you know you can trust me to be discreet. This is the only opportunity I'll have to talk to people who are way out of my league. The guests think I'm one of them."

"You are one of them." A hint of a smile softened her words.

I followed Francie's gaze as she surveyed the terrace. Although the side that overlooked Park Avenue was mobbed with guests jockeying for a clear view of the police cars and ambulance, I was more interested in the rear of the building.

"You blocked off the street, but the detectives went through the lobby to the back. Who found him? Who found Leland?"

She moved her head from side to side before speaking, as if weighing whether or not to answer me. "Mr. Vanderhof appears to have fallen from the balcony outside his bedroom. He landed on a concrete patio next to the superintendent's apartment. The super, a guy by the name of Roy Willers, was the only witness. He's lucky the ambulance got here when it did. There wasn't anything the EMTs could do for the victim, but Mr. Willers has a weak heart, and they took him to the ER. We're canvassing this building and the tenants in the building across the way to see if there are any witnesses."

Francie left me and joined her fellow officers, who were taking notes and entering contact information from the many guests. When Jonah arrived, he escorted Arabella Vanderhof inside the penthouse apartment she shared—used to share—with her husband. Her red lipstick stood out against her chalky skin, and she stumbled as she crossed the threshold. Terrence Benson, the haute couture designer whom she referred to as her special friend, didn't follow her, probably because Jonah's partner, Detective Farrow, had him cornered.

Dim lights made it difficult to read the room, but the faces of those closest to me had a look of satisfaction cloaked in sadness that the misfortune of others so often inspires. I could almost hear them thinking, *A guy like Leland, one of the richest and most powerful in the world...I guess you never know.*

Olivia and Tex broke away from a group of dancers and joined me at the deserted side of the terrace. She held up her phone and said, "The vultures are out. People are already posting about Leland's death. They think he committed suicide."

"You can always trust social media to get everything wrong." I watched as she scrolled through her feed and said, "None of this makes sense. Why would Leland kill himself? I talked to him before our performance, and he didn't seem unhappy or depressed. And I talked to him after as well. He told me to save him a dance. Does that sound like a guy about to commit suicide?"

I didn't tell Olivia, because it was probably irrelevant, that Leland appeared tired and ill, which I attributed to the stress of hosting so large a gathering. For different reasons, I hadn't told anyone about my friendship with him, but that hadn't stopped poisonous gossip about us.

Olivia tapped her phone. "Someone's been busy. A million crazy rumors are already circulating. I wonder which of these distinguished guests moonlights as a troll."

"Take your pick. It was Arabella's idea to invite influencers to the party." I was too shaken by Leland's death to stomach more updates via social media, a sentiment Tex and Olivia didn't share. They met Leland for the first time that evening and weren't as personally invested in his life, death, or reputation.

Tex pointed to his screen. "You'll be happy to know the *vanderslut* and *dancing-for-dollars* hashtags are no longer trending, but that's because the celeb chasers who attacked you are now united against Arabella Vanderhof and Terrence Benson. They're calling her the Merry Widow and him the Designer of Death. I don't know what prompted the switch, unless trolls, like cops, always treat the spouse as the most likely suspect."

Olivia poked him. "You must be the last person on the planet not to know about Arabella's affair with Terrence Benson."

A chill crept up my back, despite the warm weather. "We don't know if that's true."

She eyed me. "And if it is?"

Conscious of others close by, I spoke in a whisper. "Then Arabella and Terrence have an excellent motive for murder."

Chapter Four

A lot of people used to think I was crazy, but I can truthfully say one thing:
I gave 'em a show.
—Busby Berkeley

I was in no rush to interrogate my fellow dancers, as they'd undoubtedly talk of little else in the coming weeks. My access to the other party guests, however, would expire at the end of the evening. Would they, like me, reject suicide as a cause of death? Or would they confirm Officer Morelli's belief that Leland had killed himself?

I began by attaching myself to a group surrounding Jonathan Llewellyn Franklin III. He was a judge for the Poppy Vanderhof Choreography Prize and a close associate of Leland's. When Jonathan loudly proclaimed the death a tragic accident, others were quick to agree, possibly because his nasal whine didn't improve at close range and people wanted him to stop talking.

A thirty-something guy with creative facial hair muttered, in response to an inaudible comment from the woman next to him, "What did you expect him to say? Jonathan has a vested interest in protecting the Vanderhof name and brand."

I stayed silent, because Terrence Benson shot down Jonathan's allegation for me. The designer's languid pose made his knife-sharp response feel more cutting. "Perhaps you can explain, Jonathan, from your vast store of so-called insider knowledge, how an elderly man in frail health accidentally climbed over the balcony. He could barely get down the steps from the stage."

Jonathan's voice rose. "Leland was suffering from Alzheimer's. I think that with the excitement of the party he became confused. He must have tripped and fallen over the railing."

Terrence squinted as if trying to visualize what happened. "Yes, I can see it now. He accidentally climbed over four potted plants, leaped onto a five-foot-high barricade, and fell."

Aside from the enmity between the two men, what struck me most about their argument was Terrence's precise description of the bedroom balcony.

Jonathan's cool expression got a few degrees hotter. "It could have been suicide, but I hope that's not what killed him." With a more cheerful look, he said, "At least it was quick. He didn't suffer."

In response to Terrence's snort, Jonathan swiveled to face him directly. "I believe I'm a better authority than you. You're a lot, shall we say, *closer* to Arabella than you were to Leland."

Giggles turned to gasps when Terrence shoved Jonathan into the auction table, upending the carefully curated items. "It's a pity duels are no longer in fashion. The same goes, by the way, for the ridiculous outfit you're wearing."

Jonathan was skilled at intimidating fragile ballerinas but less confident when opposing powerful men with impeccable fashion sense. He tossed the remainder of his drink in Terrence's direction without any of it reaching the designer's elegant dinner jacket. "The truth hurts, doesn't it?"

"Not as much as getting pushed off a building." It was Terrence's exit line.

I shared Terrence's belief that Leland Vanderhof had been murdered. Nothing else made sense. And if I was right and Jonathan was wrong, there was an excellent chance the killer was still at the party.

* * *

Jonah and Detective Farrow conducted their interviews from inside the Vanderhof apartment. The rest of the police officers remained on the terrace. Most people wore a mask of horror and grief. If anyone suspected there was a killer in our midst, it wasn't apparent to me.

I hoped Marty Sherrington, the interim director of American Ballet Company, would prove a better source of information than Jonathan. She spoke in measured tones to a group of ABC board members, some of whom also sat on the Vanderhof board. Damage control was baked into her job description, and the night's events would test her ability to take charge.

Marty hit the perfect balance between sympathy and practicality. "I saw a big change in Leland after the loss of his niece, who was like the daughter he never had. We all hoped that honoring her memory with the Poppy Vanderhof Choreography Prize would help him deal with his pain, but it might have made it worse. He was quite beside himself after tonight's performance. Going forward, I propose we honor him at the fall gala."

I was impressed with Marty's resourcefulness. Her suggestion to honor Leland was a savvy move, as the purpose of the gala was fundraising.

One of the younger board members said, in a near-whisper, "Do you think he committed suicide?"

She bit her lip. "That's not for me to say. But between the Alzheimer's diagnosis and the loss of his niece, I don't think we can rule it out."

Marty may have convinced the board members of American Ballet Company that Leland killed himself, but I wasn't buying it. Misery hadn't stopped him from living. Someone else did that for him.

* * *

The number of guests continued to dwindle. Francie stationed herself at the exit door and ushered small groups from the roof to the street. No one was allowed to leave without her.

This process was slower for some of us than for others. The musicians, household help, and catering staff had to wait until the police interviewed guests who'd paid for the privilege of attending the party. The dancers occupied a less defined role, as part of our job was mingling with the partygoers after the performance, but we were classified with the rest of the for-hire attendees.

As often happened during times of stress, the herd instinct took over, and most reverted to their tribal, middle school selves by separating into distinct groups. Those who'd spent thousands of dollars for an invitation to the most memorable party of the year took possession of the tables near the bar. They had to help themselves to drinks when the bartenders abandoned their posts to chat with the waitstaff near the open kitchen.

I joined six dancers, who were huddled behind a stone planter filled with fragrant purple hyacinths. To my colleagues, Leland was a distant, benevolent figure who gave money to the company that employed us. They felt the kind of sadness one feels when a public figure dies.

To me, he was something more. Leland overrode Jonathan's reluctance to name me as one of the finalists for the Vanderhof Prize, and I owed him a debt of gratitude. He'd taken to calling me to discuss the progress of my ballet, and we met several times for cocktails or coffee. Although my relationship with the dead man was of short duration, I lamented his loss.

My rejection of his lavish gifts didn't impair our growing friendship. Leland said giving people expensive stuff was how he expressed himself, but he was amused, not offended, when I wouldn't take them. It wasn't a tough call. Fancy jewelry, like the rocks that weighed down Arabella's fingers, wasn't my style. Spending time with a man who could offer informed advice about my choreography was.

I shut my eyes to stop the tears, because sorrow, however heartfelt, was less useful than action. I peeked over the flowers to resume my observation of the guests and was surprised to see one person who remained untethered to a larger group. I elbowed Olivia and said, "Hollis looks like a lost puppy without Sierra."

"I haven't seen her since she pitched a fit over the silent auction. Maybe she's with Terrence. If so, I hope they're enjoying each other's company." Olivia wrinkled her nose. "Terrence is even less fun than Sierra and Hollis. When he did the pre-performance costume check, he freaked out over the color of my lipstick. Which was kind of annoying, because what doesn't clash with vomit green?"

I smiled at her description. Terrence's clothes were popular with fashionistas but not ballerinas. "He's got a lot to learn about making costumes for dancers. I split two seams taking a bow and had to back off the stage to avoid giving the audience more of a show than they paid to see."

While talking to my friend I kept my eyes on the remaining party guests. Like me, they looked as if the shock of Leland's death had given way to exhaustion. The exception was Jonathan. He returned to the terrace after his interview with Francie buzzing with energy.

Olivia said, with mock solemnity, "If only he used his power for good instead of evil."

I stood my ground when he beckoned, but Olivia fled. "Sorry, Leah. I know it's stupid and that he's the one who should feel embarrassed, but I can't face him."

My friend's fear, though not her humiliation, was understandable. The last time she and the former ABC director were at a party, he cornered her in a deserted hallway. Jonathan later claimed Olivia led him on. In the days that followed, she'd been reluctant to confront so powerful a man. With more clout and less to lose, I did it for her.

Despite Jonathan's current position in the Vanderhof organization, I would welcome the opportunity to do so again. His eagerness to pass Leland's death off as an accident made him a prime suspect.

Chapter Five

To achieve great things two things are needed: a plan and not quite enough time.
—Leonard Bernstein

I braced myself as Jonathan slithered closer. He examined my body with insulting thoroughness, starting at the tips of my party shoes and lingering at the neckline of my strapless dress. He stopped short of looking me in the face. Adjusting the collar of his dress shirt, which had three too many buttons unbuttoned, he said, "Where'd your friend go? We have some unfinished business."

Trying to shame him into leaving me and Olivia alone, I said, "I can't imagine why she doesn't want to see you. Can you?"

He dropped his jaw in a caricature of weary patience. "If you're talking about that ridiculous episode at the ABC gala, then you should tell her she needs to grow up. I was paying her a compliment, and she blew it out of proportion. I turn away plenty of women a lot prettier than she is."

I felt like shoving him. Not off the roof, but into the stone planter behind him. "I'm sure your wife will be delighted to hear it. Is she here tonight?"

He ignored the reference to his spouse, perhaps because she had joined the growing list of his ex-wives. "Listen to me carefully, Leah. You're a public face for the Vanderhof Prize, and what you say and do will be closely watched. Don't discuss Leland's death with any of the guests or the press. I will consult with our lawyers and send an email with details and talking points. No matter how all this plays out, it will be a public relations disaster."

He was right, but his matter-of-factness irritated me. "I'm genuinely moved by your grief."

Jonathan's lips tightened. "That kind of sarcasm is exactly what I don't want to hear. If you don't understand how important this is, I'll explain in very short words that even a high school dropout can understand."

I couldn't avoid some internal gnashing of teeth, but consoled myself with the thought *Let him underestimate me.* Plenty of others had done so and regretted it.

Like many dancers, I didn't care about education, or job security, or anything except ballet for most of my life, because when you're seventeen and standing onstage at Lincoln Center, you think it will last forever. Your brain, your mother, and everyone in the business tell you differently, but you don't quite believe it until that awful day you do. In my case, the moment of reckoning came after my second knee surgery.

Heartache over the inevitable end to my career as a ballerina had lessened, however, as dreams of becoming a choreographer took over. Securing that future was more important to me than evening the score with Jonathan. Though I longed to take a swing at his receding chin, which hung, tantalizingly, a few inches above mine, the night would not improve if one of the many police officers at the party arrested me for assault. Also, I'm a coward and better at fantasizing about physical intimidation than executing it in real life.

Jonathan, sensing weakness, put his arm around me and squeezed. A bystander would think he was reassuring me, but the vise-like grip hurt. On the plus side, however, his estimation of my strength was as flawed as his judgments about my intelligence. Using a weapon he should have anticipated, I pressed the sharp end of a stiletto heel into his foot. I didn't slam it with enough force to break any bones, which my leg muscles easily could have done. Just hard enough to let him know there were limits to how far he could push me.

When he loosened his grasp, I freed his foot. Red-faced and limping slightly, he had the final word. "If the Foundation falls short of its fundraising goals, we may find that we can only support two choreographers. If that's the case, you won't be one of them."

He stalked off, but not before tripping over Antoine Moreau. With a courteous *Pardonne-moi,* the filmmaker helped Jonathan to his feet. I wished I could overhear the brief chat that followed, but had to depend on my pessimistic imagination to guess at what Jonathan told Antoine.

Olivia returned to my side, bearing two cups of coffee. She handed me one and said, "Antoine might actually be creepier than Jonathan. Every time I turn around, he's got his camera aimed at you."

I dug in my purse for a mirror and confirmed my fears. If Antoine had secretly filmed me and Jonathan, not only had I been caught stomping on a board member's foot, but I'd done so with zero lipstick and messy hair.

I consoled myself with one of Olivia's cookies. "Antoine is doing a documentary about the Vanderhof Competition, but I didn't know he was going to be here until I saw him backstage before the show. When the Foundation made the announcement, I had this picture of myself all glammed up for the big screen, but it doesn't look like that's going to happen."

Olivia spoke so softly the most determined stalker would have a hard time hearing her. "It might cheer you up to know I overheard some banging gossip from Marty Sherrington that may or may not be true."

I warmed my hands on the coffee. "Gossip doesn't have to be true to be interesting, though Marty's a good source. She must have some great connections to have been appointed the interim director of ABC. It sure wasn't her experience that got her the job."

Olivia bent her head closer to mine. "Before the show, Terrence and Leland had a huge fight over the costumes. Leland threatened to fire Terrence. Arabella got involved for obvious reasons. She may be married to Leland, but she adores Terrence."

The designer had revealed his knowledge of the crime scene to a dozen people. This admission, however, didn't prove he'd been on the balcony when Leland was murdered. If anything, it suggested he had nothing to hide.

"If Marty thinks Terrence is guilty, we can cross her off the list of credible witnesses and him off the list of possible suspects. If Terrence were guilty, he would have agreed with any theory that took a homicide charge off the table."

Olivia yawned. "What do you think happened? I didn't know Leland well enough to judge his state of mind. I heard he has Alzheimer's."

I also yawned. We'd been going nearly nonstop for fourteen hours, and no amount of excitement could erase my fatigue. "Physically, Leland was frail. He had a hard time walking up the steps to the stage, and he didn't look well. But mentally? People keep talking about how old he was, but there are a lot of different ways of being eighty. He was sharper and smarter than the gossips trying to take him down."

Olivia slipped the last three chocolate cookies on a silver tray into her bag. "If he was murdered, who do you think did it?"

"We won't know who until we figure out why, but that's not our job."

She rubbed her eyes. "I've never known you to turn your back on a mystery. You're always in the thick of things."

"If the Vanderhof Foundation goes forward with funding me, Sierra, and Hollis, I'll need every minute between now and our debut performance to get ready. After tonight, there won't be time for any extra-curricular activities."

She yawned again. "I'll believe it when I see it."

Chapter Six

Dancing is silent poetry.
—Simonides

Tex joined us, looking remarkably fresh for a guy who began the evening by giving a killer performance in a brutally taxing ballet. Olivia squirmed away when he tried to embrace her, with a self-conscious look at anyone who might be watching. Her circumspection wasn't for my benefit but for other American Ballet Company dancers. There was no better way to destroy a blossoming romance than to become the target of gossipy colleagues.

Tex winked at Olivia and said, "It's too late to pretend you're not crazy about me." More soberly, he added, "And it's too late for Arabella to pretend she's not involved with Terrence Benson. They might as well own up to it."

Olivia instructed Tex to bring back more food. When he left, she said, "For a smart guy, Tex can be remarkably dense. No way Arabella would admit to an affair after her husband died under bizarro circumstances."

My friend hadn't suffered the effects of hate speech, but I had. "There isn't much she can do or say to make things better. Arabella's theoretical relationship with Terrence is now the business of a whole lot of people, the police included."

"You think Arabella had something to do with Leland's death." It wasn't a question.

"I don't know. The only thing I'm sure of is that Leland didn't commit suicide. Arabella was his third wife. If either of them wanted out, they'd have gotten divorced."

Olivia shuffled her feet and fixed her eyes somewhere above my left shoulder. "You must know that, um, some people think he'd tapped you as his fourth wife." She hurriedly added, "I know how ridiculous that sounds, even if you weren't involved with Jonah. The guy was old enough to be your grandfather. But stranger things have happened."

"If by 'some people' you mean Sierra and Hollis, then you're right. I suspect they started the rumors and those stupid hashtags. They can't believe a mere ballerina earned a share of the Vanderhof Prize, and telling people I had an unfair advantage was a clever move. The judges won't want it to seem like the fix is in, which will make it harder for me to get top honors. And for the record: I never accepted any of Leland's gifts, and he was fine with that."

She brushed cookie crumbs from her hands. "Then why did he do it? From the outside looking in, your relationship with Leland was creepy."

I dismissed the sudden fear that Olivia doubted me. We were friends. She knew me better than that. Thinking of the diamond and sapphire earrings I'd refused and that had ended up on the auction table, I said, "I have no idea why rich people do what they do."

* * *

Francie Morelli didn't interview Olivia, Tex, or me until she was finished with everyone else at the party. A lot of the questions the police officer asked were for confirmation of what others had told her. I figured the process of cross-checking alibis for two hundred people was in progress and didn't skimp on details, including some I was certain were irrelevant. When Jonah texted to tell me not to wait for him, I took a cab home.

After climbing five flights of stairs to my railroad apartment, I collapsed onto the bed. If my dress hadn't been so tight, I would have slept in it.

My phone buzzed with a call from my mother, who would keep calling until I picked up. I bowed to the inevitable and answered, despite bone-deep fatigue.

Barbara dove right in. "I heard about Leland Vanderhof's death, and I'm taking the next flight out of LA. I'll arrive tomorrow. Unless it's already tomorrow?" I heard the click of computer keys and, moments later, she confirmed her arrival. "Yes. I'll text when I land, and we can meet. In the meantime, I want every detail."

I was afraid of this. My mother, a crime fiction writer who fancied herself an amateur detective, had occasionally managed to insert herself into police investigations with mixed results. Previous attempts to dissuade Barbara from pursuing a course of action had never succeeded, but this time, I resolved, would be the exception to the rule.

"Don't cut short your visit on my account. The police haven't yet determined the cause of death, and Dad will be disappointed if you leave early. He misses you."

My parents were divorced but remained close friends, which was a perpetual source of aggravation to Ann, my father's second wife. It also was an unceasing source of amusement to my mother. Barbara's visit to their home in LA was made with the express purpose of getting my father to move back to New York City. I couldn't wait to hear how that went down.

My mother answered with undiminished fervor. "I already bought the ticket. And I'm tired of LA. All this sunshine makes me nervous, not to mention the toll it's taking on my skin. Ann is constantly telling me to jump in the pool, which I suspect is a metaphor. And the food! They live in an appalling health and wellness community that's enough to make a reasonable person light up a cigarette and pour some scotch. If I never see another hemp seed or bottle of flax oil, it'll be too soon."

When my phone buzzed with an incoming call from an unknown number, I let it go to voicemail, unwilling to cede the argument. "I'll be happy to see you, but don't get any ideas about investigating Leland's death."

She laughed in a way I knew well. It was the laugh of a mother comically unconvinced by her daughter. "Take a closer look at the picture you sent me from Arabella's apartment. She has every one of my books, so she already knows who I am and my methods of deduction. Call her and arrange a meeting. My agent says sales are slumping badly, and joining forces with her could be a game-changer. It's a win-win situation. We catch a killer, and

I get a contract extension with a big advance."

"I'm touched by your concern, but hooking you up with Arabella involves too many conflicts of interest. Maybe next time."

Barbara remained cheerful. "I can do this on my own, but you could make it easier for me. Think it over. Maybe you'll change your mind."

After assuring her I would never change my mind, we said goodbye.

I checked the missed phone call and found that Arabella Vanderhof had left a peremptory message demanding an immediate callback. Unfortunately, for the one person who could most appreciate the ironic juxtaposition, I would never tell my mother about it.

I called her back and said, "Arabella, I'm so sorry for your—"

Leland's widow cut short my attempt at condolences and said, "I want to hire you."

My first thought: *Could this evening get any weirder?* I kept to myself. The second I shared with her. "I'm already a Vanderhof Prize finalist. That's still on, isn't it?"

She answered with a statement that sounded straight out of a canned press release, "The program will continue, because it's what Leland would have wanted."

The rest of what she said sounded less rehearsed. "The job I'm offering you is a side gig. I want you to find out who's spreading rumors that I murdered my husband. Squash them, preferably by finding the killer. You cannot believe the insane stories I'm hearing, and my assistant appears incapable of dealing with them. If you've met Derrick, you know what I'm talking about."

My mind momentarily went blank. This was not the voice of a grieving wife who'd been told four hours ago that her husband was dead, but perhaps she knew of no other way to deal with the shock.

I felt sorry for her, as well as for her assistant. "Arabella, you don't need me for this. Go down the list of influencers you invited to the party. Those are the most likely culprits, but knowing who they are won't stop them. With so many people addicted to conspiracy theories, even identifying the killer might not be sufficient to put the rumors to rest."

She steamrolled past my objections. "Inviting the scum of the earth to the party was Derrick's genius idea. I was against it. The issue now is where we go from here. You need to feed the sharks better bait. Come up with a different story and promote it for me. If you can't pinpoint the killer, at least you can redirect the hate."

This was too much to ask. I was beholden to Arabella and the Vanderhof Foundation, but promoting false leads and investigating a suspicious death wasn't in the eleven-page contract they made me sign. Hoping to shift the burden to a more appropriate target, I told her to let the police handle the inquiry.

"The police are fools, although one of them, Detective Sobol, seems less dimwitted than the rest." Her voice got louder and her diction more precise, as if she suspected I, too, was a fool. "My husband didn't have an accident, and he didn't commit suicide. Someone killed him. And I want you to find out who did it. Is that clear enough?"

I figured that after the trauma of Leland's death, she wasn't thinking clearly and pointed out, as kindly as I could, the obvious problem with her demand. "I'm a dancer, not a detective. Hire a reputation defender to deal with the online stuff, and if you don't trust the police to investigate Leland's death, hire a PI."

An Arctic chill crept into her voice. "Don't be coy with me. I was a major investor in *Mad Music*. I know exactly what you did to catch the Broadway stalker and, almost as important, how you managed the PR nightmare that went along with it. Rest assured, I will have all the professional assistance money can buy, but no private investigator can infiltrate what goes on behind the scenes. For that, I need an insider who will report to me." The words that followed cracked like a whip. "Yes or no?"

I said what everyone else in Arabella's life had always said in response to her orders. "Yes. I'll do it."

"Of course you will. My lawyers will draw up a contract and have it to you by tomorrow afternoon. If you have any questions, you can contact them."

I understood why Arabella wanted someone on the inside to investigate, but that would only work if the killer were one of the dancers or one of the choreographers. As much as I disliked Sierra and Hollis, their only crimes, as far as I knew, were on the order of *Mean Girls*. Not *Psycho*.

I suspected the culprit was someone in Arabella's rarified social circle, and I had no entrée to that world. Worse—much worse—was the fact that I didn't trust her. Something about her words and her tone didn't ring true, which strengthened my resolve to keep my mother from interfering. There were enough complications without adding Barbara's meddling to the rest.

I told myself that I had no choice but to agree. One member of the Vanderhof Foundation board was dead. A second, Jonathan Franklin, detested me.I had to stay in Arabella's good graces.

It was Leland, however, and not his wife, I was thinking of when I consented. Arabella cared about her reputation. I cared about his. "My last rehearsal at ABC ends at six. Can we meet in the evening?"

"I will arrange to have you released early. I know your new director quite well. Marty Sherrington and I go way back, and I'll give her a call. One of my staff will make the appointment at a mutually convenient time."

* * *

The spouse is always a person of interest in a murder investigation, but Arabella's belief that Leland was killed appeared to exonerate her in the same way it did Terrence Benson. If she and her lover were guilty, they would have endorsed a verdict of accident or suicide. Or was Arabella playing a more subtle game? She could be using me as a means to distract attention from herself. As the past few hours demonstrated, a lot of people in her circle, people like Jonathan Llewellyn Franklin III, thought dancers were stupid.

On the other hand, if Arabella Vanderhof were guilty, it wouldn't be the first time a killer misjudged me.

Chapter Seven

I danced with passion to spite the music.
—Gelsey Kirkland

Grinding noises from a sanitation truck woke me from an uneasy sleep. For several dazed seconds, I was unsure which events from the previous evening were real and which were bizarre dreams. The sound of my neighbor slamming her door with gratuitous force brought full consciousness, and reality, for once, was scarier than the nightmares.

Leland was dead. Arabella was a suspect. That part was real. But the shadowy figure who pushed him off the balcony and the faceless people who pursued me? Those images were the product of my overcharged imagination.

This fractured sense of self was reflected in my current career path and schedule. For much of the summer, Ballerina Leah would spend three-day weekends in Connecticut, performing with American Ballet Company at the Vee Arts Center. Choreographer Leah would spend the remainder of the week in New York City, rehearsing dancers in preparation for the Vanderhof Prize performances.

The math was easy. Three days of dancing plus four days of choreographing equaled zero days off. What had I been thinking, to have agreed to Arabella's demand that I investigate Leland's death?

I pulled the covers over my head. The answer was the same this morning as it was last night. Rejecting Arabella could damage my chance to win the Vanderhof Prize. My inconvenient conscience was equally persuasive, if less selfish. Without Leland's kindness and faith in me, I wouldn't have been a finalist in the first place.

As always, when I'm stressed, or sad, or anxious, I took myself out of the real world and into ballet. I didn't need to play the music to enact this transformation. It's ingrained in me. I closed my eyes and took refuge in Michel Fokine's ballet, *Les Sylphides*. I imagined myself in a magical forest filled with airy sylphs in long white tutus.

This dream state was interrupted by the flesh-and-blood presence of a man in my bedroom. His invasion came as a heart-stopping shock.

The scream was out of my mouth before I could stop it.

Jonah Sobol spilled a few drops of coffee onto the night table but otherwise took my reaction in stride. "Happy to know your lungs are in good working order. Not so sure about your eyesight or your memory."

My heart was still pounding from the scare. Jonah now had the keys to my apartment, and I had his. This level of commitment would take some getting used to. "In case you didn't notice, I wasn't expecting company."

He mopped up the spilled drink and said, "You should have. I texted you twice. You didn't answer, so you now have no choice for breakfast. If you were hoping for a croissant, you're doomed to disappointment. I brought bagels."

I pulled him onto the bed. "It's not every day I get a house call from a homicide detective. Let's start with dessert."

* * *

By the time we left the bedroom, the coffee was cold, and I was starving for food and news. "What's the status of your investigation? Do you have any suspects?"

Jonah swallowed a mouthful of bagel and cream cheese. "The investigation is ongoing."

"I've seen you naked, which means you can't talk to me like I'm a member of the press. No food until you spill." I took his bagel and held it over my head.

He leaned back in his chair. "I don't want to boast, but I've bested violent criminals who have threatened a lot worse than withholding breakfast. And, as a side note, you look like you need that bagel more than I do." He circled my waist with his arm.

"Don't change the subject. What happened last night? Could you tell if Leland had been murdered?"

Two parallel lines, like inverted parentheses, appeared inside his dark eyebrows. "The condition of the body is making it tough to assess if there was a struggle. Defensive wounds, broken fingernails, all the usual evidence was obliterated by the fall. We've got two hundred alibis to sift through, and we can't discount the possibility that he committed suicide, though that seems unlikely. The distance of the body on the ground, relative to the building, suggests he was pushed. From all accounts, he was too frail to have climbed over the railing."

With a mostly steady hand, I poured fresh coffee into two cups. "Arabella called me last night."

He tensed. "She's a person of interest, Leah. I understand if you can't avoid her, given her position in the Vanderhof organization, but as much as possible, keep your distance."

I knew he'd say that. What homicide detective, let alone one who shares your bed, wouldn't insist his lover stay far away from a murder suspect? "Arabella is getting killed on social media and wants my help. She's asked me to talk with the dancers and choreographers."

Those parenthetical lines deepened. "Arabella Vanderhof can afford to employ an army of public relations specialists. What did you tell her?"

I looked into my cup instead of at him. "The woman's got all kinds of influence. With a new director at ABC, I can use a few friends in high places."

Jonah lifted my chin. "Let's go back a few steps. What exactly did Arabella say?"

I was better at remembering dance steps than words. Jonah didn't rush me. I half-closed my eyes and replayed our conversation as best I could, imitating the sound of her voice as if it were music, rather than speech.

"Arabella was an investor in *Mad Music.* She knew I'd investigated the cast and wanted me to do the same for her."

Jonah sawed through a second bagel. "Everyone on Broadway knows that. Everyone who's heard of Broadway knows that. But there's a big difference between the work you did as an informant for us and what Arabella wants you to do. If she doesn't trust me, she can hire any number of reputable PIs."

Finally, something we agreed on. "I told her exactly what you said. She's going to hire a professional, but also wants me to investigate. You don't have to be an NYPD homicide detective to deduce that she suspects one of the dancers, or someone closely involved with the Vanderhof Prize, is guilty. Which probably also means she's innocent."

Nothing I said changed his mind, a not-unexpected response. "Arabella Vanderhof is smarter than you think. Will she be paying you?"

"Yes. She said she's going to have her lawyer draw up a contract. I'm meeting her after rehearsal to discuss it. If all goes well, our next disagreement could be over dinner in Paris instead of bagels in New York."

The promise of a romantic getaway didn't move him. "Don't you see what she's doing? By paying you, she's ensuring you're on her side. I don't trust her, and you shouldn't either."

I was as irritated as one can get when the other person's arguments are better than yours. "Give me some credit. Arabella knows that everything I report to her, I'll also report to you. Happy?"

He scowled at a message that popped up on his phone. "I'll be a lot happier when this case is closed."

* * *

American Ballet Company had one final day of rehearsals at our New York studio before departing for the Vee Arts Center in Connecticut. Ten of the dancers had performed at Leland's birthday party and remained there until the early hours of the morning, but all of us were in class. The company expected no less of us. We expected no less of ourselves.

Madame Maksimova was at her usual place at the barre when I arrived. She hadn't changed much since the first time I took her class as a nervous apprentice. Her hair, as always, was coiled in a French twist. Her posture was still graceful, and her makeup stage-worthy. Madame's perfect legs, however, had been weakened by arthritis, and her gait was no longer as confident. She compensated for this frailty by using her hands to demonstrate.

The familiar routine steadied my jangled nerves. Although the individual steps at the barre never varied, the number of combinations was infinite. Madame M delighted in challenging our brains as well as our bodies, and she gave one complex sequence after another, explaining the moves in her signature mix of languages. It didn't matter what words she used, as all of ballet is in French. Go anywhere in the world, and you can follow commands to *plié, relevé,* or *jeté.*

At the end of every class, the dancers do a *révérence,* when they bow, curtsey, and applaud the teacher and the pianist. Madame acknowledged us by placing a hand over her heart. At the close of this lovely ritual, as the dancers left the room for a much-needed break, she beckoned to me.

Without preamble, she said, in her charming, accented English, "This very bad business, Lelotchka. We must talk, yes?"

"Yes, Madame. When would you like to meet?"

"I will hire a car for Leland's funeral, and we will go together. Think it best for Olga to come as well, *n'est ce pas?*"

Olga was Madame's best friend, closest ally, and secret weapon. I dropped my voice to a whisper. "Did Arabella Vanderhof call you?"

"*Da.* She phoned me at a very rude hour of the morning, but I forgive her. Very upset, which, perhaps, is to be expected. We will talk more of these things later. You, me, and Olga. We will figure this out."

I wondered at her use of the word *perhaps.* Did she doubt Arabella's innocence? Of equal interest was Madame's decision to include Olga. Madame's friend claimed to work as a cleaning lady but admitted that recent jobs had her toting a pistol, rather than soap and sponges. I was fond of Olga, despite her murky past and mysterious employment. We'd had several adventures together, but I knew no more about her life now than when we met. When pressed, she would proclaim, "I work hard, mostly for good guys. But must pay bills!"

Madame glanced at the tiny face of her jeweled watch. "We will be very efficient at rehearsal today. Arabella will not want you to be late."

I had more to say but no time to say it, as twenty dancers trooped into the studio for a rehearsal of *Don Quixote*. The irony was not lost on me. Onstage, I would dance with the title character, who famously tilted at imaginary foes. Offstage, I'd have to proceed without any clear sense of what was real and what was fake.

Chapter Eight

If anything at all, perfection is not when there is nothing left to add, but when there is nothing left to take away.
—Maria Tallchief

If the Vanderhofs hadn't been members of the Diamond Ring Supporters of American Ballet Company, Marty Sherrington might not have been so amenable to letting me skip out on rehearsals to meet Arabella. There were five tiers of donors, and giving more money earned our benefactors increasingly exclusive gifts. At the one-hundred-dollar level, they got an invitation to a dress rehearsal and first dibs at tickets for the new season. One thousand dollars bought an invitation to a studio rehearsal and lunch with the dancers. Get into the ten-thousand-dollar-and-up range, and the perks included two tickets to our gala performance, followed by a champagne reception.

Under Marty's direction, the company now offered increased, in-person access to the dancers. The initiative attracted a new group of younger fans and cost the company nothing. Assisting our patrons with a murder investigation wasn't included on the list of privileges, but the Vanderhof family tended to write their own rules.

Ballet was the only thing on my mind as I navigated the intricacies of the *Don Quixote* choreography, because it was impossible to think about anything else while you're dancing. That intensity doubles when you're in covert competition with someone like Kerry Blair, a ballerina possessed of glamorous beauty and repellent malice. Thankfully, Olivia was also at the rehearsal as the understudy. Behind us, a group of hopeful teenagers mimicked our steps, eager to get noticed.

Don Q, as we called it, was an audience favorite, and American Ballet Company performed it often. Our fans knew the steps as well as we did, and they'd scrutinize every turn, every jump, and every balance. We had to be perfect.

Madame, without moving from her chair, snapped open a fan and transformed herself from a seventy-something, arthritis-plagued ex-dancer into a coquettish señorita. She demonstrated the angle our head and shoulders should make in contrast with the fan and made us practice the move until we mastered that ten-second section of the ballet.

It was a poignant reminder of her former brilliance. Many times, I'd watched grainy recordings of Madame's performance in this role. Before my debut as Kitri, she gave me the fan she'd used for many years. It was a lovely confection of red silk and black lace and was my lucky charm.

We were at the midpoint of the rehearsal when Marty Sherrington's assistant interrupted with a message for me. I wasn't pleased to have to leave so soon. Madame was of the same opinion.

Kerry was delighted at my forced departure. Her voice dripped with fake sympathy. "Leah, are you off to another doctor's appointment? Maybe you should see my orthopedist. Older dancers swear by him."

It was no secret that my knees were on life support, and if Kerry had her way, she would have pulled the plug on them long ago. I ignored knowing looks from her friends and sympathetic ones from mine and pretended a nonchalance that fooled no one. "Thanks, Kerry. In return, I'll give you the name of a great acting coach."

It was a low blow, and I regretted the words as soon as they were out of my mouth. Critics had given Kerry's recent performance in *Romeo and Juliet* a mixed review. She'd won high praise for her technique but not for her acting.

I needn't have worried about hurting her feelings. With a mocking smile, she collapsed into a graceful heap on the floor. "Maybe you didn't get the message. Dying swans aren't coming back from the grave. May they rest in peace."

"It is the public who has not gotten the message, my dear. Every performance of *Swan Lake* sells out." Madame, who didn't look as if she was listening to us, broke off her conversation with Marty's assistant to deliver this reproof.

Kerry jumped to her feet and, with a mischievous smile, said, "I would kill to dance the role of Swan Queen."

Madame's even tone revealed nothing, other than mild interest. "We will see." To me, she said, "Unfortunately, Mme. Sherrington cannot wait. We will talk later, Leah, yes?"

I nodded, gathered my dance bag, and left.

* * *

Marty Sherrington's redesigned office had soft, indirect lighting and a desk made of glass panels that reminded me of the shelves in Arabella's apartment. Both were designed with sharp angles and translucent glass and looked like they belonged in the Museum of Modern Art, which maybe they did. My mother's books, which she'd given to the previous ABC director, now occupied a less prominent position. I didn't snap a picture of them, as I'd done in Arabella's apartment. Barbara didn't need to know the former occupant hadn't bothered to take the signed copies with him, or that Marty had piled them next to the trash can.

Marty herself looked like a work of art. I guessed her age to be about fifty. She had broad shoulders, a narrow waist, and clothes my fashionable mother would have killed for, as long as they were on sale.

The director's classically perfect nose looked pinched. "I spoke to Ms. Vanderhof this morning, and she's requested your presence at her office. Under less tragic circumstances, I would have asked her to honor your commitment to American Ballet Company, but out of respect for her and Leland, I agreed."

She was tough to read. That pinched expression indicated annoyance, but I couldn't tell if she was irritated with me or with Arabella. Marty could

37

have had her assistant deliver this message, and I waited to see if there was something more personal she wanted to tell me.

I thanked her, although if I had the choice, I would have remained with Madame and the *Don Q* rehearsal and skipped the meeting with Arabella.

"You will remember that at all times you represent American Ballet Company. We're proud that you're a finalist for the Vanderhof Prize, but your first obligation is to us. This organization is counting on you. Don't let us down."

I'd spent my entire career with ABC. Marty had been named the interim director a few short months ago. I could have given her a few pointers on how to get on, but she didn't look open to receiving advice from me. When I rose to leave, she stopped me and got to what I thought was the real purpose of the visit.

"Have you chosen the dancers who will perform in your ballet?"

I sat back down. "Tryouts are supposed to take place tomorrow. I don't know if they'll go on as scheduled, given what happened last night."

She raised both eyebrows, which preserved the perfect symmetry of her face. "It might be prudent to use people you can trust. Should you decide to do so, the company would be…grateful. We're a family. And families take care of their own, if only to ensure the well-being of all. Invite Kerry Blair to dance in your ballet. She'll bring star power to the performance."

Was her suggestion a threat or a promise? She had to know Kerry and I were rivals. Marty's voice gave nothing away, but her body language revealed worry. Underneath the desk, her legs swiveled the chair from side to side.

How many times had I been summoned to that office and had to battle an imbalance of power that never varied, no matter who sat across from me? As Madame would say, *plus ça change, plus c'est la même chose.* The more things change, the more they stay the same.

Except I wasn't the same. I kept my face as impassive as hers and did a better job of keeping my body language impenetrable. "I've spent my life at American Ballet Company. There's no need to question my loyalty."

"Indeed. Your career has already been longer than most. Let us hope that collaboration continues to work for us both."

* * *

I headed for the dressing room, where Olivia was waiting. "What was that all about? What did Marty want?"

"I wish I knew. First, she wanted me to know what a pal she was, letting me leave rehearsal early. What happened after that is anyone's guess. She said something about wanting me to pick ABC dancers for my ballet and straight up told me to cast Kerry. I'm probably overthinking this, but she questioned my loyalty and maybe wants a spy to keep an eye on me."

Olivia averted her face. "Have you already decided on the cast?"

"I've got some ideas about who I want to use, and Kerry is not on that list. It'll be easy enough to exclude her, though, since I doubt she'll attend the audition. The most annoying part about it, other than the implied threat to my dancing career, is that I would have picked ABC dancers anyway. They're the best in the world, present company included. Most of the people I want are right here."

I held up two bottles. "What do you think? Aspirin for the headache or ibuprofen for the muscle aches?"

She tapped the bottle of ibuprofen. "Take this, unless the headache is a monster. And hook me up, too. Last night's performance on top of today's rehearsals has me so sore that even sitting hurts."

I shook two tablets into her hand and palmed two for myself. "When I spoke to Arabella last night, she said she knew Marty well. I got the feeling there was a lot of history between them, though I don't yet know what it is."

Olivia stood up and stretched. "What's so surprising? As the director of ABC, it makes sense that Marty would cozy up to the Vanderhof family. That's what directors do."

"Agreed. But then, why wouldn't Marty say that?"

"No idea. But keep me posted." Olivia opened the door and stood at the threshold as if unsure where to go next. I sensed there was something else she wanted to tell me, but when I asked, she shrugged me off and left.

I figured it wasn't anything important. I stripped off my sweaty leotard, did a quick sink wash, and left the studio. Marty wanted something from me. Maybe Arabella knew what it was.

Chapter Nine

I recommend keeping in touch with life and with art.
—Agrippina Vaganova

I circled out of the revolving doors of ABC and raced to catch a crosstown bus for my second visit to the Vanderhof Foundation. The office occupied all five stories of a Beaux Arts townhouse, which was one of several on a quiet street off Fifth Avenue. Unlike the Vanderhof Music Academy or the Vanderhof Art Museum, it didn't call attention to itself.

As the bus rumbled through Central Park, I tried to recall each detail of my initial meeting with Leland, Arabella, and Jonathan, looking for clues I might have missed about tensions between them. Mostly, I remembered how nervous I was. Then, as now, my focus was on an upcoming interview, although the purpose was very different. The first time around, the visit was a final test for Vanderhof Prize competitors.

The streetscape outside the bus window blurred as images from the earlier appointment consumed me. A starched woman had answered the door and directed me to an office at the top of a long, curving staircase that looked as if it had been lifted from a Fred Astaire and Ginger Rogers movie set. Arabella Vanderhof sat behind a long table of dark, polished wood. She wore a tailored, electric blue suit that echoed the color of her eyes and clung to her slim torso. Her silvery blond hair hung in expensive waves that framed an ageless face.

She introduced me to the two men who sat on either side of her. "Gentlemen, this is Leah Siderova."

If Leland Vanderhof had any inkling of the fate that awaited him, it wasn't evident to me. He rose and extended a blue-veined hand marked with brown age spots. "We've met before, my dear. I'm a big fan."

The third judge didn't stand up. Jonathan Llewellyn Franklin III reached across the table and gripped my fingers. His greeting was a snide variation of Leland's polite welcome.

"We meet again, Ms. Siderova." He phrased it as a challenge. "As you know, only three choreographers will be named as finalists for the Poppy Vanderhof Prize. In my humble opinion, you're the least qualified. Convince me otherwise."

I was unprepared for the bone-crunching handshake, but ballerinas are skilled at masking pain. Unfortunately, my voice wasn't as obedient as my face, and I mumbled something along the lines of, *well, yes, ahem, but I, and I've always wanted to...um, yeah.*

Stage fright had been my companion for many years, and I knew how to handle the pounding heart and sweaty palms that preceded every performance. It was an essential part of what made live theater so exciting. The problem I faced, on the day that would decide my future, was that ballet, and not public speaking, was my strength. The polished speech I'd rehearsed refused to come out of my mouth, and I stumbled in an attempt to retrieve it.

Several miserable minutes later, Leland's eyes glazed over, and Arabella's polite smile drooped. Jonathan's smug expression turned scornful. His clenched fists made him look as if he wanted to punch something. Possibly me.

If I were going to go down in flames, I decided it would be on my terms and in my language. I removed the fancy, high-heeled shoes that were crushing my bunions and took off the stiff jacket my mother lent me. Without words, I began dancing the steps of a ballet that didn't yet exist. It was the only way I could get them to see the vivid images in my head.

The movement of my body unlocked my tongue. "Do you see? It's a stripped-down version of *Rebecca*, Daphne du Maurier's book. It's about jealousy, revenge, and secrets, and nothing is quite what you think it is."

Jonathan's lip curled in disdain. "A story ballet? About a book no one's ever heard of? Sounds very nineteenth-century to me. Not suitable for a prize that will honor the memory of a groundbreaking director like Poppy Vanderhof."

Leland was as enthusiastic as Jonathan was contemptuous. "I like it. A lot. We want to showcase different styles and moods, and Leah's ballet will contrast the others. I think Poppy would have loved it."

Arabella's diplomatic answer could have won her a Nobel Peace Prize.

"When Poppy directed the California Ballet, she championed an eclectic group of choreographers. Since this prize is dedicated to her, we will discuss our options and be mindful to act as she would."

* * *

Thirty-seven days later, as the curtain came down on the last act of *Swan Lake*, excited backstage chatter delivered the news that my application was successful. Although my White Swan tutu was molting feathers and I was swimming in a puddle of sweat, a flock of similarly clad and damp dancers embraced me.

Two weeks later, Leland was dead. Arabella was suspected of murdering him. And Jonathan? I didn't yet know how the third member of that ill-fated trio would execute his petty vendetta against me, only that he would.

* * *

The starched housemaid who greeted me on my first visit didn't answer the door this time. Instead, Derrick Easton, Arabella's assistant, ushered me up those marble stairs. I concentrated on not breaking an ankle on the slippery surface. Like many dancers, outside the studio or stage, I'm what my aunt Rachel would call a klutz.

I took a deep breath before entering the same room where I'd had my interview. Arabella looked exactly as she always did. Not a single strand of hair deviated from its appointed place. Although her face was bloodless, her normal hue verged on the vampiric. Diamonds flashed fire from her fingers and ears, and her black suit had not a wrinkle on it.

She pointed to the chair opposite her desk. "Sit." To Derrick, she said, "Bring coffee. And then, leave until I call for you."

If Derrick was bothered by his boss's abrupt dismissal, he kept it well hidden. Judging by the cut of his suit and the expensive-looking watch on his wrist, his salary provided sufficient compensation for submitting to her imperious commands. Arabella didn't speak again until the coffee came and Derrick went.

She sprinkled a packet of fake sugar into her coffee, took a sip, and said, "Let's get down to business. I want you to discreetly question your fellow choreographers and all the dancers present at last night's party. The goal is to determine if any of them have information that will put to rest these hateful rumors. Ideally, you will find evidence that one of them is guilty. You will report to me and no one else. I pay one hundred fifty dollars an hour plus expenses."

I'd never before been paid to investigate. Jonah's misgivings and my loyalty to Leland made me reluctant to take her money. "I appreciate your faith in me, but I'm not sure I can do what you've asked."

She placed the fragile coffee cup in the saucer. "Do you have some moral compunctions that would prevent you from helping me, a grieving widow?"

"I can't promise to keep what I learn a secret. If I find incriminating evidence, I'll tell the cops before I tell you."

Arabella regarded me with pale eyes that seemed to see right through me. "Oh, yes. You're referring to that homicide detective. Sobol. I am aware of your relationship with him."

My face got warm. Jonah and I didn't hide our relationship, but we didn't advertise it, either. "This has nothing to do with Detective Sobol and everything to do with the fact that someone close to you, and possibly to me, is a killer. This isn't a game, and you can't rig the outcome."

"You think I might be guilty. Not a good start, as it speaks to your lack of understanding, but not a deal-breaker either."

My pride was on the line, but so was my career, and that came first. "Good to know. So let me offer a counterproposal. In addition to checking alibis, I'll do what I can to uncover possible motives among the choreographers and dancers. If, at the end, you think it was worth something to you, you can pay me then. Not now."

Arabella put her elbows on the desk and rested her chin in her hands. It had the effect of concentrating her gaze on me. "Has anyone else approached you? It's only fair to warn you that if I find you're working against me, you'll be disqualified. The Vanderhof Prize will go to Sierra or Hollis."

Pride temporarily beat out ambition. "Threatening me makes you look guilty. Innocent people don't have to buy cooperation."

She laughed, the first genuine emotion I'd seen from her. "Don't be so naïve. Innocent people aren't stupider or less practical than guilty ones. Are there any other philosophical reflections you feel you must share with me?"

"No. Before I start, however, tell me whom you suspect. Don't limit yourself to Leland's enemies. Judging from those Merry Widow hashtags, you've got plenty of your own."

With a look that could freeze hot coals, she said, "I don't want my opinions to influence your investigation. If your relationship with my husband isn't enough to convince you to act, I doubt there's anything further I can say to persuade you."

Her allusion to my friendship with Leland didn't sound jealous. It sounded calculated. Almost clinical. Not for the first time, I wondered about the status of her marriage. Arabella took a delicate wafer from a platter of cookies and pushed the rest toward me. "I regret that I have another appointment. Talk to Derrick about setting up another meeting."

Arabella's refusal to answer me was as annoying as her condescending tone. I ignored her command to leave and tried again to wrest a few concrete facts from her. "One more question before I go. What's Marty Sherrington's connection to the Vanderhof Foundation?"

She choked, not badly enough that I'd have to do the Heimlich maneuver, but enough to register displeased surprise. "Marty has no connection to the Foundation, however much she might want one. She's got her hands full as interim director of American Ballet Company. Time will tell if she has what it takes to make that relationship more permanent."

Derrick walked into the room, and I wondered if Arabella had a secret button on her desk that she used to summon her assistant. It didn't feel like the right time to ask, since Derrick's task was to escort me out of the building.

I walked across the street and waited to see the person Arabella didn't want me to encounter. After five minutes, I wanted to give up. The next time I tried a stakeout, I'd do what the cops did and park myself in a car with comfy seats and plenty of coffee.

Ten minutes later, my persistence paid off. If I'd left, I would have missed seeing Sierra Younger ring the bell. I wondered if Arabella would offer her the same proposition she gave to me, and if Hollis would be a third recipient. With the promise of the Vanderhof Prize dangling in front of them, I didn't doubt my rivals would stop at nothing to secure it.

Chapter Ten

You know it is an illusion, but you see it happen; you feel it happen, you enjoy believing it.
—Edwin Denby

Leland Vanderhof was laid to rest at the Bruce Murray Funeral Home on a side street off Madison Avenue. Police barricades blocked it from traffic, although limousines carrying important people were allowed through. From behind those barriers, a crowd of curious bystanders gawked at the rich and famous.

Madame Maksimova was one of the few people at ABC, besides me, who'd received an invitation to the funeral and reception. The car she hired picked me up at my Upper West Side apartment, and we traveled together in greater luxury than I typically enjoyed.

I moved to close the window between the front and back seat, but stopped when I realized the bulky figure behind the wheel was Olga. She greeted me with her usual cheer. "Lelotchka! We are on the hunt again, yes?"

It was impossible to look at her pink cheeks and bright blue eyes without smiling. Her open, friendly face, Madame assured me, was her secret to success. "Indeed. I've missed you, Olga. Where have you been?"

"Problem in Brighton Beach. Very messy. Big cleaning job for good guys." She nodded as we zoomed perilously close to a bus.

The Brooklyn neighborhood where Olga did much of her "cleaning" was famous for more than great food and cheap shops. It was a center for Russian organized crime. I wondered who employed her and if her efforts were behind the recent arrest of a reputed crime boss.

Madame whispered, "It's best not to ask about the details. She was undercover for weeks."

"How could Olga go undercover? She's twice the size of most people. No one who sees her could ever forget her."

Madame was complacent. "It is, how you say, her superpower. Olga can vanish when she must."

I couldn't imagine anyone more memorable than Olga. "Good to know. If she can fade into the background, that gives hope to the rest of us. Though I doubt she'll be as inconspicuous today."

My companion remained confident. "Olga has arranged to work as a server during the reception. She will be spying in front of the house and behind the scenes."

I hoped she was right about Olga, as I was increasingly uneasy about my own more modest attempt to go undercover. "I'm worried, Madame. Arabella asked me to investigate the dancers and the other choreographers, but I suspect she's asked them to do the same, and that they'll be reporting on me."

Madame paled as Olga swerved around a double-parked car. "Lelotchka, you are right to suspect Arabella. She fears being charged with Leland's murder and may be using you to pin the blame on someone else. Perhaps Leland's girlfriend? I not know, but I have the suspicions."

"Leland has a girlfriend?"

She laughed at my naivete. *"Mais oui, ma chère.* Leland and Arabella have a most civilized marriage. Difficult, perhaps, for someone of your generation to understand, but quite pleasant for them. Their loyalty was to the Vanderhof Foundation. Nothing else mattered."

Neither Leland nor Arabella ever showed signs of jealousy, which I now saw in a new light. Their marriage resembled many a political partnership.

"Don't leave me hanging, Madame. Who's the girlfriend?"

"Leland was most discreet, though some say Marty was the object of his desire."

How had I missed what was sitting in plain sight? Arabella had choked when I asked about Marty's connection to the Vanderhof Foundation. Did she think I was being coy?

I tried to fit this new piece of information in with everything I thought I knew. "If that's true, Marty had no reason to want Leland dead."

Madame winced as Olga braked to avoid hitting a cyclist who decided our lane was better than his. "Leland was generous with many women. But this, you already know. There is no need to keep secrets from me."

I hadn't told her about the extravagant and inappropriate gifts Leland offered me, because I didn't accept them. Madame's jewelry box was filled with glittering gems, given to her by several husbands and an untold number of admirers, and I didn't want anyone to assume a similar relationship between me and Leland.

I stared out the window to avoid her scrutiny. Did Madame, like Sierra, suspect the casting couch and not my choreography earned me a share of the Vanderhof Prize? If I'd been less worried about myself and more aware of others, I would have asked an obvious question, one that would have led me closer to the truth before the killer struck again.

* * *

We came to a stop halfway down the block from the funeral home. It was impossible to get any closer. While Olga parked the car in an adjacent lot, Madame and I walked toward the entrance. I recognized many faces but knew very few. The mayor, both New York senators, and the police commissioner held court, encased in separate spheres of admirers and bodyguards.

Security inside the Bruce Murray Funeral Home was tight, as befitted a public figure of Leland's stature. Guards waved metal detector wands over us and examined our handbags. Even Madame didn't get a pass. We sat in the back and observed the slow-moving crowd.

Marty Sherrington arrived with her husband. If she was, as Madame suggested, having an affair with Leland, her sorrow remained hidden under a stony expression. She and her spouse neither touched nor spoke, and

I wondered if they also had what Madame termed a civilized marriage. Behind them, ABC and Vanderhof Foundation board members marched in a somber file.

An elderly woman, wearing a black, wide-brimmed hat, came next. She gripped the arm of a man who looked like a model in an ad for a pricey watch or luxury retirement community. When I asked who they were, Madame seemed surprised by the question. "That is the first Mrs. Vanderhof and her fourth husband."

Behind them, a golden-haired woman in her sixties, wearing a tight-fitting suit and sporting a colorful array of gems on her fingers, walked alone. Madame said, without being prompted, "The second Mrs. Vanderhof. I think perhaps I should not be surprised that Leland never mentioned them to you. Those marriages, unlike the one to Arabella, didn't last long."

I couldn't fault Madame for misunderstanding my relationship with Leland when I'd said so little about him, but it was time to set the record straight.

"Leland and I didn't talk about personal things. Most of the time, we discussed ballets we liked and choreographers we admired. He never mentioned any of his wives, including Arabella, and I didn't ask. What do you know about them? Were they at his party?"

Madame pressed her fingers against her mouth to cover a smile. "They were not at the party. I do not know if Arabella had any contact with them before informing them of his death. The divorces, from what I can remember, were most amiable. I presume a large sum of money changed hands, and everyone, as the Americans say, went home happy."

Organ music prompted us to stop talking, and the rest of the crowd to find seats. The service was nondenominational, and the music eclectic. Arabella didn't speak, but the mayor, senators, and Leland's college roommate did. The latter was the only one whose eulogy moved me. The others sounded as if they'd downloaded their speeches from an AI chatbot that had been given the prompt *Funeral Orations for Famous People We Don't Really Know*.

No one directly addressed the cause of Leland's death, although the mayor mentioned the Vanderhof Foundation's support of Alzheimer's research.

If it hadn't been for the excellent musical interludes, I might have fallen asleep. I grieved for Leland, but the formal procession of speakers failed to capture his vivid and generous soul. After the last of them finished, we stood for a moment of silence. The somber notes of a Bach funeral cantata accompanied the mourners as they filed out of the pews.

These were also the prime suspects in Leland's murder. Arabella was first. She leaned heavily on the arm of Leland's college friend, who looked more fragile than she did and appeared considerably more grieved. Next was Jonathan Llewellyn Franklin III and his latest girlfriend. She looked straight ahead and strode as if on a catwalk at a fashion show. He swiveled his head from left to right, in a transparent bid for attention. Terrence Benson, the designer whose name was romantically linked with Arabella's, made his way down the aisle with Derrick Easton, her personal assistant. They kept pace with each other in parallel lines, staying as far apart as the narrow aisle permitted. Marty Sherrington and her husband also kept to their lanes.

Jonathan Franklin, Marty Sherrington, Arabella Vanderhof, and Terrence Benson. Or, as I'd now come to think of them, the business partner, the mistress, the wife, and her lover. They all had the opportunity and the means to kill Leland. And the motives? When a rich man dies, there are millions of them.

Chapter Eleven

The dancer believes that his art has something to say which cannot be expressed in words.
—Doris Humphrey

We were spared a trip to the cemetery, as there would be no burial. Leland chose cremation, and at the end of the service, Olga drove us to the reception. It was held at Chez Georges, an exclusive restaurant in Tribeca that had a six-month-long waiting list for reservations. Georges himself stood at the door and ushered us to a private room above the main seating area.

The guest list was nearly the same as the one at Leland's birthday party. All the suspects were again in one place, but this time no one would escape observation. Jonah and Farrow arrived shortly after we did and stood together opposite the bar. I recognized three other officers as well. Although the NYPD contingent wore street clothes, no one would mistake them for guests, and maybe that was the point.

After queuing up in the coffee line, which was much shorter than the one at the bar, I lingered by a gleaming silver urn, next to Derrick Easton. The expression on his face, when I approached, was not inviting.

I began with flattery, which I've found is the quickest way to gain the confidence of proud men in subservient positions. "Did you arrange all this? It's quite perfect."

"Yes. But it's not like I did the cooking. I ordered the flowers, and Arabella decided on the menu." His eyes roamed the room, which made him look as though he was casing the joint, though a more likely motive was that he was seeking a better conversationalist. Underneath the impeccably tailored suit a human being surely lurked, but the stitching on his jacket had more warmth than he did.

"How is Arabella holding up? She's under so much pressure." I wanted to prolong the conversation until I could reasonably segue to the topic uppermost in my mind. Derrick, however, got there without prodding.

He rearranged a few strands of gelled hair that had the temerity to separate themselves from the rest of his glossy black helmet. "Arabella is living in a fantasy world. No one pushed Leland off the balcony. He'd been depressed for months, and I think the birthday party sent him over the edge." If Derrick regretted the unfortunate turn of phrase, it wasn't apparent to me.

I was equally blunt. "Arabella isn't the only one to think it was murder, and not depression, that caused his death."

Derrick poured sugar into his cup, sweetening the coffee but not his temper. "Arabella has all kinds of reasons for wanting Leland's death to look like murder. The biggest one is that she thinks it will reflect badly on her if it comes out that Leland killed himself. And whose fault is that? Because while he was struggling with depression after his niece's death, she was having it on with Terrence Benson. Not a good look for someone who prides herself on her public image."

Though it probably wasn't his intent, Derrick's disparaging remarks about Arabella made me more sympathetic toward her. Survivors often endured undeserved guilt, even when they weren't having affairs with hot haute couture designers.

I acknowledged the logic behind his conclusions, though I didn't think they were necessarily correct. "You're in a better position to judge Leland's state of mind, and I have to admit, I don't know anyone who would want to kill him."

"And I don't know anyone who didn't."

"*What?* You said you thought he committed suicide. Are you saying now you think he was murdered?" The whiplash of contradictory statements had me thoroughly off balance.

He examined me with the detached disappointment of an entomologist whose rare new specimen turned out to be a common bug. "Suicide at his age and in his condition is absolutely a possibility. I was simply pointing out the obvious, which is that he wasn't as popular with other people as he appears to have been with you. Not everyone was on the receiving end of his generosity."

With a curt nod, he left me and buttonholed Jonathan Franklin, who didn't look pleased to be torn from the side of his young, beautiful, but sulky-looking date.

I sipped from a thimbleful of creamed tomato soup, in which a minuscule crouton and two threads of an unidentified herb floated, and considered which potential witness to approach next. Derrick had Jonathan cornered, and Terrence was glued to Arabella's side. That left Marty Sherrington as the best remaining source of information. Away from her grand office at ABC, she might be less guarded than at our last meeting.

Madame's revelation about a possible romance between Marty and Leland worried me. Investigating one's boss wasn't a good career move. On the other hand, if the cops arrested her for murder, she wouldn't be my boss for long.

Marty greeted me with a noticeable lack of enthusiasm. I didn't take her glum expression personally, as I suspected her husband, and not I, was the source of her tension. When she introduced me to him, he took my hand and kissed it with excessive warmth and moisture. A European aristocrat might have been able to get away with the move, but not Neil Sherrington.

With alcoholic cheer, he said, "Nice spread, huh?"

Marty's smile looked as if it had been nailed to her face. She wrapped her fingers around Neil's arm and said, "Darling, you've fulfilled your obligations. It's totally fine for you to leave."

Marty's husband didn't take the broad hint. He bent down and put his face in mine. "What's the rush? The scenery's not bad, either."

Mindful of Marty's flinty glare, I didn't react to the fumes he breathed at me. It was painful, but not as bad as dancing on a broken toenail, which, for those who haven't tried it, is excruciating.

I pretended not to understand Neil's compliment and said, "Yes, the restaurant is beautiful. I've seen pictures of Chez Georges, but this is my first visit."

He let loose with a gin-soaked snort of laughter. "I was talking about you." Addressing his wife, he said, "She's adorable. Where did you find her?"

Through clenched teeth, Marty said, "This is Leah Siderova. She's a principal dancer with the company. You saw her perform at Leland's birthday party."

Her implied rebuke didn't dent Neil's mood. He pawed my shoulder and said, "So I did. But honestly, I'm not much of a one for ballet. My wife is the expert. Although you could change my mind if you wanted to." He nudged me, which caused the remaining tomato soup in my cup to slosh over the brim.

I backed away to spare Marty further mortification, but she appeared less embarrassed than I was. "Neil, go away and eat something. And no more drinking."

He saluted and said, "Yes, sir!"

Marty, with admirable aplomb, said, "Pay no attention to my husband. He has an unusual sense of humor, but he means well."

After meeting Neil the Neanderthal, I was no longer surprised to learn her name had been romantically linked to Leland's. Although he was many years her senior, Leland Vanderhof was elegant and well-spoken.

I opened with one of the artfully constructed questions that I'd prepared in advance of the event. "Leland went missing shortly before he died. Did you see anything, or anyone, who, er, looked suspicious?"

She raised her glass in a mocking tribute to my unsubtle question. "Your dancing is a lot better than your sleuthing. Are you asking if I have an alibi?"

"Yes. Arabella has enlisted me to help manage the fallout from Leland's death. As you said yourself, it's in my best interest, and yours, to ensure no one at ABC is implicated."

"I don't need you to tell me what's best for the company. In place of an alibi, I'll give you some free advice. Don't trust Arabella. Like everyone at the Vanderhof Foundation, she's calculating and vindictive. Though perhaps you've already deduced that fact?"

I wondered if Marty's resentment extended to Jonathan and Leland, or if her animosity was more general. "I don't know the Vanderhofs as well as you do, but we're all dependent on support from the Foundation. My personal opinions are beside the point."

Although Marty was evasive regarding her alibi on the night Leland died, she left no room for speculation when it came to her expectations of me. "Your future at ABC depends on me. Not Arabella. And not Madame Maksimova. You decided, without asking permission, to apply for the Vanderhof Prize. Being named a finalist made the company look good, so I didn't complain, but your day job is with us. If you fail in your obligation to the company, there are plenty of ballerinas ready to step into your pointe shoes, no matter how much money those shoes fetch at charity auctions."

Marty might be new to her role as the interim director of ABC, but she was a quick learner. There was no keener threat to a ballerina than the one she stuck between my ribs. If Kerry Blair were with us, she'd be doing a cha-cha on the grave of my dance career.

The sad truth was that each year the incoming group of dancers got younger, and I got older. Now, however, I had some leverage.

"As I'm sure you know, Antoine Moreau is making a documentary on the Vanderhof competition, and he's the hottest director this side of Hollywood. If my ballet wins top honors, I'll star in his movie. We could get a whole new group of fans buying tickets and signing up for those Meet the Ballerina events you've set up."

She had the rare ability to present a blank expression. It was a useful gift. "Yes, Leah. I'm aware of that fact. Why do you think I told you to use ABC dancers? I want the company to star and not just you."

While I was busy kicking myself for failing to understand her motives, Marty stuck another dagger into my self-confidence. "You haven't won the competition yet. You haven't even started. You also don't have as much experience as the other two finalists. Honestly, I can't ignore the possibility your ballet will flop. Our dancers, however, will shine no matter what."

"Don't be too quick to judge. You haven't seen my choreography. I'll have a much better chance of winning with your help and support."

She smiled with her mouth. "Then you agree to make ABC your first priority and to use company dancers."

"The rules require an open audition. But yes, I do anticipate using mostly company dancers, which means they too will require some flexibility in their summer schedules."

"We're on the same side, Leah, and we want the same things."

She correctly assumed I'd be too polite to question her assertion of solidarity. Marty wanted to get promoted from her temporary position. Her achievement of that ambition didn't guarantee I'd get what I wanted.

Marty repeated her warning about Arabella. "Don't trust her. She'll use you like she uses everyone else in her life. I'm telling you this for your own good."

Other than family members, and sometimes not even then, people tell you things for your own good because it benefits them. The phrase is a classic prelude to something sure to hurt.

My boss extended one more piece of advice. "Let the police handle the investigation into Leland's death. Don't get caught in Arabella's web or you'll get eaten alive."

Chapter Twelve

I feel the ticking clock...At times, I've said if I don't dance I'd rather die.
—Wendy Whelan

I was working up the courage to ask Marty about casting for the fall season when Olga interrupted us. "Ms. Vanderhof, she says to come to her now."

Marty ignored Olga, who was now dressed in an approximation of a Chez Georges uniform. "Talk to Arabella and report back to me. Don't forget what I told you."

It's always helpful when someone doesn't bother veiling her threat. The more troubling question was why she, like Arabella, resorted to intimidation. I sensed Marty was hiding something, but she was unlikely to divulge further information with a large, bright-eyed, red-cheeked Ukrainian woman looming over us.

Olga beamed at Marty. "Nice party, no? Very fancy. What you think of the food? Not bad, in my opinion, but not super. You want great food, you should go to Tatiana's Restaurant in Brighton Beach. It's my good friend who owns it. Tell them Olga sent you. Best meal of your life and you don't pay the arm and the leg."

The elegant director of American Ballet Company was taken aback by this flood of information, coming as it did from someone dressed as a server but without the deferential attitude of a Chez Georges employee. Marty mumbled a few polite words about her fondness for blini and left.

Olga said, "Lelotchka? We go now, yes?"

"""

I followed her to a small room off the main dining area. Arabella sat behind a spare desk, told me to sit, and dismissed Olga.

I assumed she wanted a progress report, but so little time had passed, I didn't have much to tell. What I had learned, I wasn't ready to share.

I needn't have worried. Arabella had commands, not questions. "Auditions for your ballet begin tomorrow. Have you thought about who you want to work with?"

If I didn't know the relationship between her and Marty was one of polite enmity and grudging collaboration, I think they were double-teaming me. I delivered the same answer I'd given not ten minutes earlier. "Yes, but it's an open audition."

"I made the rules, Leah, and don't need you to tell me that. But this is a unique situation. Hire the ABC dancers who were at my house when Leland died. You can keep an eye on them while you chat them up."

"With all due respect, if you want me to investigate Leland's death, you have to let me work independently, both as a choreographer and as your, um, your…assistant." I shrank from defining my role as her spy, and we certainly weren't friends.

Arabella said, "Don't disappoint me. I'm counting on you."

* * *

I returned to the reception and to Madame, whose smile didn't conceal the weariness that lined her face. She handed her untouched plate of food to a server and said, "Let us meet at my apartment later. We can talk and plan. You, me, and Olga. I not like this situation, Lelotchka, and I begin to worry for you. Marty Sherrington, I have not the good relationship with her. Perhaps she knows I opposed hiring her. And there is talk already about you and Arabella, that you are…" She paused and turned to Olga, who supplied the word Madame couldn't remember.

Olga said, "Pimping. That you are pimping for her." With inappropriate good humor, she added, "Also, that you are a gold digger. People here are not, I think, very nice. But what can you expect?"

I looked at the polite, well-dressed group that had gathered to honor Leland and wondered how much of what was being said about me was intended to damage Arabella. After enduring gossip about my friendship with the victim, was I now going to have to battle gossip about my relationship with his wife?

Sierra and Hollis, who'd spent much of their time at the reception cozying up to Antoine Moreau, had the most to gain from discrediting me. I hadn't capitalized on my opportunity to spend time with the filmmaker and regretted allowing my rivals to take control of the narrative. On their own, Sierra and Hollis might not wield much power, but their pull on social media, combined with their other advantages, made them formidable opponents.

I needed someone smart and tough, who would watch my back and prevent Sierra and Hollis from stabbing me in that defenseless body part. Olivia and Tex couldn't do it. They were too dependent on Marty, and their careers with ABC made them vulnerable.

Only one person had the requisite talent, loyalty, and independence. If I could convince my best friend to return to the stage, I'd have an unbeatable ally.

Gabi Acevedo answered the phone with cheerleader-level enthusiasm. "Sid! You read my mind. I got back last night from visiting the fam in Puerto Madero, and my parents came with me. I now have two very devoted, built-in babysitters. Are you free for dinner?"

Gabi was the only one who called me Sid. After my parents divorced, my mother thought her name, Siderova, would look better on a playbill than Feldbaum, my father's surname. Although American ballerinas of earlier generations often changed their names to sound Russian, those days were long past, and I resisted Barbara's attempt to rebrand me. As a seventh grader, I felt embarrassed and awkward at having to reintroduce myself with a fancy new name that no one could pronounce, including my teachers. Gabi rescued me. She started calling me Sid, which sounded cool to the middle school kids who teased me.

The sound of her voice was enough to lift my spirits. "Meet me at Madame's tonight. Seven o'clock okay?"

* * *

Madame M lived in an elegant pre-war apartment building close to two of her favorite haunts, Carnegie Hall and The Russian Tea Room. The doorman ushered me inside, and I rode a wood-paneled elevator to her Classic Six apartment, much coveted by New Yorkers. Madame's furnishings were an ode to a Russia that no longer existed, with red and gold draperies, thick rugs, and a silver samovar that rested on an intricately carved sideboard.

Olga answered the door and greeted me with a bear hug, as if it had been years and not hours since we last saw each other. Gabi rose from the sofa and, with less force but equal affection, embraced me. "Sid! Madame has been filling me in on the latest details from your life, which is a lot more exciting than mine."

Olga said, "Eat. Drink. Then, we talk." She brought a basket of sandwiches, a tureen filled with borscht, and a tray with jewel-like pastries.

Madame's eyes drooped with fatigue, but her posture remained straight. "You perhaps wish for some wine, Lelotchka? Olga will pour."

I refused the wine but accepted a cup of coffee. Much to Olga's and Madame's disapproval, I didn't drink tea, which offended some Slavic rule of digestion.

It had been a long day and, like Madame, my energy level was low. I turned to Gabi and said, "What's your schedule like for the rest of the summer? Will you be in the city?"

She crossed the room on long, thin legs and piled three sandwiches on her plate. "We'll probably head to Connecticut for a week or so to see you perform and to escape the heat in the city. Other than that, I'm at your disposal. Whatever you need me to do, I'm on it!"

"I need you to get back into your pointe shoes. Auditions for my new ballet are tomorrow at ten."

Gabi laughed. "That's a good one. Seriously, what's the plan?"

My friend had been a brilliant dancer. Her career mirrored mine, starting from when we entered American Ballet Company's school and lasting right up to the day she took a bow at her farewell performance. Following that emotional departure, Gabi got married, gave birth to Lucie, and never, to my knowledge, ever looked back.

"The plan is for you to perform in my new ballet and help me figure out what happened the night Leland died. Arabella is a suspect in his death and wants me to get information that will exonerate her. She's not asking for proof that will stand up in a court of law. More like talking points that'll help her out in the blogosphere."

Gabi polished off two of the sandwiches. "I wish I could help, but I'm out of shape. Although I still take a few classes a week, most of my workouts take place at the park, running after Lucie."

I anticipated resistance and hoped an appeal to Gabi's innate sense of justice would persuade her. "Forget Arabella and think about Leland. He was murdered, and his name, his wife, and his legacy are getting trashed. I know this isn't your problem, but I owe him, and there are all sorts of complications getting in the way of me finding out what happened. Sierra and Hollis won't give me the time of day, but they might confide in you. The same goes for the dancers they hire. You'll be one of them."

Gabi looked at Madame. "Did you know about this, Madame? What do you think?"

Madame fluttered her fingers. "It is a clever idea. Information will come to you, as it might not to our Lelotchka. No need to take risks. Except on stage. Then, you must take risks, or performance will be boring. And boring is more bad than death."

Madame's allusion to death wasn't one I would have chosen, but Gabi appeared less alarmed about the possible risks involved in investigating a murder than she was about dancing. She said, seeming to waver, "What makes you think people will trust me? They must know we're friends, right? There's a million pics with the two of us together."

"If anyone asks, say we used to be friends, but that getting named a finalist went to my head. Tell them it's like you don't know me anymore. People will eat it up."

She stretched one long leg high over her head and pretended to wince. "I'm happy to tag along as your assistant, but not as a dancer. I can't do it,

Leah. I left all that behind me, and I don't miss it."

Gabi's body told me what her words didn't. I could tell she was tempted. "This isn't *Swan Lake*. You'll have a small role, which you'll complain about to everyone who will listen. And every time you have to leave, to be with Lucie, I'll badmouth you to the rest."

My best friend, as she'd done so many times in the past, said *yes*.

Chapter Thirteen

The muse doesn't come without being called.
—Pyotr Ilyich Tchaikovsky

Fear, jealousy, deception, and revenge. Unlike the real world, ballet is great at making sense of messy emotions, which was why I chose Daphne du Maurier's gothic novel *Rebecca* as the starting point for my first major work. It captured my imagination as a kid, stayed buried in my subconscious for years, and then popped up as creative inspiration when I needed it most. My choreography wouldn't follow the plot of the book but would tap into the dark currents that drove the characters.

I mentally ran through the sequence of steps on the way to the audition. When I was one block from the rehearsal studio, I had to navigate around a long line of extraordinarily beautiful people that wound around the corner to Ninth Avenue. They didn't look like the usual crowd seeking a bargain at a pop-up shop or hoping for an autograph from a movie star. Most of the women were slender, with delicate features and tightly pulled-back hair. The men held themselves with sinewy grace. I figured they were auditioning for a model shoot or Broadway musical.

When I pushed through the door to the studio, a small guy with large biceps stopped me. "What's your number?"

I was confused. "I don't have a number."

He held up a clipboard. "Only dancers who signed up in advance can get in. If you want to try your luck, you can wait at the end of the line, but it doesn't look good for walk-ins."

My throat dried up, and my hands got sweaty. The dancers were waiting to audition for me. It was a heady, if unsettling experience. I explained who I was, and Mr. Clipboard let me in, which annoyed the people who'd secured a prime spot in front. To them, I must have looked as if I belonged in the crowd of auditioning dancers. In truth, I would have felt more at home with them than with my fellow choreographers.

A girl with black hair and porcelain skin elbowed the disgruntled-looking guy behind her and murmured, "Shut up. That's Leah Siderova." A ripple of whispers passed from one person to the next.

I avoided eye contact, ducked into the elevator, and made my way to the rehearsal space. Sierra and Hollis had their heads together when I walked into the room. They broke off their conversation when they saw me. I said hello, which wasn't an interesting enough comment to produce a response.

I shucked off a loose cotton dress, which covered up my leotard and tights. A pair of frayed leg warmers, my lucky sweater, and pointe shoes were all the gear I needed to get to work. To the music in my head, I ran through the usual series of barre exercises, watching the other two pretend they weren't watching me. Subtlety wasn't their strong suit.

Sierra was dressed in a low-cut black stretchy shirt over cherry red leggings that matched her lipstick. Hollis wore a pair of his handmade embroidered boxers over flesh-colored tights and a mesh shirt over his leotard. If the top spot was going to the person with the most creative clothes, instead of the person with the most creative choreography, they'd have left me in the dust.

Their sartorial superiority, however, didn't faze me. My whole life, I'd had to dress to impress others. This time, the dancers had to impress me, though it wouldn't be their looks or leotards that got them a role.

Sierra broke off her private conversation with Hollis to include me. "This is how we're going to run things. We'll admit the dancers in groups of twenty-five, and each of us will demo a short excerpt." She scowled, although I'd done nothing more offensive than arrive at the correct place and time. "Unless you're already planning to weed out anyone whose body doesn't fit ABC standards? If that's the case, we can rethink how to proceed."

Without pausing in my warmup, I said, "The people I choose are my business. There's no requirement that we pick the same dancers, and it probably would work better if we didn't."

As a small woman in a ballet company that prized long-legged ballerinas, I'd had plenty of bitter experiences with expectations regarding body type. Now that I was on the other side of the audition process, I wouldn't eliminate a dancer who didn't conform to the stereotypical silhouette.

Where the principals were concerned, however, it was a moot point. Gabi, Olivia, and Tex were already in. My friends' dancing, their stage presence, and their loyalty earned them a role without a tryout, but they'd have to go through the motions of an open audition with everyone else. To an outsider, the process might appear unfair, but when you're working in a small group personalities matter, and I knew I could count on them. Plus, there was that little matter of Leland's death, Arabella's insistence that I investigate, and Marty's demand that I hire ABC dancers.

Hollis put a muscled arm around Sierra's broad shoulders. "Sierra's a pro. Follow her lead, and we'll all get along fine. May the best man win."

I was certain my rivals, like me, had tapped favorite dancers for featured roles in their ballets. Sierra and Hollis headed their own companies and could choose people experienced in their styles. Whether they would use them to spy, as I planned to do with my friends, was likely.

I looked out the window at the dancers below and said, "Let's start. It'll take hours to get through this crowd."

Hollis made lazy circles on the floor with an outstretched leg. "Not so fast. We have to wait for Antoine. He wants to film the audition process."

This information didn't surprise Sierra, who wore an expression of kickable smugness, but it did me. Angry at being excluded, I said, "I didn't know Antoine was coming. We've got dancers lined up around the block waiting to get in. Who told you we couldn't start without him?"

Hollis pressed the tip of one finger to his temple. "Hm. I think it was Jonathan. Did I forget to pass along that message?"

I relieved my emotions by letting loose a series of *grand battements* and imagined each high kick hitting Hollis in a vulnerable section of his anatomy.

If he and Sierra thought this petty skirmish would intimidate me, they were right, but I'd die a thousand deaths before letting them know.

Poisonous colleagues are endemic in any competitive environment. Over the years, ballerinas, both foreign and domestic, had taken aim at me. In the end, I survived them, as I'd survive these two. I strode to the center of the studio and staked out my territory with the determination of the evil Black Swan, whose deception no one can see.

Chapter Fourteen

Antoine Moreau entered the studio with a load of equipment and a small crew. His dark hair, lightly threaded with gray, was tied in a careless ponytail, and the blue eyes that blazed onscreen were bloodshot. He wore nondescript blue jeans, a washed-out tee shirt, and a sleeveless hoodie with bulging pockets. Nothing about him suggested Famous Film Auteur. If I didn't know he'd been swanning in the South of France after winning the Palme d'Or, I'd have assumed he got his tan from working as a barista in an outdoor café.

I liked his lack of glamor and the fact that he knew to take his shoes off before entering the studio. Like me, he came prepared to work. Unlike me, he wouldn't appear on film, and I wished I'd dressed with more care. If he was expecting a Leah Siderova who looked like the ABC publicity photos, disappointment was a given. Dark circles made my dark eyes look too big, and a hasty swipe of lipstick did little to mask the pallor of too many sleepless nights.

Antoine extended a friendly hand and held mine a few seconds too long. Sierra and Hollis, he greeted like old friends.

His instructions were brief. "Conduct yourselves as if I weren't here. Later, we'll do a few interviews." His English bore only the slightest hint of a French accent that softened the consonants.

Sierra said, "I can't wait to see your vision for this film! I loved *Jazz at Night*. Absolutely fabulous." Hollis chimed in to affirm his admiration of Antoine's work.

I couldn't bring myself to add more sugar to their tooth-achingly sweet comments, although I, too, was a fan. He turned to me and said, "You look like you're ready to start."

I nodded, and the gatekeeper let in the first group.

* * *

When the dancers trooped in, Sierra claimed the first spot. She explained the organic nature of her choreography and talked at length about her philosophy of dance. The steps she demonstrated to a catchy blend of pop and hip-hop tunes weren't difficult, but they were punchy and clever. At one point, she instructed them to lie on their backs and wave their arms while thinking about the first blades of grass pushing upward toward the sun. In an act of superhuman strength, I didn't gag.

With some finagling, I ensured Olivia, Tex, and Gabi got assigned to this first group. They also didn't gag, though Gabi had a hard time suppressing a smile. Sierra complimented my friend on her ability to radiate warmth. That was true, even if Gabi's smile wasn't inspired by photosynthesis.

Hollis was next. He explained that he used his fear of math to inspire his work, which had something to do with prime numbers. It sounded very cerebral and impressive. He assembled the dancers in a complicated formation that they mostly were able to achieve, though one young dancer couldn't quite keep her body as stiff as he wanted as she jumped eleven times in each direction. The electronic score buzzed and creaked in apparent sympathy.

By the time it was my turn, I was too nervous to speak. I felt exactly as I did during my interview with Leland, Jonathan, and Arabella, and worried my wobbly voice would end up immortalized in Antoine's movie.

The solution was the same now as it was then. I skipped the talk and limited my speech to two words: *Let's dance.*

Sierra and Hollis snickered, but I didn't let them distract me. The dancers, who wore sneakers for Sierra and were barefoot for Hollis, had a brief break while the women changed into pointe shoes and the men donned ballet slippers. When they were ready, they lined up behind me as we faced the mirror.

The room got very still. As I knew it would, every distraction faded once the music began. To the strains of a Schubert duet for violin and piano, I demonstrated the steps, which I'd practiced so many times, in the studio and in my head, they were as natural to me as any other role.

We wouldn't have much time to rehearse before the performance, and the dancers needed to be quick studies. Several didn't make that vital cut. Others stumbled on the fast turns or couldn't shuck off their classical training and throw themselves into the movement. Technical skill was essential, but I wanted something more. That indefinable quality that breathed emotion through movement.

Before we began, I was concerned that I might have to justify choosing Gabi, but those worries never materialized. My friend might have lost some of her stamina, but none of her brilliance. Gabi's skinny legs ate up the space, and her expressive face and eyes demanded attention.

At the end of the tryout, Sierra and Hollis outright rejected Olivia and Tex, though not because my friends' dancing fell short. My rivals knew Olivia and I were friends, and Tex had partnered me the night Leland died.

Sierra talked about Olivia with biting disdain. "Spare me any more Dolly Dinkle ballerinas."

Hollis giggled. "Same here. Though Tex wasn't too bad. I put him down as a 'maybe.'"

Jonathan, who'd slipped in during the audition and had been a silent witness until then, said, "Olivia's an okay choice, but it would be nice to have some young, fresh faces." He spoke as if the twenty-three-year-old Olivia would soon be filing for Social Security retirement benefits.

I ignored the slight to my friends and said, "The dancers should have the skill to perform in any of our ballets. That doesn't mean we have to choose the same ones."

To this, Jonathan grudgingly agreed.

* * *

We all had to sign release forms, which gave Antoine's film company and the Vanderhof Foundation permission to use our faces, images, and names in any way they wished. No one objected, although most of the people at the audition were, in effect, working for free. For those who weren't chosen, the thrill of seeing themselves in a Moreau movie for five seconds was payment enough.

The filmmaker and his crew packed up their equipment and left. Jonathan looked at his space-age watch and informed us, with ill-concealed pride, that he was taking his supermodel girlfriend to Paradox, a famously exclusive restaurant. I'd eaten there once and wasn't impressed, but as a woman on a perpetual diet, my food choices were limited. Jonah also was no foodie, which was lucky, since on his cop's salary, a hot dog at a Mets game or a couple of slices at a pizza joint were about all he could comfortably afford.

Tex messaged an invitation to meet him and Olivia. Although I longed to hear whatever gossip they'd gleaned from the others at the audition, I had a more pressing engagement. Barbara, after a delayed flight, was home and had invited me to dinner. My mother's offer wasn't one I could refuse.

Chapter Fifteen

You never advance without losing something en passant...you lose it because
you're paying so much attention to the new thing.
—Ninette de Valois

In a city where buildings transformed, seemingly overnight, the block where I grew up had changed very little. Unlike Broadway, Amsterdam, and Columbus Avenues, where new storefronts came and went, the sole alteration in the side street where my mother still lived was how much the apartments cost.

Gerald, the doorman who'd sympathized with skinned knees when I was a kid and knee surgery when I was an adult, was on duty. He greeted me, asked about upcoming performances, and showed me pictures of his new grandson.

I admired the latest addition to his family and said, "How many is that?" I knew the answer, but didn't want to deprive Gerald the pleasure of showing me pictures of the other three. After getting a thorough update on his kids, grandkids, and a host of nieces and nephews, I took the elevator to my mother's apartment.

Barbara flung open the door and wrapped me in a hug that smelled, in the most comforting way, of cigarettes and Joy perfume.

She held my chin and examined my face, which she pronounced "terrible" and "an emergency situation." When I refused her offer of a spa day, Barbara withdrew to the bedroom and returned with a pot of face cream. "You need a full facial, but in place of that, take this moisturizer. It does wonders for dry skin."

I was grateful for the gift, though I was hungry for more than beauty advice. Barbara didn't cook and rarely ate, but she surprised me with a bag of takeout food. We sat in the kitchen, the one room in the apartment that survived her recent passion for redecorating.

I liked the kitchen exactly as it was. Rarely used copper pots hung from an overhead rack, empty canisters labeled Flour and Sugar lined the counter, and the table where I'd eaten a thousand meals sat next to a tiny window that looked out over the back of an adjacent building. Barbara opened a bottle of wine, poured two generous glasses, and plopped two plastic containers of salad on the table.

"How much have you eaten today? These salads are four hundred calories, but if you have room in your diet, I'll add a boiled egg."

My sister survived our skinny mother's lifelong obsession with her weight. I hadn't been as lucky, although my profession had a lot to do with my relationship with food. Written into our ABC contracts was the infamous Fat Clause, which served as a potent deterrent to over-indulgence in too many bagels or black-and-white cookies. Although the wording had been tweaked in response to public pushback, the intent remained the same. *Stay skinny or find another job.*

Barbara had never been a stage mother, but she did share, with other Ballet Moms, an unhealthy interest in my weight. I bypassed her question of how much I'd eaten, though I could have reported, with great accuracy, the number of calories and carbohydrates I'd consumed. After years of such calculations, I was excellent at adding three-digit numbers in my head.

The food and wine undid knots of tension. Barbara kept a lid on her simmering impatience long enough to let me finish half my meal.

She plucked a few offending croutons from her salad and said, "I spoke to Madame this afternoon. She filled me in with some details about Leland Vanderhof's death and mentioned you've already met with her, Olga, and Gabi to discuss the case. Why was I not invited?"

Her question extinguished my appetite more effectively than a dozen Fat Clauses. "There isn't much you can do, other than be my sounding board, which is something I really need right now."

She stabbed an innocent tomato with her fork. "What are your plans? I have a few ideas, but I want to hear from you before I consult Professor Romanova. Start at the beginning."

Barbara had a closer relationship with the fictional protagonist of her long-running mystery series than she did with most people. Professor Romanova used her knowledge of Chaucer and Shakespeare to solve crimes, which made her a huge hit with English teachers and librarians. *Homicide and Hamlet* and *The Merry Knives of Windsor* were among the most popular titles.

Although Professor Romanova couldn't provide insights that weren't a product of Barbara's ingenuity, I didn't debate my mother's reliance on her imaginary friend.

I fought against letting the memories overwhelm me and concentrated on concrete details. "The cause behind Leland's death is still an open question. The force of the impact on his body erased forensic evidence that would determine if Leland's death was a suicide, an accident, or murder. The usual things they'd look for, like bruising or broken fingernails, that isn't happening, at least not yet."

Barbara took out a vape pen and started puffing, which was preferable to taking our conversation outside so she could smoke a cigarette. "Why would he kill himself at his own birthday party, which also functioned as a fundraiser for his pet project?"

"That's easy. He wouldn't. There are rumors he was suffering from Alzheimer's, but I saw no sign of that. And, as you've pointed out, if he were contemplating suicide, why choose that place and time? Everyone agrees he was depressed about his niece's death, but the whole point of the evening was to celebrate the choreography prize he named in her honor."

My mother blew smoke at the ceiling and said, "The setting is a sticking point. Why would a murderer risk so many potential witnesses?"

It was a question I'd asked myself multiple times without arriving at a satisfactory answer. I offered my best guess. "Two hundred people on the terrace equals one hundred ninety-nine potential witnesses, but it also means the same number would be potential suspects. That will force a wider inquiry and, I presume, will slow down the investigation."

My razor-sharp mother picked up on the limitations of this description. "The murder didn't take place on the terrace. Madame said it happened on a balcony outside Leland's bedroom. Someone either followed him there or lured him there. If it was the first, you are correct. The killer could be any of those two hundred people. If, however, someone lured him there, it had to be someone he knew well. I hope it wasn't Arabella. Ever since you sent me that photo of my books in her library, I've been thinking of how to connect with her. It would be mutually beneficial. She gets my expertise, and I get her endorsement. Have you noticed how similar Leland's death is to the one in my book, *The Tragedy of Errors?*"

I put down my wine glass. Arguing with Barbara required a steady head. "I doubt your publisher is going to want Arabella on their marketing team. If money was the motive for murder, she'll be a prime suspect."

Barbara reached across the table and pressed her fingers against my forehead to remind me that frowning made wrinkles. "What motives, other than financial ones, are there? Professor Romanova thinks it might be romance or revenge, but you have to understand where she's coming from. The academic world is cutthroat."

I nibbled on Barbara's rejected croutons. "Professor Romanova's theories originate in your head. I suggest we concentrate on the guest list, which is made up of real people. Any number of them could have had motives I know nothing about, since I don't move in that social circle."

My mother poured more wine. "Then tell me what you do know."

I rummaged in my bag for a notebook and drew a rough sketch of the rooftop. "There was one large, open area where the stage was set up and the chairs arranged in rows for the audience, but the rest of the terrace was divided by long stone planters filled with flowers. Can anyone account for every minute of their time at the party? Probably not."

She traced a line on the paper from the stage to the apartment. "The police are better positioned to check alibis than you are. What does that detective friend of yours think?"

"His name is Jonah, which you know perfectly well. You never called Zach my doctor friend."

"I like Jonah, but a doctor is better husband material than a cop." She stopped my protest by reverting to her primary objective. "On the topic of partners, let's not forget the spouse is always the prime suspect. Introduce me to Arabella, and then we'll see what Professor Romanova thinks."

This was never going to happen. "She swore me to secrecy. I've already spilled more than I should have."

Her tone was steely. "I'm The Mom. You don't keep secrets from me."

I skated right past that one. What adult daughter tells her mother everything? "I'll keep you posted. But that's as far as it goes. You and Professor Romanova can analyze clues from your shared ivory tower, which can be accomplished as easily in LA as in New York. Dad needs you more than I do. The last time I spoke to him, he didn't sound happy."

"If Jeremy sounds unhappy, it's probably because his wife, the queen of wellness and good health, is driving him crazy. Can you believe Ann didn't want me to vape near him? The woman is a total nutcase."

A sarcastic comment about the health effects of vaping and cigarettes wouldn't stop Barbara from meddling in my life. I kept the focus on my father.

"How does Dad like his new teaching gig? Is he homesick for New York? I miss him."

Barbara dripped a teaspoon of salad dressing on her greens. "The man is a philosopher and spends his days contemplating the meaning of life. What's not to like about that?"

"I hope he doesn't decide to move there permanently. You know how much he hates winters in New York."

"He didn't give up his apartment, so that should tell you something about how committed he is to staying in Lala Land. I'm most worried about him behind the wheel of a car. The drivers in California all appear to have a death wish. Even so, the entire West Coast will heave a huge sigh of relief when Jeremy leaves. He's a terrible driver."

That was my cue. "Speaking of leaving, I've got a big day tomorrow. I'll, um, I'll call soon."

She grabbed my sleeve. "Not so fast. I want to sit in on your rehearsals and observe. You won't know I'm there. I'll be like a fly on the wall."

"Tempting, but no. With Antoine Moreau filming every minute of our rehearsals, I already have a fly on the wall. The last thing I need is my mother showing up. It'll be like the worst ballet cliché come to life."

Barbara accepted my refusal without trying to convince me otherwise. It wasn't a good sign.

Chapter Sixteen

*If age someday grounds my feet and wilts my port de bras, what vestige of the old
life will be left?*
—Sascha Radetsky

I was eager to begin rehearsals for my new ballet but had to wait until I
returned from ABC's new summer home, at a refurbished performing
arts center in Connecticut. Dinner with Barbara prevented me from
traveling with Olivia and Tex the previous evening, which meant I had to
board an early morning train.

Leotards, tights, and pointe shoes took up most of the room in my small
suitcase. I managed to jam a cocktail dress, a cotton skirt, two tank tops, a
sweater, and a swimsuit into the bag, although the swimsuit was unlikely to
get a workout. My schedule wouldn't leave much time for dips in the lake or
the pool, whose heavenly blue water gleamed from promotional brochures.

When I leaned over the bed to kiss Jonah, he opened one eye and said,
"Don't engage in criminal activities while you're outside my jurisdiction."

I sat on my suitcase and tugged at the zipper. "Don't worry. I won't have
time for anything except ballet."

He sat up. "I wish I were going with you. Don't go for any solitary walks in
the countryside. Stay close to Olivia and Tex and keep an eye on Madame."

"Olga will protect Madame. I can take care of myself."

Jonah swung his legs over the bed and pulled me close. "If anything seems
off or suspicious, your first call is to me."

I showed him the pepper spray Barbara gave me after a previous adventure.

As befitting a woman as stylish as my mother, the metallic finish was the color of antique silver.

"If you're in danger, it's usually best to run and scream. And don't forget, you'll get more attention if you yell *fire* instead of *help*." Jonah handed back the flask. "I hope you never have to use this. But if you do, don't spray yourself."

He brushed a loose strand of hair from my cheek. "I wish you didn't have to go."

My phone buzzed with a message from my driver, who was minutes away. I rushed out of the apartment and down the stairs, but had to stop halfway. Mrs. Pargiter, the neighbor who knew my schedule as well as I did, was waiting in the hallway. She wasn't alone. Farley greeted me with a wagging tail and yips of pleasure. Mrs. Pargiter growled.

I'd adopted the dog a few months earlier with the understanding that we would share him, but Mrs. Pargiter wasn't good at sharing. She said, "I suppose you'll want Farley back when you get back from wherever you're going."

I scratched the tiny mutt behind his ears. "Yes, I do. I miss him. I'll let you know if anything changes."

Her eyes brightened with interest. "Like another murder?"

"You can't hope for too much as yet, Mrs. Pargiter."

She sniffed. Her sense of smell was as good as Farley's. "Tell that nice Detective Sobol I made cookies."

Mrs. Pargiter's opinion of Jonah was much higher than her opinion of me. "Tell him yourself. I'm sure he'd love to see you and Farley."

* * *

Sometimes, the climb down the five flights of stairs was harder on my knees than the reverse trip, and that morning was one of those times. My heart also ached. I hated leaving Jonah and Farley and felt a twinge of regret for Mrs. Pargiter as well. Underneath my elderly neighbor's disapproving exterior beat the heart of a lonely woman, who rarely left the house before

Farley and I entered her life. Like my new ballet, our relationship was a work in progress.

I checked the license plate of the waiting car before exiting the vestibule. When the driver saw me, he clicked open the trunk without getting out. I heaved the suitcase inside and waved to Mrs. Pargiter, who was at her post by a window that overlooked the street. Not much got by her, and she wasn't above yelling at loiterers to move along.

A small black sedan that had been idling across the street pulled out of its spot by a fire hydrant and followed us, which didn't set off any internal alarms until we zoomed through a yellow traffic light. The sedan stayed on our tail, although the light had turned red. A storm of honking ensued.

"Did you see that?" The driver took one hand off the steering wheel to fan himself with his cap. "Takes all kinds, but that was a close one."

It happened too fast for me to immediately connect the idling driver across from my apartment building with the reckless guy tailing us. I tried to get a good look at the person behind the wheel, but after risking bodily and vehicular damage to stay close, he remained a car length behind. I took out a pocket mirror to keep him in sight without letting him know I was watching, but a delivery guy on an electric bike peeled out of the bike lane and swerved back and forth, obscuring my view.

Speeding through a red light occurred often enough in New York City that my driver forgot about the incident two blocks later. There were no injuries, no cops, and no apparent witnesses, other than my cabbie and me.

I was uneasy but not scared. An army of early risers strode the sidewalks, and the route to Grand Central didn't require back-alley maneuvering or deserted streetscapes. At 59th St., I lost sight of my stalker, if that's what he was.

I looked right and left after exiting the cab, and when I got inside circled a pillar and watched as a stream of people stepped through the doors. A group of chattering tourists entered, all wearing identical red T-shirts, followed by a trio of women in exercise gear. A procession of business types carrying briefcases, messenger bags, or backpacks followed. Most people milling about under the starry ceiling were traveling into the city, and more commuters exited than entered. Nonetheless, I wouldn't be alone when I boarded the Metro-North outbound train to New Haven. It was a well-traveled route.

After ten uneventful minutes, I gave up sleuthing and used the rest of the time before departure to buy a cup of coffee and compose myself. The trip to the station had rattled me. My driver had made several unnecessarily risky moves, weaving in and out of traffic in a manner that qualified as cinematic, though it did nothing to alter the destination time.

The back of my neck crawled with the uneasy, and possibly imaginary, sense that someone was watching, but the problem with identifying a potential stalker was that many people were, in fact, covertly examining me. I wasn't famous enough for instant name recognition, but more and more, my face was familiar enough that I could almost hear passersby thinking *Where do I know her from?* My star turn on Broadway had yielded the unexpected benefit of a side gig, as a model for expensive jeans. Pictures of me mid-leap, hair flying, now adorned city buses and electronic billboards.

When the platform number for my train flashed on the list of departures, I followed a clutch of people, none of whom appeared to be motivated by any desire beyond timely transportation. I sat in a window seat and hoped the rhythmic pulse of the train wouldn't put me to sleep. Before I left my apartment, I'd looked forward to a nap. Now, with the prickly feeling of unseen eyes on me, I feared one.

The door separating my car from the one in front opened with a clatter and loud chatter, as Sierra and Hollis entered. They looked as startled to see me as I was to see them.

After a whispered consultation, which held up a family of four behind them, they sat in the seats facing mine. Sierra said, "I guess you could call this a lucky coincidence. We have work to do, and if we get it done now we don't have to meet later."

I had a book in my backpack, downloaded episodes of my favorite detective series on my phone, and a list of choreographic problems that needed work, but with Sierra's beady brown eyes and Hollis's unnaturally large blue ones watching me, I couldn't concentrate. Without pretending pleasure, I agreed to her proposal. We could get some of the most pressing paperwork sorted, which was my least favorite part of the Vanderhof Prize required duties.

We worked on our individual submissions before collating information about schedules and staff. It didn't occur to me, until thirty minutes later, to question why they, too, were going to New Haven.

Sierra flushed with pride. "Marty Sherrington wants us to do a workshop for the ABC dancers. If me or Hollis gets the top prize and is featured in Antoine Moreau's film, we'll get the chance to stage our work for the company." With an evil smile, she added, "If that happens, you're welcome to audition for a role."

The conductor checked our tickets, which interrupted daydreams of stomping on her instep. When he moved on, I told Sierra my schedule was full and silently hoped this was true. Casting for the fall season had not yet been released.

She gnawed on a thumbnail and spat out the half-moon her teeth had detached. "Audiences are tired of the same old stuff you guys trot out every year. When I heard ABC was doing *Don Q* again, I was, like, are you kidding me? It's positively medieval. They should retire those warhorse ballets."

Don Quixote was choreographed in the nineteenth century, but I didn't correct her, because the larger point she was trying to make irritated me more than the error. "If you don't know—and you should—that ABC mostly does modern works, there's no reason for us to talk about programming. But here's a news flash: no matter what Marty says, she isn't going to ditch ballets that attract sold-out crowds. People come to see a great show, and we give it to them. No one needs a two-hour lecture to understand and enjoy them."

Hollis squinted, as if unable to get my medieval self in focus. "And that is why you, with your Schubert score and pointe shoes, and," he paused to laugh, "storyline that's straight outta some dead writer no one's ever heard of, that's why you don't stand a chance."

Sierra smacked her lips. "Hollis is right. Without Leland's vote, you might as well give up. I think we all know what he saw in you."

I didn't answer Sierra's taunt, because I wanted my choreography to speak for me. The debut performance of my ballet would either justify the decision to award me a shot at the Vanderhof Prize or confirm the doubts that lived online and inside my head.

Everyone knew my two rivals had talent. I'd seen it for myself. But I couldn't let her insult to Leland go unchallenged.

"Sierra, you've outdone yourself. I thought you were a typical, jealous, insecure schemer who'd stab her rivals in the back to get ahead. I didn't think you had it in you to trash a dead man. Leland was your benefactor, as well as mine."

She lifted her hand as if to slap me. I didn't think she'd follow through, but I grabbed her wrist, just in case. "We are required to maintain a strict code of conduct. You've now disqualified yourself from the Vanderhof Prize."

Her face turned an unhealthy shade of purple that contrasted poorly against her orange and red hair. "It'll be my word against yours. Hollis will back me up."

Hollis was torn. Although he claimed to be math-phobic, it was clear he understood his odds of winning would improve without Sierra. I could almost see his mental gymnastics as he tried to determine which path benefited him most.

Sierra turned from him in disgust. "Forget the whole thing." She chewed at a ragged cuticle, drawing blood from it and, thankfully, not from me. "If I were you, I'd be very, very careful."

"You're right to fear me. My competitors have never fared well." I squeezed past them and took a seat in the back of the car.

When the train pulled into New Haven, I retrieved my luggage and headed toward the exit. Again, I felt eyes on my back, although this time I knew who was watching. A threatened slap was the probable extent of Sierra's potential for violence, but I was nervous, nonetheless. I hid behind dark glasses, but sweat rolled down the sides of my face and my back, a traitorous river of fear.

Chapter Seventeen

I had to learn that slower is faster... It's like preparing for a jump.
You can't rush. You must summon the appropriate energy.
—Edward Villella

Derrick Easton descended from a different car on the same train that brought Sierra, Hollis, and me to New Haven. I didn't know he was on board, but he knew we were, as the Vanderhof Foundation required us to file our travel plans in advance of the trip. I didn't blame Arabella's assistant for strategically avoiding our company. If I could have, I would have done the same.

He'd arranged for a van to meet us at the station and directed the driver to a wood-paneled restaurant that proclaimed its pizzas the best in the world. After placing our orders, Derrick left to take care of unspecified errands. By the time he got back, Sierra was polishing off her second slice. The driver and Hollis wolfed down three, and Hollis wrapped two more in a napkin for the road. With real regret, I skipped the world-class pizza and ate a salad, dressing on the side. Form-fitting tutus don't leave much room for meals with the size and heft of a triangular stone slab.

We trooped back to the van. If Derrick noticed the lack of conversation, he kept it to himself. Without apology, he communicated only with his phone until we arrived at the residence hall for the Vee Arts Center. It was located in a bucolic setting that seemed worlds away from the city.

Hollis and Sierra opted for a walk about the grounds, but I didn't have that luxury. I left my bag with the receptionist and followed rough-hewn signposts to the open-air theater. Madame sat in a chair at the edge of the stage as she directed a group of corps dancers.

I wore a leotard and tights under my dress and needed only a pair of pointe shoes to start warming up. The stage overlooked an expanse of greenery that ended in a dense forest. Along the sides, tall trees shaded dirt paths.

The sense that I was being watched returned, but I shook it off as a paranoid delusion. Rehearsals were open to all the artists in residence, and dozens sat on the grassy knoll. Antoine Moreau arrived shortly after I did, weaving in and out of the spectators, his camera in tow. These commonsense explanations could not, however, quench the troubled sense that a predator lurked.

ABC was one of many companies that would perform over the course of a summer-long season. Orchestras from around the country and the world, as well as a local theater group and opera company, were among the offerings.

Kerry Blair, who never met an attention-grabbing move she didn't like, incorporated a cheeky wave to the onlookers as she pirouetted offstage. When she came back for a choreographed curtsey, she was greeted with applause and wolf whistles.

The informal party atmosphere elicited a glare from Madame. She whispered to Olga, who sat by her side. Olga rose from her chair and approached the revelers. I couldn't hear what she said to them, nor could I see Olga's habitually smiling face when she said it. Their reaction was predictable. Red-faced, they approached Madame and apologized. Olga gave the ringleader an approving slap on the back, which knocked him off his feet.

Madame walked to the center of the stage, where she gave Kerry and Horace notes on their performance. "You are too careful in your solo. Be more wild and, um, what is word?" She frowned and said, "Reckless. Reckless and mischievous. Like when you came out after. You must look like a rebel while you dance. After, you again become prima ballerina. You have it the opposite way around."

Kerry nodded soberly at the criticism but glowed when Madame called her a prima ballerina. It was the highest praise, and I hoped it would soothe

Kerry's jealousy. She longed—as who would not?—to dance Kitri on opening night, but that honor was mine.

My knees and neck were stiff from the train ride, and my head wasn't yet in ballet mode, but the clock was ticking. The weary corps de ballet dancers sat in the shade while Tex and I worked through some of the rough spots in our pas de deux. I was feeling a bit rusty and was sorry to have had to miss the previous rehearsal.

I was late for my big entrance when the fan I needed for my solo went missing. Madame, with fraying patience, called for the stage manager, who called for the prop master, who called for Bobbie York, the costume mistress. Bobbie blamed me for losing the fan and stormed off to find a replacement.

The delicate, red silk confection had been a gift from Madame, and I was distraught over its loss. Kerry, with a simpering look, offered me hers. Through gritted teeth, I thanked her, and we resumed our places.

It didn't go well. Tex was an excellent and thoughtful partner, but even he couldn't mask my wobbly balances, which were so brief they barely registered. I fell off pointe during my pirouettes. The fan Kerry gave me got stuck and refused to open.

Most of my colleagues looked away, which was the harshest criticism of all. The only bright spot was that Antoine and his camera crew were taking a break and weren't there to record the fiasco.

Madame halted the trainwreck of my second attempt to dance the role of Kitri. "What is the problem, Lelotchka? You were brilliant at the last performance. It looks now like a different person dancing. Your knees? Are you in pain?"

"No, Madame. I should have done a longer warmup, but I'm fine." My knees hurt, but that was no excuse. They always hurt.

She lowered her voice. "Maybe you are too tired. It is not necessary for you to push yourself. Kerry is ready."

Kerry was always ready. The woman couldn't wait to dance on the ashes of my career, but as long as I remained above ground, I would fight to keep my place in the company. I said, with all the confidence I could muster, "I'll be fine to dance tonight. Don't worry. I won't let you down."

Madame looked doubtful. "Rest while we rehearse the opening. Kerry will stand in." She walked to the first row in the audience, and Olga moved to the wings.

Derrick emerged from the shadows in the rear of the stage, approached Olga, and said, "Are you part of the tech team? Or a member of security?" He closed the distance between them. "I know I've seen you before. Remind me where that was."

She winked at him. "Olga is very good with cleanup. You need help?"

Madame had been right about Olga. Our imposing friend did blend into the background. Derrick must have seen her at the reception for Leland's funeral, but he didn't connect the server at Chez Georges with the woman in front of him.

Her friendly expression didn't budge. Neither did she. "I am good friend to Madame Maksimova."

Derrick regarded her height, girth, and smile. "Show me your ID."

It would take a lot more than his dour face to alter Olga's cheer. "Yes, sir! This is no problem for Olga! I am here to assist the great and famous Madame Maksimova. Will give you this ID of which you speak as soon as the dancers finish rehearsal."

It was a hot day. Derrick, always so cool and unflappable, wiped his forehead with a monogrammed handkerchief. "You're coming with me."

I stepped between them when Derrick extended his hand in the direction of Olga's well-muscled arm. My friend was kind to most people, including officious meddlers like Derrick, but her response to bodily threats wouldn't go well for her opponent. Olga reacted to verbal abuse with philosophical indifference. Physical threats would unleash military-style force.

My brief intervention gave Derrick time to consider the unwise decision to engage in a fight he couldn't win. He backed off and said, "I'm contacting security."

Olga, her good humor restored, said, "I am security!"

This wasn't strictly true, but was close enough to the truth to pass. Derrick stalked off the stage, knocking over two ballerinas precariously perched on one knee.

The lively music that Minkus wrote for *Don Quixote* stopped. Madame, who was focused on the corps dancers, had a sharp edge to her voice. "What is happening? Why all the chitchat? Dance, please. Not talk."

Derrick edged around a group of women dressed in wilting practice tutus. When Madame spotted Arabella's assistant, she said, "Mr. Easton. Rehearsals in progress. No interruptions, please."

Her reproof didn't impress him. He pointed to the wings and said, "Are you aware of the fact that there is an unauthorized person here?"

Olga lumbered onto the stage. "I try to explain, but this nice gentleman, he is not understanding Olga. I tell him I will get a card of ID later."

With the discipline bred into them after years of training, the dancers were silent, although a few smiles broke through. For them, it was an amusing break in the middle of a sweaty and strenuous rehearsal. Madame was an exacting taskmaster, and age hadn't dimmed her eyesight. One tiny error was all she needed to insist the dancers repeat their steps a dozen times. And then, another dozen times.

Madame folded her arms. "Dancers, you take five. Not six. Five." She waited for the stage to clear and said, "Mr. Easton, please to get off the stage. You are Ms. Vanderhof's assistant. Olga is mine. If you want her to have an ID card, you will so kindly arrange to get her one."

Derrick didn't wilt, but the tip of his nose and ears turned pink. "I will check with Ms. Sherrington. If everything is in order, your assistant may stay." He turned on his heel and, not realizing Olga was standing close behind, crashed into her. The force of their collision didn't alter Olga's position, but Derrick was knocked backward.

Olga rescued him from an ignominious fall, but Derrick didn't thank her. Surrounded by suppressed laughter, he left with the little dignity he had left. He was a proud man who endured Arabella's dictatorial manner but was no match for Olga.

Derrick wasn't the only one to retreat with a bruised ego. I slunk backstage to rehearse a role I'd learned as a teenager. Having given Kerry's fan back to her, so that she could rehearse the part that I hoped was still mine, I pantomimed flipping a fan open.

I forced myself to concentrate, to analyze each step. Was I favoring my right knee over the left? Was my back arched enough in those wobbly balances? Heedless of my surroundings, I hit my elbow on a shoulder-high packing case. A gleam of red satin caught my eye.

It was my missing fan, cut into ribbons.

Chapter Eighteen

...when I left the stage door and sought my orientation among real people I was in a wilderness of unpredictables in an unchoreographed world.
—Dame Margot Fonteyn

A thousand things can go wrong during a live performance. The music cuts out. The curtain gets stuck. Instead of a few snowflakes falling from above, a blinding blizzard descends. Worst of all is when you're the source of your own catastrophe. At some point, all of us have slipped, tripped, or flubbed a pirouette. It's humbling and scary and explains why dancers combine practical measures with wishful thinking in their attempts to ward off disaster.

Like my colleagues, I've invested random objects with magical properties. The beautiful fan, which had been my lucky charm for every performance in *Don Quixote*, was now a sorry mess of ripped satin and lace. The damage felt personal, like I'd lost a friend and not a stage prop. I wondered how I'd missed seeing it during my earlier, frantic search. Had the person who slashed it hidden it before I arrived? And then, perhaps, placed it in the open where the impact of finding it would hurt even more? The white plastic spokes, ripped from red silk, were like bones against blood. It hurt me to look at it.

I was, as was no doubt intended, intimidated. But to what end? My inquiry into Leland's death had barely begun, and Arabella was unlikely to have told anyone she was using me to investigate.

I used a tissue to place the pieces in a plastic prop bag to avoid smudging possible fingerprints, but I was less sure about what to do next. Without a more direct threat against me, the death of a red satin fan wouldn't interest the local police. I could report it to whoever was in charge of security at the Vee Arts Center, but beyond that, there wasn't much I could do. Ballet was rife with tales of a bygone era, when competitors slashed their rivals' costumes and poured ground glass into pointe shoes. I thought those days were past.

* * *

Bobbie York would never win points in a contest for Miss Congeniality, but she was an excellent and efficient costume mistress. By the time our rehearsal break ended, she had a replacement fan for me. It molted rusty sequins when I flipped it open.

She rummaged in her workbox and said, "I'll refurbish it before tonight. In the meantime, try not to lose this one."

I drew her aside and opened my bag to show her the mutilated fan.

She reacted with predictable rage. "Give that to me. I'm reporting this obscenity to Marty Sherrington. We won't tolerate this kind of behavior. It's grounds for dismissal."

I stopped her from touching the fan. "Lower your voice. Tell Marty, but don't tell anyone else."

Her mouth dropped open. "We have to find the person who did it before they inflict further damage."

Bobbie had never been a friend or ally, and she tended to speak before thinking. I didn't want to confide too much, but I also didn't want to leave her unprepared for any future vandalism by confiding too little.

I settled on an appeal to our mutual self-interest. "Antoine Moreau is here. Do you want this episode, which will make both of us look bad, to end up in his movie?"

Her anger flamed hotter. "Do you think I was the target? That someone is trying to make a fool of me?"

Bobby was sensitive, a trait that was of little help in situations that required

91

discretion. "The fan isn't company property. It belongs to me. If I wasn't the target, my next best guess is that it was Madame. Everyone knows the fan was a gift from her."

With a sour look, she said, "Have it your way. I'll tell Marty and see what she thinks."

* * *

As the *Don Q* rehearsal wound down, the temperature abruptly dropped, and the sky grew dark. An electronic alarm rang out in a series of ear-shattering blasts that terrified me. The decibel level was high enough to herald the end of the world, but Tex explained it was an emergency warning system that indicated lightning and not an imminent apocalypse.

We ran to the safety of the residence hall. On the way, we passed tiny, soundproofed practice huts from which musicians emerged, clutching their instruments. Swimmers from the nearby lake, carrying colorful beach towels, raced up a dirt path.

Everyone who wasn't a dancer made a beeline for the bar and restaurant. The company stayed together, waiting for instructions. Mother Nature made the final call, as rain and hail pounded against the windows. Ten minutes later, the lawns and stage were soaked, and the dirt paths dissolved into muddy pools.

I pretended to be disappointed but was secretly relieved. The day's accumulation of stresses that began with a possible stalker, continued on the train ride with Sierra and Hollis, and culminated with the dismemberment of my precious fan, had robbed me of energy and confidence.

I declined Olivia's tepid invitation to join her and Tex, figuring she wanted some alone time with him. Ice for my knees and a hot bath for the rest of me would soothe my physical ailments. The emotional hurt, including that humiliating outing as Kitri, would remain until I erased it with a performance that would prove my career wasn't over.

Arabella, however, had other plans for me. She owned the grandest of the Gilded Age mansions that circled the lake and informed me, via text message, that I was to report to her in thirty minutes.

The weather provided a better excuse than any I could come up with. **Can't go. Lightning alert.**

She didn't miss a beat. **Alert lifted. Rain stopped. SHORT WALK.**

The all-cap ending to her text annoyed me. A short walk along a dark road was challenging for a city dweller like me. Also, while I'd packed a swimsuit and a pair of spike-heeled shoes dyed to match my cocktail dress, I hadn't bothered with such frivolous items as boots, a rain hat, or an umbrella.

My relationship with Arabella, which should have been purely professional, was now tied up with the investigation into her husband's death. I was beholden to her, and she knew it. With Jonathan Franklin firmly opposed to awarding me anything more valuable than a one-way ticket home, self-interest dictated compliance.

Those considerations, however, held less weight now than they did in the hours following Leland's death. Although sympathetic to Arabella's plight, I was already weary of the burden that our unequal partnership exacted upon me and anxious to sever that tie. Jonah and Detective Farrow were excellent and experienced investigators, and the pursuit of justice belonged with them. I checked the calendar and counted off the days until I would be free of Arabella and subject only to the whims of ABC's interim director, a fickle crowd, and the frailties of my own body.

What was the worst that could happen if I refused to accede to Arabella's demands? Sierra or Hollis would win the Poppy Vanderhof Prize and be featured in Antoine Moreau's documentary. There were worse fates. Getting this far exceeded my modest choreographic ambitions, but there was nothing like competition to bring out the best, and the worst, in me.

Ambition and pride had the final say. I skipped the ice packs, showered briefly, and dressed in leggings and a sweater. At the last minute, I remembered to take the pepper spray.

The receptionist who'd looked after my luggage when I arrived stopped me. She spoke in a motherly tone, though not in my particular mother's tone. Barbara preferred staccato pronouncements to gentle suggestions. My mother also didn't own sensible shoes.

"The weather is so bad, my dear. If you must go out, let me get you an umbrella and a raincoat. Wait right here."

She returned with a flashlight, a yellow plastic jacket that could have doubled as a camp tent for three people, and a huge umbrella with the Vee Arts Center logo printed on it.

I thanked her and peered into the black night. Arabella's house, which she described as being on the topmost part of a hill, gleamed through the dark tree line. I pointed to it and said, "I'm not going far."

She nodded. "Ms. Vanderhof's estate. A lovely lady and such a tragedy about her husband."

I wouldn't have described Arabella as lovely, though she did possess a brittle charm.

The receptionist said, "Keep to the main road. There's a back way that's shorter, but unless you know the area, it can be confusing."

She needn't have worried. Even in broad daylight, I wouldn't have chanced a walk through the woods, which was filled with creatures possessed of more than two legs. As for that "main road," it may have qualified as a major artery in the wilds of Connecticut, but to me it looked treacherous. Once I passed through the gates of the arts center and its widely spaced lights, a moonless sky obscured the way forward, and I had to use the wavering beam of my borrowed flashlight to avoid falling into a shallow ditch that bordered the path.

I stopped when I heard footsteps behind me. Hoping for a companion, I turned around but saw no one. Were there bears in the woods? Did bears attack at night? I didn't wait to find out and ran as fast as I could, toward the blazing lights of Arabella's house.

Chapter Nineteen

Dancers aren't pompous. They're too tired.
—José Limón

I arrived at the Vanderhof mansion out of breath. When no one answered the bell, I pounded on the door. Still no answer, but someone had to be home. Every light was on. A fresh downpour of rain, accompanied by hailstones that cracked against my umbrella, added to my misery. What was keeping Arabella?

I pressed my ear against the door and jabbed the bell again, but howling winds prevented me from hearing if it was in working order. The fogged-up glass panels didn't let me see past the foyer, and I circled the house to the back door. Motion sensors triggered spotlights along the path. Although earlier I'd wished for more light, I felt exposed and vulnerable under the harsh glare. The feeling of being watched, which had rattled me since the taxi ride to the train station, persisted.

The back door didn't yield better results than the front one. My text messages and phone calls failed, and I was on the verge of giving up when I spied a half-open window and called Arabella's name. She didn't answer.

The window was low enough for me to haul myself up to it. I threw one cautious leg over the sill but was too nervous to commit to entering the house. Concern for a fellow human being wasn't enough to overcome memories of every scary movie I'd ever seen, where the heroine ignores menacing music and is knocked unconscious and then locked in a terrifying torture chamber.

A creaking sound that could have been harmless or the footsteps of a serial killer helped me decide my next move. Abandoning altruistic impulses in favor of self-preservation, I jumped off the sill and onto a thorny tangle of greenery. Years of balletic leaping and (mostly) landing on my feet enabled a relatively graceful move. I didn't feel the pain of the impact until hours later.

A sudden gust whipped through the trees and turned my sturdy umbrella inside out. I kept it for use as a weapon, as it was too windy to use the pepper spray, and I was mindful of Jonah's warning about not blinding myself.

Every other minute, I checked to see I wasn't being followed. Behind me, the lights of the Vanderhof house glowed through the mist, but there were no visible markers ahead. The fog deepened, and I found myself on the wrong path, much narrower than the one that had taken me to the estate. The arts center was situated in a valley that protected it from the elements but kept it shrouded in darkness. In other words, I was lost.

Intent on navigating the way forward, I should have been more mindful of the ground below. It might have stopped me from tripping over a root and sprawling into a tree. My hands took the brunt of the impact and, after backing off, I stumbled into a patch of wet greenery. For a woman who ventured no further into Nature than the paved walkways of Central Park, it was a wide-awake version of several favorite nightmares.

The fall zeroed out what was left of my shaky sense of direction. I turned in a slow circle and tried to find the path. Unfortunately, like Arabella, it had disappeared. I used the Vanderhof house to orient myself, but ended up in a dense patch of woods.

A snapped twig alerted me to the presence of someone else in the forest. Taking my chances with a possible animal or human predator, I yelled, "Whoever you are, I'm lost. Can you give me a hand?"

The long, low hoot of an owl was the only answer. I snapped off the flashlight and, as quietly as I could, felt my way through the trees. If whoever was out there wanted to find me, I'd make them work for it.

* * *

How I made it back to the Vee Arts Center remained a mystery. I felt as if hours had passed, but I lost all sense of time when I lost my sense of direction. It was probably no more than thirty minutes. Fear of a stalker made me highly attuned to every sound, which is what saved me. When faint laughter echoed through the forest, I followed it to its source. Had the wind not died down and the rain stopped, I could have been wandering all night.

The kindly receptionist, aptly named Clara Love, greeted me with a concerned frown. "Glad you made it back so soon. How is poor Ms. Vanderhof doing?"

"I don't know. No one answered the door, and I'm worried something happened to her. I couldn't get my calls or texts to get through, but I'll try again now."

Clara, without asking more questions, used her desk phone to make a call. She hung up after leaving a message for Arabella and picked up a walkie-talkie.

"Jen? Get Red and head back to the residence. I got one of those ballerinas here. She was supposed to meet Ms. Vanderhof, but no one's answering the door. I called the landline, but no luck there, either."

Two kids, presumably Jen and Red, entered the reception area. Underneath yellow slickers with orange armbands, they wore the navy blue shirt and pants that marked them as members of the security team. Both had light freckles, dark red hair, and backpacks. They seemed excited, like we were off to crash a party instead of trying to locate a missing woman.

Jen spoke first. "I called my dad. He's on his way. He said it could take a while, so me and Red will check out the house."

My inconsistent courage made a brief return, and I said, "I'm coming with you."

Jen, who looked no older than a high school freshman, said, "Thanks, but we'll take it from here."

I introduced myself, though my name carried no weight with them. "I'm Leah Siderova, and I'm a friend of Ms. Vanderhof's. If she's sick or hurt, she'll want someone she knows with her."

Calling myself Ms. Vanderhof's friend was a stretch, but labeling myself a reluctant employee was a less persuasive argument.

Clara *tsked* her disapproval of this plan. "You're soaked and shivering. You need a hot drink and dry clothes. Let the twins take care of Ms. Vanderhof. Their father, Teddy Perryman, is the chief of police."

Although I'd earlier wavered about a continued commitment to Arabella, abandoning her felt wrong. I'm not claiming I would have braved a second walk through the woods by myself, but I was less hesitant about a return visit accompanied by Jen and Red. They were young but large and confident.

The receptionist, thwarted in her effort to spare me another go at pneumonia, gave up. "Stick close to the twins. They've been working summers here since high school. They know this place inside and out."

"How long ago was that?" To me, they looked about thirteen.

Red drew himself up to his full lanky height. "We're sophomores at New Haven College."

Jen was fairly dancing with excitement. "We're wasting time. Let's go."

When we exited, they turned left instead of right, and I remembered Clara telling me about a shorter, more direct route to the Vanderhof house. My two guides stepped lightly along a path too narrow to admit more than a single person but, thanks to their high-powered flashlights, they had an easier time of it than I'd had on the deceptively titled Main Road. The hike, however, remained treacherous. Low-hanging branches slapped me, and gnarled roots coiled like snakes, ready to take down unwary ballerinas whose feet belonged on expensive, made-to-order, Marley dance floors.

A hairpin turn brought us to the edge of the Vanderhof estate. The interior was as brightly lit as before and as silent. The oppressive atmosphere seemed to get to Red and Jen, and their cheerful banter dwindled and then died. I hung back as Red tried the doorknob, which didn't budge.

At the open window, Red gave Jen a boost. She climbed inside and called out, "Ms. Vanderhof? Are you okay?"

The crack of branches against a window was the only response. Jen opened the back door for me and Red. Taking cautious steps, we searched every room of that beautiful house. We also checked the exquisitely neat and well-organized closets, which my mother would have loved. Barbara was forever reorganizing her clothes but had yet to achieve the precision of Arabella's minimalist collection. I waited in the kitchen while Jen and Red descended a steep staircase to the basement. If a psychotic serial killer captured them, someone would have to get help, preferably without succumbing to starvation and torture first.

When they returned, Jen said, with an officious air, "No sign of a struggle." She turned to me. "Could you have mistaken where or when Ms. Vanderhof wanted to meet?"

"No. There was no mistake. I didn't want to come out in this miserable weather, but she insisted. You should call in a missing person report. Or an APB. Or whatever it is cops do when someone disappears."

Neither sibling made a move to do so. Red leaned against the marble countertop. "Are you sure it was Ms. Vanderhof who left the message? Maybe one of your dance friends pranked you, and they're in the bar having a good laugh at your expense."

Twenty-four hours earlier, I would have dismissed his suggestion as absurd, but the memory of my pretty fan, cut to ribbons by a malicious person or persons unknown, stopped me.

"Arabella texted from her phone number, which means if someone pranked me, they did it with her phone."

Jen peered through the window. "Did you ask the housekeeper if she knew where Ms. Vanderhof was?"

When I replied in the negative, we tramped down yet another dark and muddy path toward the housekeeper's cottage. On the way, we passed a pool surrounded by lavish plantings and a building, constructed along the same architectural lines as the house but smaller. I stopped and said, "Who lives here?"

Red pointed to the large rectangular doors on the side. "No one. It looks like a guesthouse, but it's a garage. Mr. Vanderhof had a bunch of fancy antique cars."

The garage doors were locked. Jen swept her flashlight across the driveway, which had a faint imprint of tire tracks on the wet ground.

I bent over them and said, "It looks like the last person to drive this way headed to the main road."

Red, without looking, said, "How can you tell?"

"If it were the other way around, the tires would have left muddy tracks. These are clean."

The wind quieted enough for us to hear the sound of a motor. I pressed my face against the garage window. It was too dark to see inside, but a terrible suspicion of what we might find possessed me.

I banged my plastic flashlight against the window. The glass cracked but didn't break. I turned to Jen. "We have to get inside. Give me your flashlight."

She handed it to me. I used two hands to swing it like a baseball bat. A spider web of cracks radiated from the blow, along with a faint smell of gas.

Blinding headlights stopped me from giving the window another whack. Jen cried, "Dad!" as a burly guy in a police uniform got out of the driver's side of the cop car. He rushed past me to check that his kids were unhurt.

I grabbed his arm. "I smell gas. I think someone might be inside."

His deputy rammed the butt end of a pistol into the window, which shattered it. He reached inside, unlatched the narrow side door, and flipped on the overhead lights.

I was terrified that Arabella Vanderhof had met a similar fate as her husband, but the crumpled body they dragged from inside an antique sports car wasn't hers.

It belonged to the third member of the Vanderhof Foundation board, Jonathan Llewellyn Franklin III.

Chapter Twenty

...the dance of the future is the dance of the past, the dance of eternity.
—Isadora Duncan

The police officers turned off the car, flung open the wide, rolling garage doors, and pulled Jonathan onto the driveway. They didn't attempt to revive him. It was clear from Jonathan's staring eyes and the stench of death that surrounded him that he wasn't going to recover consciousness with a dramatic intake of air, the way victims sometimes did on TV.

Perryman crouched over the body. "Do you know him?"

The weak chin, petulant mouth, and slight body were both familiar and foreign. It was as if a wax dummy, dressed in absurdly fashionable clothes and high-topped sneakers, had been placed there by a stage designer with a macabre sense of humor. Jonathan's skin was an unhealthy pink. The sight and smell of him, combined with the lingering odor of gas, was too much for me to swallow. I sped around the corner and threw up a protein bar and two cups of coffee.

When I returned, Chief Perryman exhibited a singular lack of sympathy. "Well? Who is it?"

My throat burned with bile, and talking was painful. "His name is Jonathan Llewellyn Franklin III. He's a friend of Arabella's." There was so much more I could have said about him, but I'd save it for Jonah.

The second officer had a pen poised over a small notebook. "Next of kin?"

"His mother lives in New York. I can't recall her first name. His younger brother is the architect, Melville Franklin." Melville was famous, but neither cop appeared impressed.

I boxed up my emotions for release at a later date and, from a distance, took careful note of the scene. Six cars, polished to a high gleam, were parked in parallel lines and faced outward, in an evenly spaced row. The seventh was where Jonathan had breathed his last. At the farthest end was room for an eighth car. The empty, rectangular space was cleaner than the area around it.

I wondered if Jonathan had been knocked unconscious before being placed in the garage. Or maybe he passed out and his death was an accident?

When Perryman moved away from the body, I got the answer to the last of those questions. His gloved fingers were stained red from a gash behind Jonathan's head.

With no expectation that he would answer, I said, "What killed him? The blow to the back of his head or the carbon monoxide?"

The police chief stared at me. "That's for the medical examiner to decide."

Showing more emotion might have earned me his sympathy, but not everyone responds to violent death the same way. Later, I might fall apart, but doing so then wouldn't help Jonathan or the detectives who'd investigate how he died.

"How long do you think he's been dead?" Cops can be cagier than coroners when it comes to estimating the time of death, but I figured there was no harm in trying.

Perryman's lips tightened. "How do you know him? Were you friends?"

"Jonathan is on the board of the Vanderhof Foundation. I'm a finalist for the Poppy Vanderhof Choreography Prize, and he's one of the judges. We knew each other professionally."

He remained noncommittal. "I'll get to you in a minute. Stay here. Don't go back inside the garage."

Perryman's caution was unnecessary. Although the smell of gas had faded, carbon monoxide was odorless. I didn't know how long it would take for the air in the garage to reach safe levels.

The police chief drew his kids aside to talk to them. They were clearly shaken. Jen's shoulders shook with the force of her sobs. Red pretended he had something in his eyes, which leaked tears. When Perryman finished consoling his kids and giving them instructions I couldn't hear, he returned to me.

"Why were you here? And what made you look inside the garage?" His voice had an angry edge to it, perhaps because I'd involved Jen and Red in this mess. I guessed the twins' usual evening consisted of strolls along the grounds of the arts complex, interrupted by an occasional complaint about late-night noise or after-hours dips in the pool or lake.

When I told him what brought me to the estate a second time, he scowled and said, "Not one of you thought to call me first?"

Jen held up her phone. "We did. You said you'd be back soon, so we figured we'd check out the house and wait for you here. We didn't think—we didn't know—" The rest of what she said got drowned in a fresh wash of tears.

Perryman awkwardly patted his daughter's back. "After what happened last summer, you should have known better than to investigate on your own."

His reference to a previous episode made me wonder what other secrets the Vanderhofs harbored, aside from infidelity. Neither the cop nor his kids answered my question about last summer's incident.

Seemingly unaware of his boss's reticence, the deputy piped up, "Mr. Vanderhof's niece died. She drowned in their pool. The death was an accident, but, well, you know how people talk."

Indeed I did.

* * *

A van pulled up the driveway, and a team of white-suited crime scene techs took over. They set up bright lamps, around which swarms of insects buzzed. Perryman told me to return to the arts center. I didn't contest his order, but I didn't leave, either. Aside from a burning curiosity that kept me rooted, I was afraid to chance another lonely walk through the woods. What if the killer were still there?

The deputy walked down a dark path to the housekeeper's cottage. Before he left, Perryman's helpful second-in-command brought us bottles of water, which soothed the ache in my throat and helped clear my head. When he returned, he was accompanied by a woman in her fifties. Her silhouette was much like Arabella's, though her hair was brown and her forehead deeply lined. I was surprised the noise and activity hadn't roused her. Maybe, like me, she'd been too scared to explore.

The housekeeper's face was white and strained. She looked at Jen and said, "Not again?"

Jen's voice was hoarse. "Not a drowning. It's um, his name is Mr. Franklin. H-h-he's dead."

The housekeeper crossed herself. "This house is cursed. My grandmother used to say the ghost of Millicent Vanderhof came out of her grave at the full moon."

I broke in to observe we couldn't know if there was a full moon, given the thick clouds. Also, although we were in the middle of the woods, campfire-style ghost stories were not a productive subject for discussion. A real murder had been committed that evening, one that was scary enough on its own terms.

I stuck out my hand. "We haven't met. I'm Leah Siderova, and I had an appointment to meet Ms. Vanderhof earlier this evening. Any idea where she might be?"

She grasped my hand with cold, wet fingers. "I'm Greta Bromley. I got no idea where the latest Mrs. Vanderhof is. My hours are Monday to Friday, from nine to five, and in my off hours, I keep myself to myself."

I looked back at the house, every window still bright. "Then you haven't seen her today?"

Greta shrugged. "It's the weekend. I heard her car a while back but paid it no mind. There's a back road off the estate from my house, so I don't travel this way unless I have to."

The hostility with which she delivered these pronouncements was unmistakable. Less clear was whether her resentment was relevant to the tragic events still unfolding.

I pivoted to a different topic, hoping to jar loose any bit of information that might prove helpful. "Do you—did you know Jonathan Franklin? He was a business partner and friend of both Leland and Arabella."

"I met him, if you can call it that. He was here often enough but wasn't one to stop and chat." Greta leaned closer. "Ask me about Terrence Benson. There's plenty I could tell you about him."

I had no patience for her eyebrow-wiggling. "Are you referring to his supposed affair with Arabella?"

Greta's lips parted to reveal large teeth. "I never said that, but, as you obviously already know, he and Arabella are *very* good friends. It wouldn't shock me if, after a decent period of mourning, the third Mrs. Vanderhof ended up the new Mrs. Benson."

Chapter Twenty-One

The minute a dancer walks off the stage it is forgotten.
But the moment it is executed, it is art.
—Doris Humphrey

Jen and Red watched my conversation with Greta without appearing to hear any of it. The siblings wore identical, shell-shocked expressions, and the housekeeper's words moved them so little we might as well have been speaking a foreign language. Their indifference to Greta's revelations might also have been because they didn't know Jonathan and Arabella as well as I did. Or, perhaps more accurately, as well as I thought I did.

Back in New York, plenty of people would certainly take note. The evolving drama now included the suspicious deaths of two Vanderhof Foundation board members and the disappearance of the third. As if that weren't enough, lurid details about the private lives of all three would provide enough copy to keep gossips busy for years.

When I pressed Greta for more information about Arabella, the housekeeper said, "I don't think you understand what I'm trying to tell you. This is the *Vanderhof* estate. Around here, that means something."

Her perspective challenged my assumptions about the Vanderhofs' marriage. In New York, Arabella was so closely associated with Vanderhof Enterprises and the Vanderhof Foundation, I didn't think of her as separate from her husband's name and legacy. Despite rumors of infidelity on both sides, they were a team.

With a proprietary air, Greta placed her hand on the edge of a stone fountain. "This house has been in the family for generations. The latest Mrs. Vanderhof didn't step foot in the place until she decided to turn the local summer camp into a high-class hangout for her overdressed city friends."

Wrapped in the extra-large yellow raincoat the receptionist loaned me, I was confident the housekeeper wouldn't classify me as an overdressed city friend.

I followed Greta's lead and asked about Leland. "There was a lot of talk after Mr. Vanderhof died that he might have committed suicide. I never saw any indication that he was unwell, but I heard he was diagnosed with Alzheimer's."

Greta sighed, and I got a whiff of garlic and whatever nightcap she'd drunk. "Don't you believe a word of it. Arabella Vanderhof killed that poor man as surely as I'm standing here next to you."

I didn't want to lose her confidence, but I couldn't let the accusation go unchallenged. "Arabella doesn't believe Leland committed suicide or that he accidentally fell. A guilty wife would be pushing either of those stories, but she isn't."

"Sounds to me like Arabella has you wrapped around her little finger. But if I were you, I wouldn't believe everything I hear."

Greta's condescending tone grated on me. "I was at Leland's birthday party and saw Arabella after he died. She was devastated. No one's that good an actress."

"I disagree. Some people are that good, especially a pro like her. Did you know Arabella was an actress before she married Leland? She pretends to be this high-class lady, but she used to flog Alka-Seltzer and Pepto-Bismol. I'm not saying the woman had much success. I think her only legit role was a bit part in a failed soap. I bet she didn't tell you about that."

Never would I have guessed the elegant Arabella, whose aristocratic nose always looked as if it were avoiding a faintly unpleasant smell, had spent her youth pursuing a career onstage. I figured she, like Leland and Jonathan, had been born to privilege.

Greta's ghoulish pleasure set my teeth on edge. When she moved closer to examine the crime scene, I took advantage of the relative privacy to text

Jonah. Police Chief Perryman had yet to conduct a formal interview with me, and Jonah needed to know what happened as soon as possible.

If I hadn't feared eavesdroppers, I would have phoned him instead. When reality delivers horrors that an overactive imagination hasn't anticipated, texts are a poor substitute for human contact.

I kept my message brief: **Jonathan dead. Arabella AWOL. CSI here.**

The text failed to send. I wandered up the hill, hoping for a strong enough signal to connect me to civilization. My third attempt was successful. The phone flashed with his message, **I know. On the way. You ok?**

Worried that he might be with his partner, I kept the message short and impersonal. **I'm fine. Is Farrow with you?**

No- be there in 85 min. Meet u at the arts center.

Since Detective Farrow wasn't in the car with Jonah, I sent a line of hearts and a nervous, bared-teeth emoji. I didn't, however, return to the arts center. That would be like exchanging a front-row seat for standing room. I'd paid the price. Might as well see the show.

* * *

I climbed a few feet higher, which afforded a better view without getting too close to the crime scene. Jonathan's wasn't the first dead body I'd seen, but I wasn't inured to the sight or smell of death. Jen and Red sat farther away, on a bench next to the pool. Greta paced up and down the path near the house. The harsh lights the cops had set up allowed me to see the housekeeper more clearly.

Although she'd spoken disparagingly about the overdressed city people Arabella brought to the arts festival, Greta's clothes had an urban flair. My mother, the most stylish person I knew, wouldn't have rejected the cropped pants or chunky jacket.

I clambered down the muddy slope to resume our conversation. Although I knew the answer to my question, I asked it anyway. "Is that outfit a Terrence Benson?"

She shoved her hands into two deep pockets. "What of it? You think because I'm a housekeeper I should dress like a slob?"

Her prickliness didn't offend me as much as it might have under other circumstances. "Don't be so touchy. Five minutes ago, you were slamming Terrence, but you're wearing a jacket with his initials on the collar."

Her shoulders dropped a few inches from their tense position beneath her ears. "Arabella gives me her castoffs. No point in me throwing out perfectly good clothes, no matter whose name is on them." She lifted a corner of my plastic poncho and said, "I predict you'll be getting an upgrade soon enough."

My clothes and lifestyle didn't interest me as much as hers. "Do you also work at the Vanderhof's New York apartment?"

She put a tissue to her mouth and coughed unconvincingly into it. "Sometimes. Not if I can help it."

Greta walked back to her cottage in the woods. I didn't follow her. There were many more questions I could have asked, but I wanted more time to reflect upon what she told me before talking to her again. I had the uncomfortable feeling that while I'd been interrogating her, she'd been in control the whole time.

Chapter Twenty-Two

The artist must be ecstatic about something.
—Ted Shawn

Arabella's disappearance in the wake of Jonathan's murder was certain to refocus attention on her possible role in her husband's death. She didn't answer repeated texts or phone calls, and that scared me. I had no way of knowing if she chose to remain silent or if someone was silencing her.

I walked back up the hill, where the reception was better, and called Jonah. "How much longer before you get here? There's still no sign of Arabella. I'm jumping out of my skin with worry, and now that I've met her creepy housekeeper, I'm even more stressed."

"Leah, we've got it covered. I've got eyes on her apartment building and the townhouse where she has her office. There's an APB out as well. We'll find her. Already talked to Perryman. He said her car is missing from the garage."

I strove to speak with a similar measure of calm, but couldn't manage it. My voice, always less disciplined than my body, shook. "Something drove her away, and that something must have happened right after she texted me. I know it's not much to go on, but maybe you can get some idea of how far she might have gotten since then. Every lamp inside her house is on, so it must have been a hasty exit. I don't know if she was rushing away from something or toward something, but I'm scared."

The faintest sound of a sigh escaped him. "Don't talk to anyone other than the cops. Perryman's deputy will escort you back to your room, where you will lock the door and not open it to anyone except me."

My legs were shaking, my head was aching, and I was fresh out of courage. "Hurry up. I-I need you."

Jonah, with an exaggerated New York accent, said, "Could you repeat that, please, for the record? I want to enter it as evidence."

The warmth of his voice stilled my shivering body. "I'll save it for the in-person interview."

* * *

Perryman's deputy corralled Jen, Red, and me and drove us to the Vee Arts Center. The residence looked much as I imagined it must have when it was still a camp, with wood beams, lamps fashioned from twigs, and deer heads fixed to the walls. Guarding the stone fireplace was an eight-foot-tall stuffed bear, standing on its hind legs, wearing a hunting cap and carrying a fishing pole in its huge paw.

When we walked inside, Clara rushed from behind the receptionist's desk to greet us. She spoke first to Jen and Red. "I talked to your father. He said to go up to your rooms but to call if you need him."

The deputy, who'd been mostly silent since his incautious reference to the drowning death of Leland's niece, said, I'll keep watch on the place until morning."

Clara nodded her approval. "In that case, I'll get you some hot cocoa, unless you want coffee."

He agreed to coffee and said, "I'll do a perimeter check first."

Clara handed him a walkie-talkie and turned her attention to me. "You look like you're about to keel over. I can get you something stronger than coffee if you like. How about a whiskey? Or a glass of wine?"

"I wish I could, but the cops are on their way from the city and will want to talk to me. I'll take you up on that coffee."

Clara went into the back room and returned with two foaming cups and a tin of butter cookies on a wooden tray. I sank onto a plush, plaid sofa and patted the seat next to me. "Why don't you take a break?"

She gave the sofa a long look. "I guess that's okay. I don't think anyone will mind if I sit for a while."

I knew, without looking at the nutritional information on the side of the tin, that each butter cookie weighed in at one hundred calories and packed fifteen carbohydrates into four small bites. I mentally added up the day's damages and nibbled on one. Not eating invited questions about ballerinas and food, and I had more serious topics to discuss.

The ABC dancers, Antoine Moreau and his film crew, and Sierra and Hollis, all left the rehearsal at the same time and remained in the lobby until we knew the performance would be rained out. My exit from the residence hall, an hour later, got the receptionist's attention, and I hoped anyone else who left had done so as well.

I began with the process of elimination, which proved to be a fortuitous choice, as Clara appeared to have already thought it through. She got a faraway look in her eye and said, "I have a picture in my mind of who came in and out, but I don't know most of the names. No offense, but you ballerina types look alike to me."

I took out my phone and paged through the camera roll. Clara identified several American Ballet Company dancers who left the building, including Olivia and Tex. "I was busy taking phone calls, so I can't swear there weren't others who came in or left. On a night like this, you'd think they'd all eat here."

I unearthed a PR photo of Sierra, Hollis, and me accepting the Vanderhof Prize. The choreographers were unmissable. Sierra had flaming orange and red hair. Hollis, tall and dark with round blue eyes, wore embroidered boxers on top of his leggings. Clara didn't remember seeing either leave the arts center. I was disappointed but not surprised to have to strike them from the list of suspects. Jonathan Franklin championed their work, and his death was a loss to them, not a gain.

The cozy atmosphere in the lodge and Clara's comforting presence didn't lessen the dread that had shadowed me since I left the city. With that dread came loneliness. I could no longer deny a change in Olivia. She wasn't the kind of person who would abandon a friend in need, but perhaps she thought it better for her career if she kept her distance from me.

Clara cleared her throat, and I realized she was waiting for me to speak. I put away my phone and concentrated on the one person whose movements were central. "When was the last time you saw Jonathan Franklin? Did he check in here before going to Arabella's house?"

The receptionist poured two plastic containers of creamer into her coffee. "I gotta be honest with you, Leah. I knew who he was, but never met the gentleman. The higher-ups stay at the Mayflower Hotel. It's right in the center of town. Very fancy."

I should have thought of that. It was where Madame Maksimova and Olga were staying. "Tell me about Greta, Ms. Vanderhof's housekeeper. I met her this evening."

Clara picked at the crinkly paper lining inside the box and took her time choosing a cookie that was covered in sugar crystals. "Greta? Yes, er, Greta. What about her?"

"Housekeepers can become almost a second family to the people who employ them. Did she ever talk to you about Arabella? Or Leland?"

Clara stood up and swept crumbs off her plaid shirt and khaki pants. "Greta and I are not friends. I hardly know her, and when she's here there's no reason for us to spend time together. Most of the time, she's at the Vanderhof's New York apartment. Didn't she tell you that?"

"No. She left that part out."

I knew Derrick was on duty the night Leland died. I didn't know if Greta was. The niggling sense that Arabella's housekeeper had controlled much of our conversation returned with greater urgency, and I wondered what other things she'd led me to believe that weren't true.

Greta accused Arabella of killing Leland. The housekeeper didn't strike me as a reliable source, but guilty or innocent, Arabella had to know her departure and her silence would make her look guilty.

So why did she do it?

The only reason to run was if she also was in danger.

Chapter Twenty-Three

I was all personality and no talent.
—Ruby Keeler

Clara returned to her post behind the reception desk, and I retreated to my room. I didn't want to meet anyone who might ask unanswerable questions or be forced into small talk when my head was aching and feelings were raw.

I bolted the door, took off my shoes, and swallowed two aspirins. Next, I rubbed a magical and extremely stinky ointment on my feet and calves. With my head and muscles somewhat soothed, it was time to review the events of this violent night while they were still fresh in my mind.

Jonah, for the next hour or more, wouldn't be available. He texted to tell me he'd arrived at the Vanderhof estate and would call later. Too restless to rest, and too lonely to remain disconnected, I considered calling Barbara.

Although scientists may not have proved the existence of mother's intuition, there was no getting around the fact that when I need her, Barbara knows it. This included the times when I wished her maternal antennae were less attuned to me, but on that night, I seized the phone the second her name popped up.

With eerie prescience, she said, "Leah, I couldn't sleep. Is everything okay?"

Tears I'd suppressed for hours poured out. "Jonathan is dead. He was—he was murdered. I was there. I-I found him."

Her *Oh no* came out in a long sigh. "Sit tight. I'll be on the next train out of Grand Central. Rest assured, I've already got Professor Romanova on the case."

Though gratified by Barbara's quick offer to help, nothing good could come of my mother and her fictional sidekick inserting themselves into a murder investigation. "Please don't. I appreciate the thought, but I'm an adult. I don't need my mom to rescue me, especially since I'll be back in the city on Monday. We can talk more than."

Undeterred, Barbara proposed a second plan of attack. "If you don't need me in Connecticut, I'll start investigating on this end. Not to speak ill of the dead, but Jonathan Llewellyn Franklin III has plenty of enemies in New York City. Between his real estate shenanigans and the mess he made at ABC, the cops will have their hands full trying to figure out who did the deed." She continued talking over the click of computer keys, "Have you spoken to Arabella? This would be the perfect time for you to introduce us."

Barbara wouldn't rest until she finagled a way to meet Arabella, even if it was over the body of a dead man, but I now had the perfect excuse to put her off. "That's not possible at this exact moment, since she's missing."

The clacking stopped while my mother digested this new roadblock to her plans for Arabella. "I did not see that coming. What did the police say? Maybe you'd better start over and tell me everything."

I tried giving her a concise summary, but Barbara was a stickler for details and interrupted several times. When I finished, she said, "Don't trust anyone. That includes the housekeeper, the receptionist, and your fellow dancers. Especially Sierra and Hollis. In the meantime, I'm on the case."

"You've already done plenty by listening to me. I don't know what else you can do."

"I can find Arabella. She doesn't know it yet, but she needs me and Professor Romanova. Don't you worry about a thing."

Although I knew it was impossible to prevent Barbara from executing whatever madcap plan she was cooking up, I threw out one final plea. "Is there anything I can say that will stop you?"

"Nothing comes to mind. I'm your mother, and I know you better than you know yourself. Can you please trust me?"

I had more to say, but my phone was buzzing with alerts. When Barbara ended our call, I stared at the line of messages. How had news of Jonathan Franklin's death gone viral before his body was cold?

I called Gabi, who answered with a cheerful hello and an update on Lucie's potty training.

I was stunned that my best friend wasn't getting a similar inundation of news. "Are you under a rock? My phone is about to explode."

"What's blowing up this time? I have to tell you, Sid, my life is way more exciting with you in it."

In a few short sentences, I told her of Jonathan's death. Unlike Barbara, she didn't interrupt.

"Let me get right back to you." I heard her shout *Mami! Toma Lucie!* before the line went dead.

Gabi called back a few minutes later. She sounded a lot less cheerful. "Speaking strictly from a PR perspective, which is the only one that counts these days, it looks as if Arabella is the one with a target on her back. The comments I saw about you were positive. Check out the borderline weirdo who calls herself litpicker. She's getting some real traction, reposting your videos and saying what a great artist you are. It all feels performative and at the same time kind of disturbing. I guess what I'm trying to say is that I can be at the arts center early tomorrow. My parents are fine with me leaving, and Lucie will love getting spoiled by them while I'm gone."

The panic that had me reeling for the last few hours receded. There's nothing more comforting than a friend who will put her life on hold because you need her. "You don't have to leap into action this second, especially since we need to keep up the fiction that we hardly know each other. What I need is advice. Help me figure out what to do, other than go home, give up my chance at winning the Vanderhof Prize, and reserve a spot on the unemployment line."

I could hear the smile in her voice. "You always did love the dramatic roles. But before you go all Anna Karenina on me and jump in front of a train, let's think this through. I want to know how the story of Jonathan's death hit so soon. Who spilled?"

She'd latched onto the same detail that worried me and to which I had no answer. "Obviously, the cops aren't posting on social media. That leaves the housekeeper or the receptionist. I pick the housekeeper, because I like the receptionist."

This argument didn't convince my cautious friend. "Plenty of criminals are likable people. You have to look trustworthy to be a successful conman. The same goes for homicidal maniacs. Every time I read about a serial killer, the neighbors always say what a nice guy he was. Is there anyone else you can talk to who can help you identify the person who squealed?"

I would have smacked myself in the head if I didn't already have a headache. "Yes. I was so upset about not being able to contact Arabella, I wasn't thinking straight. I'll call Derrick Easton right now. He's Arabella's assistant and can weigh in on the housekeeper and other potential squealers."

I ended the call with Gabi and hit Derrick's number. At the fourth ring, he picked up. "What is it, Leah?"

His tone was not welcoming, but it never was. "I'm sorry for calling so late, but I can't reach Arabella. I'm worried about her. Do you know where she is?" I held my breath, hoping for an affirmative answer.

"How should I know? I have a personal life and don't appreciate after-hours calls. I'm not on duty twenty-four seven."

His answer sounded like the one Greta gave me. "This is an emergency, Derrick. Surely you've heard by now of Jonathan Franklin's death. If you know where Arabella is, please tell me."

"I can't tell you what I don't know. Call nine-one-one for an emergency. Not me."

Was there a cautious tone under the angry one? I wasn't sure. More telling was his lack of interest in the disappearance of his boss. A guy who didn't ask questions was a guy who already knew the answers.

He ended the call when I asked where he was staying. Derrick had come up on the train with us. He wasn't at the Vanderhof estate, and I didn't remember seeing him at the residence. Assuming he didn't return to the city, he had to be at the Mayflower Hotel. I wondered if a nondisclosure agreement made him cagey or if secrecy was intrinsic to his personality.

I took out a notebook. As the daughter of a writer and a college professor, I learned early about how to make writing a natural outgrowth of thought. Leaving the house without a book, paper, and no fewer than three pens was a deadly sin in the Siderova-Feldbaum family, one that would be compounded if I used the Notes app on my phone.

After some deliberation, I reordered my list of suspects so that Derrick's name was back on top. Despite his protests, he knew more than he was telling me.

Without reporters, influencers, or two hundred attention-grabbing people to provide mostly inaccurate information, I was unprepared for the tsunami of notifications that continued to light up my silenced phone. I braced myself for cruel comments. These were plentiful, but I could find few that were directed at me. Jonathan got countless tributes from people in the dance world, which would have pleased him. When he was the interim director of ABC, before he was forced out, the comments were much less kind.

All the hate went to Arabella, though no one, as yet, appeared to know she'd gone missing. I found the anonymous fan Gabi mentioned, who hid behind the tag @litpicker. She wrote that I was her "fave ballerina" and that I had to "dance my way out of a gilded spider web." I wondered who penned the metaphor, as the profile picture was a question mark in front of a book.

The mysterious alchemy of social media, which crowns and drowns people with breathless speed, was on my side. Depictions of me as a scheming gold-digger switched to a sympathetic portrait of an injured innocent, and Arabella Vanderhof was now the woman every troll loved to hate. The reprieve should have made me feel better, but it didn't.

Online relationships weren't real. The person who killed Leland and Jonathan was.

Chapter Twenty-Four

Without expecting to find much of value, I followed a trail of social media breadcrumbs. What I learned sickened me. Many posts portrayed Leland's party guests as murder suspects, their photos faked to look like mug shots. Arabella topped the list of clickbait victims, which included designer Terrence Benson, award-winning filmmaker Antoine Moreau, and ABC director Marty Sherrington.

Glamorous models like Jonathan's girlfriend were spared censure, as was I. That my name was linked with those professional beauties gave me no pleasure, although it had delighted the admins at ABC. The day after Leland died, the head of our PR department congratulated me when views of my dance videos quadrupled.

After many minutes of fruitless scrolling, I quit following the influencers' accounts. They were a dead end of doctored images. I turned to posts from guests with a more modest following.

A search for photos that included Derrick or Greta yielded zero results, possibly because Leland's friends didn't take pictures of the help. Making the whole exercise more frustrating was the fact that people who posted may not have done so until hours after the photos were taken. I did find an unflattering shot of Leland being led from the stage. In the background, I could make out Antoine Moreau, whose lens was focused on two blurred figures.

The circumstances surrounding Jonathan's murder were quite different from the ones that defined Leland's. Although the Franklin family was as storied as the Vanderhofs, Jonathan died at a deserted estate in the wilds of Connecticut, and not at a crowded party on the Upper East Side. Six people, and not two hundred, knew what happened: two teenage security workers, two cops, Arabella's housekeeper, and Clara Love. Who among that group had the audience and the appetite to ignite a second firestorm of half-truths and conspiracy theories?

* * *

Jonah texted before coming up to my room. When I heard his footsteps, I flung open the door, pulled him inside, and wrapped my arms around him. For those few minutes, I concentrated on the smell of his skin. It was a mixture of soap and citrus and some other scent that was uniquely his, a little musky, a little bitter, and with something sweet underneath.

His embrace was too brief. "We have to talk."

Desperate for comfort, I snaked my leg around his, trying to tumble him onto the bed. "I'm a dancer. I talk with my body."

Jonah stayed planted to the ground. With his index finger, he traced the outline of my lips. "I'm on the clock. We might have time later, after I meet with Carina, for you to try some other moves. I promise not to fight too hard. Now, though, we have to talk. With words."

"Who is Carina?"

He got a self-conscious look on his face that I did not like at all. "Carina Russo is my new partner. Farrow's mother is sick, and he's taken a leave of absence to be with her."

For many reasons, I was sorry to hear about Henry Farrow's replacement. "That's awful. Please give him my best and tell him I hope he's back soon." I also hoped Carina Russo was a stodgy, middle-aged woman with six kids and bad breath.

Jonah sat at the desk and questioned me about my trip to the Vanderhof estate. He was a good listener. When I finished, I asked if he'd heard from

120

Arabella.

He scratched a few notes before answering. "No. Perryman thinks she killed Jonathan, panicked, and did a runner. So does Carina."

Rich people, in my limited experience, didn't run from trouble. They hired a team of lawyers to make it go away. "It's way too soon to make that judgment. Arabella had no reason to kill Jonathan. And if she did, there are less risky ways to do it. A more logical explanation is that she ran away because she was scared. Maybe she witnessed the murder."

Jonah rubbed bloodshot eyes. "Your theory doesn't explain why she's not answering her phone or why she didn't call the police. The only tire tracks on her property appear to have come from her car."

"That doesn't mean she was the one driving it. The killer could have forced her into the car. Or drugged her." My knees ached after trekking through the forest, and I stood up to relieve the pressure on them.

"That leaves open the question of how the intruder got there. Perryman's deputy called the three cab companies that service this area and came up empty. No cars were sent to the Vanderhof estate, and there was no sign of a struggle at her house or in the garage."

A thrill of fear crawled up the back of my neck. "The killer must be either staying at the arts center or hiding at the arts center and got there on foot. What doesn't add up is that Arabella told me to meet her and then killed Jonathan. Why would someone planning a murder invite a witness?"

Jonah shook his head. "Her phone and purse are gone. Her car is gone. According to the housekeeper, so is her luggage. The doors were locked. There was no sign of a struggle. Those facts indicate she left of her own free will. Kidnappers generally don't wait for their victims to pack before they go."

I also had facts. "Arabella enlisted my help. The reasons behind that might be complicated, and I'm not saying they were all unselfish, but it's the strongest proof we have that she's innocent. As for what happened tonight, what do you make of the fact that all the lights in the house were on? It was like she wanted someone to investigate."

Jonah's eyebrows, his most reliable indicator of stress, drew closer together.

"Arabella didn't enlist you. She hired you, which in her mind might be the same as buying you. Maybe she thought she could feed you information that you would then give me."

I remembered Arabella's reference to my relationship with Jonah, but that proved nothing. *Unless,* a traitorous voice whispered in my ear, *all that talk about my skills covered up her real motive, which was access to inside information about the NYPD investigation.*

Jonah's dark eyes had depths that were difficult to plumb, even for me. "Arabella doesn't know you, Leah. And she might be running scared. But keep this in mind: You don't know her, either. If she went along with the idea that Leland committed suicide or that he'd had an accident, it might have backfired. She's smarter than you think."

I shook off my doubts about Arabella's motives and said, "I admit that's one possible explanation. But there are others. Fear could have driven her away, or she could have been lured out of the house on some pretext. After Arabella left, there were no witnesses, and her absence makes her look like a prime suspect."

Weary of this back-and-forth argument, I pulled him out of the chair and onto the bed. Two breathless minutes later, a rap on the door broke our embrace. A low, throaty voice asked, "Can I come in?"

Thanks to Jonah's restraint, we were still dressed. After tucking in my shirt and straightening the blanket, I opened the door. Jonah resumed his seat in the chair by the desk and pressed a pen to his notebook. He wore an impassive expression, and his eyebrows were firmly in place, though his skin was a warmer tone than usual.

Carina introduced herself and stepped inside. Disappointingly, she was no middle-aged mom. Jonah's new partner was almost as tall as he, with long legs, auburn hair, and clear green eyes, the kind that can never be mistaken for blue. She refused his offer of the chair and leaned gracefully against the door.

She had a piece of fabric balled in one hand. "I hope I wasn't interrupting anything."

Jonah laughed and said, "It's not what you think." He took the thin scrap of frayed red silk and turned to me. "What is this, Leah? A friend's idea of a joke?"

I realized the two detectives thought the strip of fabric was left on the doorknob for the same reason college kids do it, to ensure privacy while having sex. Never having gone to college, I didn't know if that was a real thing, but apparently it was.

My heart was thumping. "That's part of a fan I use onstage. Madame Maksimova gave it to me." I sat on my hands to keep them from shaking. "Someone stole it and slashed it. I found most of the fan backstage, but whoever did it must have kept this as a trophy to taunt me with."

Jonah's voice was hard-edged. "When did it happen?"

"It happened at rehearsal today." After a moment, I amended this timeline. "Actually, I'm not sure when it happened. I discovered it today. Someone could have wrecked it any time after Bobbie York unpacked the costumes yesterday afternoon."

Carina was amused. "What's up with you dance types? I'd rather hang out in a room full of pickpockets than figure out how ballet works." She fingered the trailing red threads. "You think someone is jealous of you?"

Jonah slid the remnants of my beautiful fan into an evidence bag. "I doubt this has anything to do with the murders, but you never know. Could be petty vandalism from a jealous dancer. Could be something more. A message, maybe? Leah was close to both victims."

Carina spoke as if I weren't in the room. "You got that right. Leah was close enough to Vanderhof that he left her a pair of earrings any woman would kill for. Not to mention that apartment. I'm jealous, and I don't know her or him."

"What are you talking about?" I heard what she said, but didn't understand how it related to me.

Jonah, unlike his new partner, addressed me directly. "Leland Vanderhof added a bequest to his will shortly before his death. In it, he left you a pair of diamond and sapphire earrings and the deed to an apartment in the Vanderhof Building."

I felt as if I'd stepped through a modern-day looking glass and landed in an upside-down world. "When were you going to tell me? For that matter, why didn't anyone else say anything? Do you think that's the reason Arabella wanted to see me tonight? To tell me about the will?"

Another thought struck me. "I didn't know about the bequest, but Greta does. She said something to me tonight about how I'd soon be wearing nicer outfits. Was she also a beneficiary?"

Carina twisted a lock of her long, auburn hair. "You bet. Her and Derrick Easton, to the tune of fifty thousand bucks."

Jonah didn't comment on my unexpected windfall. Carina, however, wasn't done.

"Might want to stick close to a friend, if you have any you can trust." She picked up a battered pointe shoe. I itched to grab it from her.

Her words inflamed yet another fear, one that had been simmering for a while. Was Olivia still a trusted friend? Maybe the problem was mine, and I was seeing complications where none existed. Either way, I'd make it right.

Chapter Twenty-Five

Dance is like life. It exists as you are flitting through it, and when it's over, it's done.
—Jerome Robbins

On the morning after Jonathan Franklin died, members of the local police force came to the arts center to interview the dancers. The victim's close association with American Ballet Company and his position on the board of the Vanderhof Foundation connected him to nearly everyone there. My presence wasn't requested or required, as Jonah and the odiously beautiful Carina had interviewed me the previous evening.

Still shocked by the murder and so much else, I had no appetite for social contact or food. Coffee, however, was a necessity, and I brought some from the lobby to my room. I could claim that I wanted to clear my mind and organize my thoughts, but behind those reasonable excuses was a bigger truth: I was scared. The creeping sense that someone was watching filled me with dread. I also feared that others would learn of Leland's bequest. The local cops, as far as I knew, didn't view me as a murder suspect, but the rest of the world might. I shuddered to think what Sierra would say and do once she found out.

Other than my quick trip to the lobby, I didn't leave the safety of my room until Olivia and Tex knocked on the door. When I opened it, Olivia said, "A million wild stories are making the rounds at breakfast about you hunting down Jonathan's killer."

Tex gave me a lopsided smile. "What Olivia means is that we're up to date on the rumors. We're here to find out what really happened before we have to get to rehearsal."

He held out a bag of pastries. "I thought you might be hungry after last night's adventure."

Perhaps they didn't yet know about Leland's bequest. If so, I was in no rush to share that information with them. "First, tell me what people are saying."

With callous cheer, Olivia said, "The gossip is banging. According to your bffs, Sierra and Hollis, Arabella killed Jonathan and booked. And then, you tried to track her down. Though Sierra hinted that since you and Jonathan didn't get along, maybe you're the one who offed him."

Tex stuffed a cherry pastry into his mouth. "Olivia is being kind. They also said you helped cover it up."

She delivered a discreet kick to his shin. "Don't listen to him. It's not as bad as all that. All your friends shut down Sierra and Hollis and defended you. The company has your back. No worries there."

He moved out of range of her legs and said, "You're not doing Leah any favors by making things sound better than they are." With an apologetic glance, he said, "Not everyone was on Team Leah. Kerry was the loudest voice against you. Olivia and I stuck up for you, but not a ton of other people jumped in. They didn't pile on, but they weren't putting themselves out there, either."

I guessed as much. We all knew that at ABC, few people will care if your personal life is in ruins. Not your colleagues, who stand to gain if you falter. Not the front office admins, who care only about the bottom line. Not the audience, who pays to see you dance.

No matter what happens in our private lives, dancers can never miss class, never miss rehearsal, and never stop trying to be perfect. I did all those things, and despite the discipline that had been bred into me, my emotions remained raw. Stuff still hurt.

I drank coffee to avoid their pitying looks. "Did anyone suggest a motive? Are there any other names that came up?"

Tex bit into a glazed donut. "Most of us never met the Vanderhofs, except at a fancy party. To us, they're donors who get a big round of applause at ABC fundraisers, and the rest of the time they do whatever super-rich people do. Kerry thinks Arabella killed Leland, and then Jonathan threatened to turn her in, so she bumped him off as well. It makes sense to me."

Olivia peeled the paper lining off a blueberry muffin. "I think she's guilty, and you would too, Leah, if you weren't taken in by her money, and the Vanderhof prize, and all that other stuff. Innocent people don't leave the scene of the crime. Arabella's probably miles away by now. If I had a private plane and a pile of cash, you wouldn't catch me staring down a murder charge. I'd be sunning and swimming in an exotic location where they'll never find me."

With an easygoing grin, Tex said, "Me and Olivia are gonna shut up now and let you do the talking, since you're the one with the inside dirt."

Desperate to set the record straight, I once again relived the horror of the previous night.

Olivia latched onto one of the bits I'd left out. "What did Jonah tell you?"

"Not much. The cops will know more after the medical examiner does the autopsy." I zipped my bag and said, "We better get going. Hell hath no fury like Madame when a dancer shows up late to class."

Tex patted my back and quoted one of Madame's favorite sayings, "Death is no reason to miss class if you are not the corpse."

With that grim reminder, we left the arts center and headed toward the amphitheater. I didn't tell my two friends about the fears that plagued me, but ignoring them didn't make them go away.

An unknown enemy ripped apart my fan. Someone followed me last night. And someone killed Jonathan. The question that haunted me and gave me bone-shaking shivers was this: Did the person who destroyed my fan and my confidence also murder two people?

* * *

The route to the stage followed a meandering path from the residence. Several cops accompanied us, and others were stationed at the amphitheater.

Two stood guard in front of where the audience would sit. The rest pulled aside members of the stage crew, presumably to question them.

Backstage chatter about the latest victim was subdued. Jonathan Llewellyn Franklin III was not a popular man. The company survived his short stint as its interim director, but the loss of trust remained, however hard Marty Sherrington tried to paper it over with talk about the Franklin family's generosity.

Olivia summed up the general mood. "It's tough to know what to say. Jonathan didn't deserve to die…"

Kerry spit out what no one else would. "But it'll be great to never see him again."

Olivia clapped her hand across her mouth, as if she'd been the one to utter Kerry's cruel words. When my friend recovered, she said what the rest of us were surely thinking. "I wonder who did it. The cops interviewed all of us, but they can't possibly suspect one of the dancers killed him."

Kerry looked down her perfect nose at Olivia, who, like me, was one of the smallest ballerinas. "Isn't it obvious? Arabella Vanderhof did him in." She shifted her supercilious glare to point in my direction. "Why don't you enlighten us, Leah? Or doesn't your boyfriend know anything either? The cops don't seem to have made much progress in solving Leland's murder."

I was so used to Kerry's spitefulness it had lost the power to move me. I lifted my shoulders in a *who-knows?* shrug and said nothing.

This irritated her more than the cutting comments I could have used to fend off her malice. "We know you're hiding something, Leah. Drop the innocent act."

"Good acting is what gets you out of the corps de ballet and into the spotlight. You should try it." I took a replacement fan from the props table and swished it open.

Her voice rose an octave. "Acting is what has-been dancers lean on when they're losing their edge."

I let her have the last word, because I was distracted by two other rivals, more deadly than she, parked in the front row. Sierra and Hollis sat next to Marty Sherrington, and the three were chatting like best buds. Was Marty, like Arabella, playing us against each other? And if so, to what end?

Chapter Twenty-Six

*It is only perfection in the foundations that can lead to mastery of the whole.
Talent is work.*
—Galina Ulanova

Madame, assisted by Olga and the cane I knew she hated, walked onto the stage to begin class. Her eyes were red and her hands trembled, but her voice was strong. "We have tragedy, but show must go on. Is not a cliché. Is truth. We will respect the death of Mr. Franklin with a ballet performance that will bring honor to him. Is what we do, *mes chers danseurs.*"

When Madame was tired, her English gave way to a heavier reliance on Russian and French. She articulated the final syllable in "ballet" as the Russians do, pronouncing it *ballyette,* and substituted her usual address to us, "my dear dancers," with the one she used during her years at the Paris Opera Ballet. The precise definition of her words may not have been clear to the newer dancers, but all of us understood the underlying meaning.

No one was better than Madame at uniting the company and inspiring us to work together. I noticed, however, with some dismay, that she didn't look directly at me. Our relationship went far deeper than that of coach and protégée. She'd become, in addition to my teacher, a friend and ally.

A sick feeling rose in my throat. There could be only one reason for Madame to avoid me. I'd bombed yesterday's rehearsal. My contract was up at the end of the summer, and a half dozen dancers were itching to take my place. Had Marty Sherrington instructed Madame to give me The Talk?

There was no worse situation than to be on the receiving end of a Talk.

Chats, unlike Talks, are good. Chats tell us we're getting a promotion or a lead role. Chats are about great reviews or exceptional performances. Talks are never good. They fall under two major categories. One is the Fat Talk. The other is the Farewell, or Retirement Talk.

During these, the company informs ballet dancers who know no life outside ABC that their services are no longer required. If you're important enough, they'll schedule a farewell performance, where you'll get showered with bouquets, a fitting reminder that you've attended the funeral of your career.

The discussions are rarely a surprise to the dancer or anyone else in the company. One day, you get the cast list for the new season and learn that a younger dancer's name appears instead of yours. You might find yourself relegated to minor roles or not performing for long stretches. Some older dancers prolong the agony. Others announce their retirement before the company does it for them. Age isn't the only factor, as injuries can end a career before it's properly begun.

Mirroring my black mood, the dark clouds of yesterday returned. They hovered over us, like a brooding commentary on the course of human events below. I ignored flicks of pain from my left knee, tossed back my head, and leaped onstage as I'd done a thousand, thousand times. The effect of this grand entrance, however, was lost when the now-recognizable sirens, warning of lightning, blared over the music. We raced backstage to collect our bags ahead of a second day of rain.

A golf cart pulled up to the stage to transport Madame back to the arts center. She insisted I ride with her. As the driver bumped us over the rutted path, she said, "We must talk. Come to my hotel with me."

When we arrived at the residence, I helped Madame out of the golf cart and said, "Can this wait an hour or two? I've got a few things to take care of first."

I wanted to make up for the regrettable decision to avoid my fellow dancers. The unexpected break in our rehearsal schedule would enable me to give an edited version of what happened, one that might silence some of the wilder stories now in circulation.

She cleared her throat. *"Nyet.* I fear not, Lelotchka. Now is better." Madame waited for me to change into street clothes, and when I returned to the lobby a taxi was waiting to take us to the Mayflower Hotel. I held an umbrella over our heads as fat raindrops began to fall.

The Mayflower had an old-world elegance very different from the rustic lodge where the dancers were housed. We arrived in time for tea, which the menu informed us was a featured attraction at the hotel since its opening in 1914. Next to champagne, it was Madame's favorite beverage, but she knew I preferred coffee and ordered both.

The waitress brought two silver pots and wheeled a tray to our table laden with sandwiches, delicate pastries, and crystal cups of fresh fruit. Madame, who prided herself on maintaining the same weight since girlhood, chose the fruit. I declined the offering, not because of dietary concerns, but because the knots in my stomach made eating impossible.

The coffee was hot and strong. I downed half a cup, which propped me up enough to face whatever headwinds were coming in my direction.

Madame stirred her tea and said, "Marty Sherrington, she is questioning me about you. She disapproves very much of your investigation into Leland's death. Marty also thinks maybe you want to give up dance to choreograph. These two things together, they are not good." She cocked her head at me. "I am *neprosty.* No, that is not right. I am *inquiète,* that is, how to say unquiet? Worried? English is not giving me the word I am feeling."

Marty knew Arabella had summoned me to discuss Leland's murder, though, to my knowledge, she was still in the dark about Leland's bequest. But the new director's message wasn't about murder or money. It was about me.

I kept my back straight and head high, as Madame didn't approve of slouched shoulders or slumped spines. "Is this Marty's way of telling me ABC won't renew my contract?"

"Perhaps. That day comes for us all. Has it come for you? With a different person in power, the answer would be no. But Marty Sherrington has what they call an agenda." She made a *pfui* sound, an indication of her low opinion of our interim director.

The pity in her eyes took my breath away, but I didn't allow grief to master me. "Don't worry about me, Madame. This wouldn't be the first time that someone wrote an early obituary for my career. Was it yesterday's rehearsal that prompted Marty's doubts? I saw her watching us today, but didn't see her then."

Madame dropped her teaspoon with an angry clink. "I do not know what goes on in the mind of Marty Sherrington, but your knee injuries are no secret. Not so easy to come back, if you are again hurt, and the role of Kitri needs steel."

Those traitorous knees stiffened, but I didn't let the pain show. I slapped a cheerful smile on my face and said, "Tell Marty I've never been better. If she wants to make herself useful, maybe she could find the person who vandalized my beautiful fan."

Three lines that creased her forehead deepened. "We think alike, Lelotchka. I tell her this, but she used it against me. Against us. Marty thinks it happened because you are involved with murder investigation. In her mind, if you go, the problems also go."

I thanked Madame for the coffee and rose from my chair. "I suspect Sierra and Hollis are at the bottom of this. I saw them talking to Marty earlier today."

Madame placed an arthritic hand on mine. "Tread carefully, dear Lelotchka. I am your friend, and I fear for you. Your career, yes, but also your safety. This might be the right time to choose what you will be in future. Ballerina? Choreographer? You also have the talent for investigation."

"I don't want to choose. I want everything."

Her tone was gentle. "This you will not get."

"I know. But I'm going to try." I looked through the window at the ceaseless rain. "I guess there's no performance tonight, but I want to be ready in case the weather clears."

Madame's eyes misted over. "There is no need. If we have performance, you will not dance Kitri." She tried to soften the blow. "But you will dance Mercedes. Is fantastic role for you. Always, you bring down the house. Next weekend, we shall see. Marty said perhaps you can alternate with Kerry."

Kerry and I were already scheduled to take turns dancing as Kitri and Mercedes. To an outsider, the change in dates would be inconsequential. A non-issue. But to lose the distinction of an opening night, starring performance, was a blow. It was as clear an indication of my decline as a banner headline: *Star Ballerina Upstaged by Conniving Rival.*

I could not let that happen. Somehow, some way, I'd rewrite that headline to read *Leah Siderova Triumphs in Don Quixote.*

Chapter Twenty-Seven

Someone need not be perfect to be a great dancer —
feeling a soul is more important than what the body can do.
—Marcia Haydée

When I exited the Mayflower Hotel, a doorman whistled to the first cab lined up along one side of a circular driveway. He held his umbrella over my head as I climbed into the car, though there wasn't much he could do about the ankle-deep puddles. I told the driver to take me to the arts center and instructed my sore heart and wounded pride to shut up and quit bothering me.

The woman behind the wheel was the same driver who took Madame and me to the hotel. She turned the wipers on high and said, "We haven't had a month like this since I don't know when. It's a killer for us locals. We depend on the summer trade."

I agreed that the rain was unusual and unfortunate. It was preferable to talking about other recent events that were too terrible to think about, let alone discuss.

The driver glanced into the rearview mirror and said, "You up here for the performance? If so, you might want to get yourself a rain check. The whole weekend looks like a washout."

I was pleased to stick with the weather as a topic. "Yes. I'm here for the performance."

She stopped at the town's single traffic light and turned to face me. "No way! You're that ballerina! Saw your picture in the newspaper this morning."

Shock kept me silent. I hadn't expected news of Jonathan's murder to appear in print so soon. "Do you have the paper? I haven't seen it."

She passed me a thin, tabloid-sized newspaper. "They got your picture right there on the front page, but *The New Trafford News* is a weekly. You want something more up to date, you get yourself a *New Haven Daily*."

Relieved that my chatty driver's interest in my identity was unconnected to my troubles offstage, I thanked her for the paper and read *The New Trafford News*. After checking out the photo of me and Tex on the front, I flipped through articles about an upcoming Fourth of July celebration, signups for kids' sports teams, and a recipe for corn chowder that would have eaten up three days' worth of allotted calories.

This pursuit took me to the gates of the arts center. As we rumbled over the dirt road, the driver said, "I wasn't going to bring it up, 'cause it's bad for business, but you musta heard about the murder at the Vanderhof place."

Lulled into thinking I was going to escape questions about Jonathan's murder, I was caught off guard and fumbled for an answer. "Yes. Yes, I did. A real tragedy."

"Did you know the guy? People are saying it was Ms. Vanderhof who killed him, but I don't believe it. Why would a rich lady who just lost her husband kill someone?"

"I don't believe she did."

I wasn't being coy, or loyal, or anything other than honest. Arabella had many unpleasant qualities, but if she'd wanted to kill Jonathan, she would have planned it better.

The car was moving so slowly, I could have walked the distance from the gates to the front door in less time. I tapped the half-open window between us and said, "You can let me off here. I need to stretch my legs."

The driver, a comfortably rounded woman of about forty, with curly hair and a white smile, obligingly came to a stop. I paid her, and she handed me her card. "Terry's Taxis. That's me. Anytime, day or night. It's a family business. No call for you to get an Uber. We'll get you where you need to go, and it'll cost you a lot less money."

I put the card in my purse and plowed through the puddles to the residence hall. The rain had slowed to a fine mist, but growls of thunder continued. I braced myself for the inevitable catty comments about Kerry taking over my role at the opening night performance.

The lie I planned to tell wasn't entirely divorced from the truth. I would claim the decision to step aside was mine, because my knees were acting up and I didn't want to risk another injury. This would fool no one but would allow me to save face.

These plans were rendered irrelevant when my phone pinged with a text message canceling the evening performance. Two hours earlier, the postponed opening would have been a bitter disappointment. It now felt like a stay of execution, although the relief was short-lived. It didn't matter if the change in cast hadn't yet been made public. Kerry would surely have broadcast the news the second Marty told her.

I skirted the bar and avoided shouts from a group of friends by pointing to my watch and acting as if I were late for an upcoming appointment.

Olivia followed me to the elevator. "What's so important that you don't have time for a drink? The performance was canceled, and we're drowning our sorrows."

"I'd love to, but I'm swamped. Going all out with an Excedrin dinner and a gallon of water before I head back to the city."

She struck a pose, raising both arms above her head. "Are you sure? Tex is with me. Together, we're one hot ticket."

I pretended to consider her invitation. "Hot? Some say not."

"Rude." She laughed and, in a softer tone, said, "How are you? You don't have to talk about anything, unless you want to."

I couldn't share the pain that gripped me, even with someone who knew me as well as Olivia. "I'm fine. Great. Really, really good. No worries whatsoever. If I didn't have a million things to do, I'd join you."

When she didn't answer, I filled her silence with truthful-sounding assurances. "I hate punking out on you, but my to-do list is out of control. I've got to finish choreographing a ballet that proves I was worthy of the Vanderhof Prize, find out who trashed me to Marty, and, oh yeah, figure out why Arabella summoned me to her house, where I found a dead body and a benefactor who's gone missing."

The elevator doors opened. I didn't ask Olivia to join me, but she stepped inside and said, "It'll kill the party if I leave, but for you, anything."

When we got to my room, I started packing. My friend pushed aside a stack of clothes to sit on the bed. "It's not like you to run away. The old Leah would be downstairs, working the crowd, and worming secrets out of people who won't know what hit them. What's gotten into you?"

"Coming here was a mistake. I should have taken a leave of absence from the company to concentrate on choreography. It would have spared me the humiliation of losing out on the opening night spot to Kerry. I can't face her or anyone else right now." The larger threat to my career I kept to myself.

"When you're finished boo-hooing, think about what I'm going through. You were younger than me when ABC promoted you to principal dancer. I'm stuck. If I left for another company, maybe I'd get the chance to prove what I can do, but then, I'd be giving up the dream I've had since I was five."

The bitterness in her voice took me aback. "You're a wonderful dancer, and your time will come. Be patient."

A resentful stranger took the place of my trusted friend. "You think you have problems? Kerry is obviously in line for a promotion. I'm still waiting. But if I wait too long, some long-legged teenager will take my job and I'll be out of work and out of luck."

My friend wasn't wrong about anything except her assumption that nothing could be done to improve her situation. "Talk to Madame. If it wasn't for her, I wouldn't have gotten the chances I did."

Olivia's voice hardened. "That's ancient history. I wasn't around then, but Madame says all the time how things are different now. It's not the same company as when you were René Vernier's golden girl. Madame M trained you, but he made you."

This was true. René Vernier founded ABC and led it for many years. One of his last official acts was to arrange a splashy debut in *Swan Lake* when I was twenty-two. After he retired, ABC had a series of short-term leaders, most of whom sought a more uniform look for its dancers than the eclectic one René championed. If any of the subsequent directors had been in charge when I was Olivia's age, my career might have taken a very different path.

I survived many leadership changes, as well as two knee surgeries, but reviews of my dancing now invariably included both acclaim and a cautionary note. Critics praised me for still having *It*, that intangible quality that made for exciting performances, but the implication was clear. When you still have it, the days of losing it aren't far off.

Olivia had always looked out for me. I should have done the same for her. Should have understood, without being told, that underneath her joking, she was hurting. If I hadn't been so wrapped up in myself, I would have known that.

She cut off my response, correctly anticipating what I would say next. "Marty Sherrington doesn't know I exist. And I'm not asking Madame M for anything. If you hung out more with the rest of us, you'd know she's on her way out. Marty is going to schedule Madame's retirement to coincide with the opening night gala."

The floor beneath me shifted, and I sat down hard. Madame Maksimova was as fixed in her position at ABC as the Empire State Building on 34th St. "I don't believe it. She's been with the company forever. She would have told me if she was leaving."

Olivia's face crumpled. "There won't be an official statement until September, but I think she's guessed what's coming. Haven't you noticed how cranky she's been in rehearsals?"

I had, but I attributed her irritability to arthritis. "How do you know this isn't more spiteful gossip?"

Her eyes were damp. "Sierra Younger bragged to a bunch of people that Marty offered her a job as interim coach. As bad as things are now, they'll be a million times worse with Sierra in charge. She keeps calling me Dolly Dinkle. Who even says that anymore? You'd think she'd go with a new insult."

My breath eased, and strength returned to my legs. "Now I know it's a lie. Marty would never replace a ballet legend like Madame with a wannabe who couldn't get on pointe if her life depended on it."

"Leah, it's time to face facts. You think preserving René Vernier's legacy is part of ABC's grand mission. It's not. Madame is too old school for Marty. She wants new blood."

Panic, confusion, anger, and fear would all have been appropriate reactions. I didn't feel any of them. Olivia's revelations crystallized and made clear what I had to do next.

I resumed packing and said, with deep regret, "I let you down, and I'm so sorry. But I swear, I'll make it up to you."

She braced herself against the door. "What are you going to do?"

"I'm going to find Arabella. She's at the center of every bad thing that's happened since the day I got that cursed Vanderhof Prize."

"What if you can't find her?"

"I'll make her come to me."

Chapter Twenty-Eight

The beautiful always retains the freshness of novelty while the astonishing soon grows tiresome.
—August Bournonville

I fished Terry's Taxi business card from my purse. She was thrilled to get a fare on that miserable evening and promised to get me to the station in time for the next train.

Olivia kept fighting my decision to leave. "If you walk out now, it'll confirm every rumor that you're too weak to dance. And when news about Madame's forced retirement hits, it'll be even worse."

Everything she said made sense in the world we used to inhabit. But that framework was history. One thing, however, still held true.

"You're my understudy for Mercedes. It's a great role, and you'll get the chance to show what you can do." I reminded her of our favorite joke, from the show *42nd St.,* 'You're going out a youngster, but you gotta come back a star!"

We'd mocked that line a thousand times, but Olivia didn't smile. "Nope. Not like this. I'm sorry if what I said made you feel like you had to bow out. I won't let you do it."

Her protests didn't hide the upswing of hope in her eyes. I didn't blame her a bit. I'd feel the same way. I kept my tone light. "You're not the boss of me."

She blocked the door and said, "I'll come with you."

In the transitional, transactional world of a competitive ballet company,

I'd found not one, but two true friends. I assured the one I almost lost that the second would have my back. "Gabi will help me in New York. You hold the fort here."

Olivia opened the door, and we rode the elevator together. "What can I do?"

"Tex is our best secret weapon. He's well on his way to becoming a legit star, and Sierra and Hollis will want him in their circle and on their side. Tell Tex to keep his distance from me. People know we're friends. But we're also onstage partners. He wouldn't be the first guy to trash-talk his ballerina behind her back, and if he does that, he'll earn their trust and we might learn something important."

Her dark eyes mirrored the stress in mine. "Leave it to me. And Tex."

I was on the cusp of telling her to be cautious in how much she confided in Tex when I decided to trust both of them to do the right thing. Giving up control was hard, but cramping their efforts before they started wouldn't help.

My genial cab driver, who'd ferried me from the Mayflower Hotel to the arts center after the disastrous meeting with Madame, entered the lobby. "You ready?"

I hugged Olivia and picked up my bag. "As ready as I'll ever be."

* * *

Although I had the luxury of solitude on the trip back to New York, memories of Leland and Jonathan haunted me. With no seatmate and no distractions, I stilled their competing voices and paged through my notes, trying to make sense of the baffling and violent episodes that had hurt so many.

These reflections didn't make for a pleasant trip, but, as the train pulled into Grand Central Terminal, some of the tension receded. I was home. Whatever challenges the city held, they would be in a setting that offered multiple escape routes and reliable cell phone service. No backroads and no dark forest, but as I passed through the doors of the train station, I remembered the uncomfortable feeling I'd had of being watched.

142

On this trip, however, no one inside the station or on the street gave me pause, and I felt free. Only Olivia knew where I was. Soon enough, I'd email Marty and Madame about my decision to skip the performance on the following evening, but for the moment, I reveled in anonymity. I texted Jonah my change in plans and asked if he was back in the city. Like me, he preferred conversations to texting and didn't ask for an explanation. **On my way to yr place.**

* * *

As I dragged my suitcase up the stairs, it occurred to me that the Vanderhof Building, where I now owned an apartment, had an elevator, a doorman, and a host of other amenities. It did not, however, have Mrs. Pargiter, who was on hand to greet me. My neighbor waited until I was nearly at her door before unhooking the chain lock that allowed a three-inch peek into the hallway. "Detective Sobol just got here. He has Farley. We have to watch his weight, so no snacks."

"Who's on a diet? Jonah or Farley?"

Mrs. Pargiter answered with great seriousness. "Farley. Detective Sobol is free to eat the cookies I made him."

I thought we were done, but she had more instructions. "Bring him back tomorrow morning. Farley, not Detective Sobol. We have a play date with Betty Boop that we don't want to miss."

Mrs. Pargiter would never favor me with the attention she lavished on my boyfriend, but thanks to the dog we shared, the situation between us had improved to the point that not every word out of her mouth was a complaint. I agreed to all she said and asked who Betty Boop was.

"Betty is Mr. Kim's new rescue dog, which you would know if you hadn't been off gallivanting to who-knows-where."

The word gallivanting, as I understood it, didn't match the torturous road I'd traveled, but I was too tired to justify my absence. After thanking her, I climbed to the top of the stairs, where Jonah and Farley were waiting.

The warmth of my lover's arms, accompanied by joyful yips from Farley, didn't erase the burdens that followed me from New Haven to New York. For a brief interlude, however, fears about Jonathan's murder, Arabella's disappearance, and the imminent implosion of my career receded.

I started to talk, to tell him all kinds of important things, when Jonah pulled me into the bedroom and stopped my words with his mouth. Heat from his embrace burned through me. Locked in his arms, we paused only to shut the door on a bewildered Farley.

The night was warm. Sweat and desire bonded us together. When Jonah's work phone chirped, I tried to detach myself from him, but one-armed, he kept me close. It was oddly erotic to hear him speak so evenly while feeling his body connected to mine.

The moment passed, as I knew it would, after hearing Carina's distinctive, husky voice on the other end of the call. Jonah let me go and told her, with all the emotion of a mailman delivering a package, "Yeah. Be there asap."

He stood up and rummaged in the pile of clothes on the floor. "Something's come up. I have to go."

I propped myself up on one elbow. "Will you be back tonight?"

He caressed my bare shoulder and kissed it. "You know the drill. Can't tell yet when I'll be done."

With no expectation that he'd take me up on the offer, I said, "Tell me where you're going. Maybe I can help."

"Maybe you can, but not tonight. What's your schedule like tomorrow?"

"After a morning ballet class, I'm going to run a few errands."

If he hadn't been in such a rush to leave me for his beautiful new partner, I would have been more explicit.

Chapter Twenty-Nine

The problem is not making up the steps but deciding which ones to keep.
—Mikhail Baryshnikov

The negative aspects of having a homicide detective as a boyfriend included late nights, an unpredictable schedule, and having to decode emotions from someone accomplished at hiding them. The positive side included insights that watching detective shows couldn't provide.

I learned quite a lot about effective interrogation techniques when I became the prime suspect in a murder case, which was how Jonah and I met. Most of what I knew came from him, but ballet gave me skills that proved unexpectedly useful. Cops have all kinds of tools to help them read people. Nail-biting, throat-clearing, and repeating questions before answering them are some of the basic tells.

Dancers, however, can detect signals telegraphed by an angle of the arm or placement of the feet. Those instincts enable us to control the movements of our bodies in ways that are more powerful than speech. The following day, I called Jonah before putting my skills to the test.

The tone of his voice told me he wasn't alone. I said, "I'll keep to yes-no questions. Have you and Carina interviewed Derrick Easton?"

"Yes."

I figured as much. Arabella's assistant had refused to tell me where he was on the night Jonathan died, probably because he didn't want to admit he'd left Connecticut earlier than he was supposed to. "Did he have any info on

Arabella? Any idea where she might be hiding out?"

"No."

"Did you believe him?"

"No comment. I'll get back to you later."

When a homicide detective tells you he'll get back to you later, a return call could happen in ten minutes or ten hours. Before conducting my next rehearsal, I had to make use of the little time I had to find Arabella.

After an early ballet class, my first stop was the townhouse where the Vanderhof Foundation had its offices. When the door opened, I expected to see the starched receptionist who greeted me on my first visit. I also wouldn't have been surprised if Derrick did the honors. I wasn't prepared, after an unusually long wait, to see Greta, the housekeeper at Arabella's Connecticut estate.

Her expression was tranquil, but she'd had time to compose herself. Greta's eyes told the real story. They were red-veined and puffy. Too little sleep was the probable cause.

She acted as if we hadn't met at all, let alone at the scene of Jonathan's murder. "The office is currently closed. Please call if you wish to make an appointment."

I stuck my foot in the door. "What are you doing here? I thought you were still in Connecticut."

"I could ask you the same thing." She spoke with admirable self-control but was careless enough to step back. I slid inside and said, "We both have our reasons for being here. It wouldn't surprise me if we wanted the same information."

Instead of waiting for an explanation, I surprised her and myself by bolting up the stairs. She followed, but not fast enough. "Where do you think you're going? Stop right there!"

I opened the polished wood door to Arabella's office without knocking. Derrick Easton was behind her desk.

He clicked his tongue in disapproval. "Shouldn't you be at the arts center?"

"Get Arabella. Now."

Rarely did I issue commands, and when I did, I always softened them with a *Would you please* or an *If you don't mind*. I deleted those polite intros with Derrick, because I wanted to convey strength. His posture, like Greta's, revealed a level of discomfort that was greater than an unanticipated visit from a very small ballerina could adequately explain. Arabella's assistant tapped his fingers at the bottom of the laptop, but he didn't make contact with the keys. Greta made slight gestures with her right hand in the way people do when they're talking, but she said nothing.

He rose from his chair and said, "Arabella isn't here. I'll give her the message when I see her."

Derrick walked to the door. I slid past him and behind the desk. On the computer screen was a picture of a sun-kissed lake surrounded by mountains. He reached over and closed the lid. "This is outrageous. I'm calling the cops if you don't leave immediately."

I could tell he was bluffing. "Don't bother. I'll call them. They're looking for Arabella, and I think you know where she is."

"I don't. And if I did, I wouldn't tell you." He exchanged a glance with Greta, one I couldn't decipher.

Greta's pupils dilated, and she said, in a more conciliatory tone, "Let me make you a cup of tea, and I'll explain."

Since Derrick's lips were closed in a stubborn line of resistance, I accepted the invitation and followed her down a long hallway. The townhouse, which Arabella and Leland used as an office for the Vanderhof Foundation, appeared deserted. We walked down marble steps and into the marble kitchen, which was large enough to accommodate an army of chefs.

The silence unsettled me. Where was the starched receptionist? Or the Vanderhof Foundation office workers, who'd tenanted those empty rooms at my previous visits? Greta's jittery movements further unnerved me, and I pondered escape routes, even as I tried to stifle my unhelpful imagination.

No one knew I was there. It was a mistake with an easy fix. I took out my phone and confirmed that Jonah could see my location, although that precaution was unlikely to help if Greta and Derrick decided to make me disappear as thoroughly as Arabella Vanderhof had. I sent him a text to be on the safe side.

His answer left no room for misinterpretation. **Leave.**

I did the next best thing. In a concerned voice, I told Greta, "I can't stay long. Detectives Sobol and Russo are expecting me. I told them I'm here."

This information had no apparent effect on the housekeeper. She turned her back to me and clattered about, taking cups and saucers from the cupboard and milk and lemon from the fridge.

In the cheerful, bright kitchen, I sat next to glass doors that looked out on a brick patio, furnished with lounge chairs and a picnic table under a striped awning. The backyard was bordered by other buildings. When Greta placed two steaming cups on the table, I suggested we sit outdoors.

She didn't budge. "Not a great idea. We have rats. The whole block is infested."

Rodents topped the list of things that terrified me. The next items, like fear of heights and fear of failure, didn't come close. I'd rather face a killer than a rat, which sounds irrational but isn't. You can reason with a person. You can't reason with a rat. If I ever had to go face-to-face with one, I was sure I'd pass out before getting bitten and dying of rabies, hopefully before regaining consciousness.

Without further argument, I sat across the table from Greta. I pretended to sip the tea, but when her back was turned, I spilled half into an aspidistra plant. According to my mother, nothing killed those.

Greta looked at me as if waiting for an answer, but I hadn't heard her question. She said, probably for the second time, "You shouldn't get yourself worked up over Ms. Vanderhof's disappearing act. She's done it before, you know. She'll resurface when she's ready. I told the detectives the same thing."

I added a spoonful of sugar to the remaining dregs of tea. It wouldn't matter how many empty calories I tossed into the foul-smelling brew, as I wouldn't be drinking any. "Did someone die the last time she disappeared?"

Tea dribbled out of the housekeeper's mouth. "No! What are you saying? Ms. Vanderhof has her own way of dealing with things. You'll see. Keep doing what you do, that dancing thing, or choreography, or whatever. Trust me, she doesn't want you poking into her affairs."

"The last time we spoke, you acted like you hated her. You told me you worked at her country estate and left out the part where you also worked at her office and penthouse. What else did you lie about or cover up? Were you at Leland's birthday party?"

She picked up her cup and saucer and dropped both into the sink. "Are you always this rude?"

The muscles in my back tensed. In those few beats of time, a creeping sensation that we weren't alone took possession of me. The kitchen was bright. No one was on the patio. As far as I knew, the only other person in the house was Derrick.

And yet, the walls in that beautiful kitchen felt as if they were closing in on me.

Chapter Thirty

Movement begins to negotiate the distance between the brain and the body
And it can be surprising what we learn about each other.
—Bill T. Jones

I wondered if the creepy sense that I was being watched was the result of an electronic eye or a human one. Nothing concrete spelled out danger, but I hurried to ask my questions and leave.

Without expecting much from Greta, I said, "Who told you about Leland's will? When did you find out you were a beneficiary?"

"What's that? When did I find out?" She scratched her head as if trying to summon the answer from her memory.

"Stop playing for time, Greta. I know you know."

She stuck out her chin. "I've known for ages. At least five years, probably more. Why do you think Derrick and I stuck it out this long? If it was up to Arabella, we'd'a gotten nothing. Leland made sure we were taken care of."

Greta's phone buzzed. She looked at it but didn't respond.

I slipped the rest of my tea into the uncomplaining aspidistra plant and asked for another cup. The second Greta's back was turned, I checked the message on her phone. It was from Derrick. The top line, in a font three times the size on my phone, said **Get rid of her.** It was impossible to see the rest of the text without unlocking the screen, but it was enough.

I didn't think Derrick wanted Greta to get rid of me permanently, but I wasn't brave enough to stay long enough to find out. And yes, maybe I would have accomplished heroic things if I had the courage of Superman and the wicked resolve of the Black Swan. I'll never know, because the sense, the smell, of danger was too strong for me to ignore. I jumped out of my seat, skated across the highly polished floors, and muttered an excuse about being late for something. When I was safely out of the townhouse, I ran down the block like a woman with two perfectly functioning knees. I didn't look back and didn't stop until I reached the corner, where I stepped in front of a burly guy with a briefcase and stole his cab.

It was an unforgivable breach of taxicab etiquette. For one scary minute, I thought he was going to pull me out of the car, but he desisted, perhaps because of the unfairness of the fight. He was twice my size, but I was three times as determined. When he slammed the door, the driver shot across two lanes of traffic to make the turn.

I called Jonah and said, "Can you meet me? Like, now?"

"Yes. Where?"

"Let's meet at the Figaro."

The swiftness of his response moved me more than a thousand *I love yous*. Without explanation, he understood the urgency of my need without tedious explanations.

* * *

Café Figaro was one of my favorite places in the world. The restaurant smelled of coffee, sugar, cinnamon, and citrus. The family who owned it was like a second family to me.

When I entered, Mrs. Pizzuto enveloped me in a hug. "Where have you been? Me and Mr. Pizzuto, we missed you. We saw your picture in the newspaper, and Mr. Pizzuto, he says, Well, Leah, she's busy, but I said, What are you talking about? Not too busy to visit old friends? I'm right, no?"

The warmth of her embrace reminded me of what I'd been missing. After hours—no, days—of being on my guard and acting a part, and worrying what other people were thinking and feeling, coming to the Café Figaro was like coming home. The restaurant was full, but Mrs. Pizzuto plucked a Reserved sign off a back table that she saved for family members and pulled out a chair.

She didn't bring a menu or ask what I wanted. After patting me on the shoulder and telling me I was too skinny, she brought a double espresso with a thick layer of foam and a platter of fresh fruit.

The strong coffee restored me, and when Jonah arrived, I was embarrassed at my irrational flight from the Vanderhof office.

Mrs. Pizzuto brought Jonah a cup of coffee and a plate of cannoli. She picked up my left hand and frowned at Jonah. "When are you going to make our Leah an honest woman? Say the word, and we can have the wedding here. I will make you a wedding cake like you wouldn't believe."

Jonah laughed. "Please, Mrs. Pizzuto, don't hold back. Tell us what you think."

He was teasing, but she was serious. "I think that when two people are in love, they don't talk, talk, talk. They get married. Have babies. What, you have a better plan?"

"No. That sounds fine to me." He picked up a napkin, twisted it in a circle, and put it on my finger. "What do you say, ballerina girl?"

"I say, let's eat." Talk of marriage made me nervous. Three self-described commitment-phobic ex-boyfriends married other women after dumping me. I understood why, but the experience had made me skittish. Dating a ballerina sounds glamorous, but most guys end up wanting a predictable schedule and future. I didn't want to jinx what I had with Jonah.

I waited until he vacuumed up the cannoli before telling him about my visit to the Vanderhof office. Skipping over the part where I'd felt threatened, I said, "Are Greta and Derrick on your list of suspects? They benefited from Leland's will and could have worked together to plot his murder. If Jonathon suspected them, that could have been their motive to kill him as well."

I steeled myself for a disapproving reaction, but he listened and took notes without comment. Every few minutes, he looked at the opposite wall, which was decorated with photographs of me. They were the work of Mrs. Pizzuto's daughter, who used them as part of her portfolio when she applied to college. The kid had talent. She got a full scholarship to art school, and I became an honorary member of the Pizzuto family.

I preferred the studio portraits, where my hair, makeup, and pointe shoes were without blemish. Jonah's favorite picture was the one I liked least. It was taken in Central Park, against one of the rocky outcroppings that dotted the landscape. On that cloudy day, my hair was loose and tangled and my tights a ragged mess. But it was the expression the camera's eye caught that bothered me. In it, my eyes looked too big, my cheeks too thin. I looked haunted, like some pathetic lost girl. I tried so hard to present a confident front, and this side of me was one I preferred to keep hidden.

I tugged at Jonah's sleeve to get him to look at me and not the imposter in the picture. He picked up the piece of napkin that he'd twisted into a ring and smoothed it out. I expected him to tell me to quit meddling.

But Jonah surprised me with a question I didn't see coming. He leaned back in his chair and said, "What's your plan for finding Arabella?"

I didn't have any ideas that rose to the level of being called a plan. "Derrick had a picture of a lake resort on his laptop. I think he and Greta know exactly where Arabella is, but are afraid to spill. Assuming Arabella hasn't been abducted, we could ask some of her friends if she's got a favorite vacation spot or retreat."

Mrs. Pizzuto, who knew what we wanted before we did, brought more coffee and a plate of pignoli cookies, warm from the oven. With a smile, Jonah told her, "You would have made a great detective. How did you know this is a three-dessert problem we're working on?"

When Mrs. Pizzuto left to attend to other customers, Jonah said, "Arabella's disappearance effectively releases you from any promise you made her. You can, with a clear conscience, quit."

"That's true, although I didn't need this latest development to convince me. On the night she disappeared, I'd already decided to bow out, whatever the cost. Now, I'm not so sure."

Jonah said, "Don't think I didn't notice that in the list of errands you shared with me, you didn't mention a side trip to the Vanderhof office."

My face got hot. "I didn't hide what I was doing. I texted you."

His face stayed cool. "You texted me after the fact, when it was too late for me to stop you or suggest a less risky strategy. How can we continue without that basic level of trust?"

The coffee turned bitter in my mouth. "I trust you, but it's not fair of you to pretend we're on an equal basis. Do you expect me to check in with you every time I make a move?"

"Yes. Because this isn't a ballet where you know the end before you start. It's literally life and death." His mouth was set in a grim line. "And now, I feel like we're back to where we were a year ago, with us working at cross purposes instead of together."

I locked up all the sloppy tears that threatened a jailbreak. If I didn't cry after Madame's End-of-Career-Talk, I wasn't going to do so now. Ballerinas who can't control their emotions in public end up getting eaten alive by scheming competitors like Kerry and hotshot choreographers like Sierra and Hollis. And, maybe, by people like Arabella Vanderhof as well.

Jonah frowned at me. "What are you thinking? When you get that look on your face, I can't tell what's going on inside you."

I couldn't bring myself to tell him how badly his words hurt me, any more than I could tell him about how badly I'd danced in rehearsal. A discussion about the choreography competition offered a way to talk about my career without having to relive the humiliation of getting pushed aside by Kerry.

"Three people founded the Poppy Vanderhof Prize for Choreography. Others sit on the board, but Leland, Jonathan, and Arabella were the driving force behind it. Who knows what'll happen without them?"

He closed his notebook and signaled to Mrs. Pizzuto to bring the check. "Would delaying the prize and all the hoopla be so bad? From where I'm sitting, it seems like the right move."

"It would be a disaster for me. Everyone thinks my career as a dancer and choreographer are independent of each other, but they're not. I'm pretty sure the reason I got the Vanderhof Prize was because I had a bigger name than the other applicants. Sierra and Hollis have thrown it in my face over and over again, and you know what? They're probably right."

Jonah's dark, hooded eyes fixed on mine. "I don't believe it. I think they picked the best they could find, ballerina girl. And that's you. But even if all you're telling me is true, what's the harm in performing with ABC until the

Foundation sorts things out?"

Talking about emotions and problems worked fine for a lot of people, but not for me. I felt worse, not better, because saying the words made it more real. "I'm in a ballet version of Catch 22. I got the finalist nomination because of my dance career. But Marty Sherrington has made the future of my dance career dependent on getting the top prize."

He stood up and paid the bill, over Mrs. Pizzuto's strenuous protests. She thought she still owed me for posing for her daughter in Central Park on a cold and damp day. When he returned, he said, "In that case, let's find Arabella."

Chapter Thirty-One

People tend to look at dancers like we are these little jewels, little cardboard
cut-outs, and yet we have blood and guts and go through Hell.
—Susan Jaffe

I sat with Jonah at his kitchen table and reviewed a list of people who were in the vicinity of the Vee Arts Center when Jonathan Franklin died and Arabella disappeared. My lineup of suspects had Greta and Derrick as strong contenders, but I kept going back to Sierra and Hollis, for reasons that had nothing to do with a possible motive for murder.

Jonah clasped my hand to quiet a nervous tap dance my fingers were executing on the tabletop. "I don't doubt Sierra and Hollis are hiding something. Same with Derrick and Greta. Everyone lies, but it doesn't mean they broke any laws. None appears to benefit from Jonathan's death."

A slow, hot rage built inside me. "I think Sierra and Hollis tore apart my fan, and then, to rub salt in the wound, retrieved what was left of it to hang on my doorknob. They've been trying to intimidate me since the day we met."

The anger subsided as I realized how I could use my rival choreographers' actions against them. "Sierra and Hollis have been cozying up to Marty Sherrington, hoping to get hired at ABC. If I can prove they stole the fan, it'll drive a stake into the heart of their ambitions. It might also disqualify them for the Vanderhof Prize."

His voice was gentle. "Assuming you're right, how much energy do you want to invest in getting revenge against them? When this case is resolved, nail them if you can."

Logic was on his side, but I wasn't. The dismemberment of an inanimate object paled next to fatal attacks on two people, but what if they were connected?

Since we had no evidence as yet to link the events, I copied from Jonah's notebook the names of people who stayed at the Mayflower Hotel. These included Derrick Easton, Antoine Moreau, Marty and Neil Sherrington, and two others whose presence surprised me. "Why did you include Madame M and Olga?"

"They're not suspects, but they are potential witnesses. Not much gets by Olga." Jonah leaned back in his chair and, as was his habit when he was thinking things through, studied the ceiling for answers.

I hadn't spoken to Madame since our post-rehearsal meeting at the Mayflower Hotel Tea Room. "Did anyone have information about Arabella?"

Jonah tossed his pen on the table. "According to Derrick Easton, this isn't the first time she's gone off the grid. He said when she's feeling stressed, she goes to some high-end retreat, where she can recover from the pressure of having more money than a small country. He must have been checking it out when you interrupted him."

"Greta said the same thing to me. I don't trust either of them." I wished I knew something more concrete to use against Arabella's housekeeper and assistant.

I told Jonah about the cryptic text Derrick sent Greta *Get rid of her,* but had to admit it fell short of conclusive evidence for anything other than his desire to, well, get rid of me.

Jonah flipped through his notebook. "Derrick isn't the most likable guy, but he's been working for Arabella for years and claimed the first time she went AWOL and he reported her missing, it almost got him fired."

I looked over his shoulder at his neat handwriting. "Where did Arabella go last time?"

He turned the page and read, "Kämp Spa and Wellness Clinic in upstate New York."

I looked it up, and there it was. The same place I saw on Derrick's laptop.

Jonah tried to tamp down my excitement. "Carina contacted them, and Arabella's name isn't on the register. If she came incognito and in disguise, she still would have had to use a credit card with her name. Believe me, Leah, we're doing all we can with the resources we have. I've combed through—"

His phone interrupted us, as it so often did. This time, however, it wasn't work that took him away.

When the call came in, he left me in the kitchen and walked into the bedroom. I would never eavesdrop on a conversation Jonah didn't want to share with me and therefore didn't follow him and press my ear against the wall. On the other hand, I saw no reason not to stand a few feet away and hold my breath.

I heard him mutter, "Yes. No. I didn't forget. I'll, um, I'll be there in an hour. Something came up at work. Okay. I love you too."

I returned to the kitchen before he could catch me lurking and called out, "Is everything okay?"

He stuck his head in the doorway and said, "I forgot I was supposed to be someplace tonight. Wait here for me. I won't be late."

"Is this about the murder case? Or Arabella?" I tried to keep a dispassionate tone and expression, but it was a challenge. With how many people did he end conversations with *I love you too?*

Jonah stomped into the bedroom and yanked a pair of pants and a shirt from the closet. "I promised my mother I'd go to a party at the neighbor's house. Don't ask me why."

I was relieved that his *I love you* wasn't intended for a different girlfriend. If he wanted to go to a party without me, well, fine. We were two independent adults with lives that extended beyond our relationship.

Jonah rubbed the stubble on his chin, and I followed him into the bathroom as he turned on the shower. Speaking over the rush of water, I said, "Since you won't be here, I'll ask someone else to help me find Arabella."

He pulled the shower curtain aside. Although I was still dressed, in a tank top and shorts, he grabbed me and pulled me in with him.

I gasped as the cold water hit my warm skin. "Let me go! What are you, some kind of polar bear?"

"Nope. I'm not a polar bear any more than you're a spy. Did you think I didn't know you were listening in? Here's a lesson for you, before you make the same mistake with someone who doesn't love you as I do: Don't attempt to surprise people on their own turf. I know every breath of air, every tiny creak in the floor. You might as well have been wearing combat boots and flashing a light ahead of you."

There was no way to maintain dignity while standing in wet clothes. I stripped them off and said, "What's the price of admission to this hot-ticket party at your mom's house? It must be high, since you didn't invite me."

He turned off the water and handed me a towel. "These are my mother's friends. You'd be bored to death. Trust me, I'm going to be bored to death. I won't be long."

On a different night, or at another time, having Jonah abandon me for a party at his parents' house might not have hit so hard. But I'd spent days in a paranoid muddle about my career and my future and, at this vulnerable juncture, that same insecure perspective shook my assumptions about our relationship. Jonah had met my parents many times. I'd never met his.

I stalked back to the bedroom and said, "Is your mother still trying to hook you up with the girl next door?"

The pause before his answer was as eloquent as a *yes*, but what he said was, "Leah, be reasonable. You weren't supposed to get back to the city until tomorrow, and this isn't your type of scene."

I finished toweling off and pulled fresh clothes from a drawer he'd emptied for me. "What is my type of scene? And don't tell me it's hanging at some glam party, because you know I hate them."

My days and nights were so busy, it never before occurred to me that I hadn't met many of Jonah's friends, other than a few coworkers. Most of those interactions tended toward the investigative rather than the social.

Jonah's schedule was as packed as mine, and tougher, because it was more unpredictable. For some couples, those limitations might be problematic, but I wondered if not being able to see each other as much as we wanted to was part of the reason we'd lasted so long.

Discussions about marriage never got more serious than the paper napkin ring he fashioned for me at the Café Figaro. My track record with men, as my mother frequently observed, wasn't good.

The bond I shared with Jonah was different from the epic failures that littered my past. I didn't care when Matt told me he was a confirmed bachelor and six months later, wed a woman he'd started seeing before we broke up. Shortly after their destination wedding, they moved to a Brooklyn brownstone and started having gifted children. I didn't understand, until events made them plain, that when Matt said he didn't want to get married and have kids, what he meant was he didn't want to get married and have kids with me.

My pride suffered a minor blow, but my heart didn't break. His disloyalty hurt, but I spilled more tears over my knee surgery than I ever did over him. Zach was the next man to enter my life. He also left me for another woman, in his case, his ex-wife.

But Jonah? I couldn't bear losing him. Not to the girl next door and not to Carina Russo, his new partner.

He seemed to hear what I didn't tell him and said, "Get dressed, and you can see what you're not missing."

I kissed him and told him to give my regards to his parents.

Jonah hesitated. "Are you sure?"

I pushed him out the door. "Positive. I've got work to do."

His dark brows formed a single line. "If you're planning any more trips like the one you took today to see Arabella, I'm going with you."

"I don't need to leave the house to get this work done. Now leave, before I change my mind."

With a look that said he didn't quite believe me, he left.

* * *

I got to work. If Arabella had voluntarily gone into hiding, perhaps the reason for that decision, and a clue to where she was, lay in her past and not her present. I had a vague memory of hearing her say she'd trained as a dancer, but I didn't know about her career as an actress until Greta told me.

What had Greta said?   She mentioned a commercial for something stomach-related and a stint on a soap opera. I flipped through my notes and found it. Alka Seltzer and Pepto Bismol. Pre-Vanderhof, Arabella's last name was Hellman, although I didn't know if that was her unmarried name or a stage name. Hours of random searches turned up nothing, other than an astonishing number of YouTube videos of old TV commercials. My deep dive into shows from the 1990s was similarly futile. I scanned the cast members for daytime soap operas like *General Hospital, The Young and the Restless*, and *All My Children*.

My best bet was to wait until morning and ask Jonah to check marriage records for an Arabella Hellman. He could surely get it done faster than a civilian like me. I turned out the light but couldn't get my brain to stop buzzing. Jonah predicted a boring party and an early exit, but at midnight, he hadn't returned.

And then, inspiration struck. I jumped out of bed and searched for evening soaps. After scrolling through episodes of *Dynasty* and *Knots Landing,* I combed through TV series of a later date and found Arabella in the pilot of a short-lived dramedy called *Subway Stops*. It followed the lives and loves of four women and was a less successful version of *Sex and the City*. The show lasted only one season, but there were pages of photos on Picture-It. Although Arabella was much younger, that aquiline nose, platinum hair, and thin lips were unmistakable.

So was her stage name: Arabella Sherrington.

Marty said she and Arabella were old friends and shared a long history. She didn't tell me she'd married Arabella's former husband.

Chapter Thirty-Two

Choreography is simpler than you think.
Just go and do, and don't think so much about it. Just make something interesting.
—George Balanchine

Jonah didn't return until two am. The second I heard his key in the lock, I jumped out of bed.

He held up one hand, as if to head off a complaint. "I wanted to get back sooner, but couldn't get away. And then, there was an accident on the BQE, which—"

I drew him back to the kitchen table. "That doesn't matter. I hope it was fun." Neither statement reflected my true feelings, but discussing Arabella's former marriage to Marty's current husband couldn't wait.

Jonah poured a glass of water and gulped it down. "We know about the marriage. Carina doesn't think it's relevant to this investigation, but I don't agree. It's made me take a closer look at Neil Sherrington. What if two women dumped him for the same guy? That had to hurt. The second murder could have been collateral damage. Neil and Marty were at the Mayflower Hotel when Jonathan died. They alibied each other, which doesn't count for much."

It was difficult to separate the facts from the rumors. "I never saw much affection between Marty and Leland. I'm also not convinced a flirtation with an eighty-year-old man would drive Marty's very laid-back husband to commit murder."

Jonah said, "Neil is always in the background but never out of the picture.

How well do you know him?"

"We only met once, at the funeral reception. The guy was all over me, and I was worried Marty would start to hate me the way Bobbie York does, and for the same reason. It's bad to have the costume mistress think you're angling for her husband, but fatal if your boss thinks you're making a play for hers."

He refilled his glass with tap water. "Was Marty resentful or angry?"

"If she was, I couldn't tell. But she's got a great poker face and could have been seething underneath. Maybe Neil is the reason she wants to get rid of me." Realizing I'd said too much, I rushed to cover up. "I've heard Marty wants to fire Madame, though she hasn't gone public with an announcement. Olivia said ABC is planning a big retirement celebration that Madame will pretend she wants but will break her heart."

Jonah put his hands on my shoulders. "Why didn't you tell me about this earlier? You spent all afternoon talking about Arabella and half the night searching for clues, but you never mentioned the thing you care about most."

Unable to stay still, I started pacing, a habit I'd had since childhood. This need for movement was what drove Barbara to enroll me in a ballet class. Ballet did help tame that unquenchable energy, but when I was upset, the urge for a physical outlet returned. "I'm more worried about Madame than I am about myself. ABC is her whole life. This will kill her."

Jonah didn't try to stop my restless trek. "It won't kill Madame. But it looks as if it's killing you."

I tripped over a nonexistent break in the floor, a dead giveaway to how I was feeling. "My role with the company isn't important compared to everything else, so let's concentrate on that. It makes sense that the same person who murdered Leland also killed Jonathan. Who benefits from their deaths? Love and money are supposed to be the prime reasons for murder. How do they figure in this case?"

Although it was late and we were both tired, we returned to our accustomed places at the kitchen table. Jonah said, "Love and money are a good start, but there's also ambition, revenge, and blackmail."

Arabella's failed marriage to Neil Sherrington, which an hour earlier had seemed so important, now felt less so. "Aside from Derrick and Greta, if we think money was the motive, my vote goes to Terrence Benson. Although he's rich and successful, with Leland out of the way, he can marry Arabella and get into a whole new tax bracket."

Jonah yawned. "He's not as flush as you might think. We checked his financials, and they're not good. Terrence invested a ton of money in a third store right before the pandemic hit. If he'd parked his money in residential buildings, he'd be sitting pretty, but he's had to sell his other two places at a loss to keep his design business in the black."

The designer had been twitchy and temperamental before the performance at Leland's birthday party, but I'd worked with plenty of artists who were a lot worse. "Terrence had the opportunity to kill Leland, but what about Jonathan? If he was at the arts center, I didn't see him."

"Terrence claims he never left the city but has no alibi. Said he was working at home on costumes for the Vanderhof Prize choreographers."

I sighed, thinking of the costumes Terrence had designed for ABC's most recent ballet. "He might be the darling of Paris and Milan, but his designs for ballerinas are among the worst I've seen."

Jonah said, "They looked pretty good to me. Especially yours."

"Flattery will get you anywhere."

He gave me a long, lazy smile. "I'm thinking the bedroom."

* * *

I woke up to an email glut that included a High Importance message from Derrick Easton. In it, he informed me, Sierra, and Hollis that the board of directors had conducted an emergency meeting and voted to proceed with the Poppy Vanderhof Choreography Competition as planned. He would be the new director of the program and report to Marty. Greta was now a special assistant. A new slate of judges would be appointed shortly.

I hoped the new judges would be impartial, but I was prepared for the opposite to be true. The dance world, like the social sphere that included families like the Vanderhofs and Franklins, was small. Everyone knew, or knew of, everyone else. If favors, friendships, and divided loyalties played a role in the judges' decisions, it would surprise no one.

I read the email to Jonah and said, "Derrick and Greta now have the best motive of anyone to have killed Leland and Jonathan, and maybe Arabella as well."

* * *

Although I was weary from too little sleep and too many warring ideas inside my head, I headed to the rehearsal studio hours before my scheduled time slot. The Vanderhof Foundation's largesse provided the choreographers with all-day access to a practice room but only a two-hour rehearsal with our dancers. This wasn't enough time for a novice like me. I was still figuring out the logistics of how they would enter and exit. This was the kind of thing I took for granted when someone else was choreographing.

Antoine Moreau was an almost invisible presence, and his camera crew was equally discreet. They were so skilled at blending in I almost forgot they were there, which was, I guessed, the intended effect. Other onlookers were more intrusive. Sierra, Hollis, and their dancers lingered on the sidelines. They whispered, pointed, and reacted to an inaudible comment by Sierra with muffled laughter.

I suppressed my anxiety about transferring the images in my head onto a group of flesh-and-blood people. Clapping my hands three times, as Madame did, I spoke with as much authority as I could muster. "Anyone not in my ballet has to leave or be silent. I don't want any distractions."

This wasn't my usual mode of behavior or address, and I surprised myself, as well as Sierra and Hollis. Their dancers apologized and left. They were used to being told what to do. My rival choreographers, however, didn't budge. I stood, my hands on my hips, and waited. When they didn't leave, I said, "You're wasting my rehearsal time. I will redeem the lost minutes from your sessions."

Sierra, with insolent slowness, picked up her bag and sauntered toward the door. Hollis followed, and after pointedly ignoring Olivia, whispered something to Gabi, who nodded and laughed. I was pleased to see that Gabi had infiltrated their closed circle, but didn't, by so much as a flicker of a smile, acknowledge what happened.

All in all, I felt pretty good about how I handled the situation until I realized Antoine Moreau had filmed every bit of it. I could see it now: a clip of me clapping my hands and giving orders like, well, like a million other choreographers who were a lot higher on the food chain than I was.

Hashtag me miserable.

Chapter Thirty-Three

To dance is to take part in the cosmic control of the world.
—Havelock Ellis

At the end of my rehearsal, I left the studio to change into street clothes. Gabi was about to enter the elevator when I stopped her. She held the door open and said, "We need to talk, but I have to get home before Lucie and my husband forget I live with them. I'll call later."

I was disappointed, as I was impatient to pump her about what Hollis had whispered in her ear. He shared with Sierra an unpleasant sense of humor, and I didn't put it past either of them to brag about destroying my fan.

With Gabi unavailable, I cast about for a different confidante, someone with knowledge of the major players but without a personal agenda. Because Jonah wouldn't be free until the evening, I called Barbara. My mother's ability to slice through thickets of nonessential information and get to the heart of complicated relationships was exactly what I needed.

Barbara answered a millisecond before her voicemail picked up. "Leah! Darling! How lovely to hear your voice."

Something about her tone seemed off. The words were familiar, but she sounded different. Guarded, which she never was.

I checked the time and said, "Are you free for dinner? Let's meet at the Lincoln Center Diner, and we can debrief. A lot has happened."

Barbara, who was a fast talker, even for a native New Yorker, was slow to answer. "I'd love to, but I've got plans."

"What's his name?"

The sound of her vape crackled in my ear. "Who, darling? I don't know what you're talking about."

"Barbara, please don't make me jump through hoops. Who is he, and what's his name? Unless this is another online hookup? If that's the case, take Aunt Rachel with you, and don't let him in the house."

With apparent sincerity, she said, "I swear there is no man in my life. I simply have plans with a friend. A female friend."

I gave up. "Enjoy your evening. What about tomorrow? I can stop by after ballet class."

The hiss of her vape got louder. "So tempting! But I must decline. I'm under deadline to deliver *The Gaming of the Clue*. It's getting so tiresome coming up with punny names for Shakespeare plays, but I do like this one. Professor Romanova is in fine form. I think my agent will be pleased. I'll send it to you."

This had never happened before. There was nothing my mother liked better than to ponder solutions to real-life murder cases while quoting obscure passages from Shakespeare, Chaucer, and her fictional amateur sleuth. I was at a loss as to what she might be hiding and told her so. "The last time we spoke, you couldn't stop talking about Leland's death. And now Jonathan Llewellyn Franklin is also dead, and you're not interested in meeting? I'm not buying it. What's up?"

"Leah, my darling, always the drama queen! I'll call tomorrow. Or maybe the next day. Don't worry and, well, don't worry. And, um, don't come by the apartment. I'll let you know when I get back."

"Where are you?"

After a long pause, Barbara said, "I'm at a writers' retreat in a town in the Adirondacks that I can't quite remember the name of. Rustic, but charming, and the scenery is spectacular. I should be home soon. So, like I say, don't call me. I'll call you. And don't come to my place, because I won't be there."

I heard tinkling noises and what sounded like the hiss of steam, followed by a splash of water. "You sound like you're at a spa."

She laughed with an unconvincing *ha-ha*. "I wish! Gotta go!"

* * *

I took the subway back to my apartment. The crush of too many bodies in too small a space was uncomfortable, but not as uncomfortable as the conversation with Barbara. Most writing retreats were located in rural areas where people got inspiration from Nature. My mother loathed the outdoors and claimed too much fresh air gave her hives. She preferred wine bars, cafes, and the Lincoln Center Diner. When she was writing, you couldn't blast her away from her desk.

When I got home, I contemplated my next move. Jonah was working. My mother was involved in some activity she didn't want to share with me. Olivia and Tex had left rehearsal together and didn't look as though they'd welcome a third. Gabi was with her family.

I was hungry and opened a can of soup, because cooking anything more elaborate was beyond my capabilities. The oven got so little use, I stored extra leotards and tights in it. The air was hot and sticky, and I opened all the windows.

My brain, as well as my body, needed a break, and I began reading Barbara's latest mystery. Professor Romanova, for the tenth time, stumbled over a dead body and called the hunky police chief, who found nothing unusual in the fact that an English teacher discovered a murder victim every September.

I was deep into the book and a quarter way through the soup when my phone pinged with a text. I didn't recognize the sender's number. There were no words to accompany the picture, and it took a minute for me to identify the object in the photo. When I did, goosebumps popped out on my arms, despite the heat. The photo was a close-up of my mutilated fan. Thin white sticks with remnants of red silk looked like fingers dipped in blood.

I closed the windows, turned on the air conditioner, and forwarded the text to Jonah, who said he wouldn't be home for hours and not to leave the apartment. I felt like a sitting duck. A sitting cooked duck, as the air conditioner wheezed, coughed, and died.

My phone brightened with a call from another unfamiliar number. I stared at the screen. Should I answer it? Ignore it? I swiped right but didn't say anything. Let the caller make the first move.

An accented voice on the other end said, "Leah? Is this the phone that is Leah?"

I was so relieved to hear a familiar person on the other end, the phone slid in my sweaty hands. "Hello, Antoine. What can I do for you?"

"You can allow me to take you to dinner. I'm staying at a friend's apartment a few blocks from you. Would you like to meet at Sami's?"

I looked at the congealed soup. The heat in the apartment kept it from getting cold, but it didn't appeal. The choice between dinner in an air-conditioned restaurant with an award-winning filmmaker and melting in a fifth-story apartment waiting for another creepy text was easy.

I said yes. It didn't cross my mind to ask how he knew where I lived.

Chapter Thirty-Four

Ballet is the one form of theater where nobody speaks a foolish word all evening,
nobody on the stage at least.
—Edwin Denby

I headed toward Broadway and my dinner with Antoine, feeling a lot more secure in my neighborhood than on the wooded paths at the arts center. A beacon of safety, should I need one, was right down the block. Mr. Kim, the owner of the bodega on the corner, was a self-appointed, one-man neighborhood watch.

I stopped by the store to say hello to him and to pick up some of the zero-sugar, probably unhealthy, but delicious candies he stocked for me. A small, curly-haired mutt with dark, intelligent eyes that looked a lot like Mr. Kim's greeted me from behind the counter.

I stroked the dog's silky fur and said, "You must be Betty."

Mr. Kim nodded and took three boxes of licorice candies from a drawer beneath the cash register. "You haven't been here in so long, I had to hide them so I didn't run out."

I thanked him and said, "It's good for you to have company."

His cheeks turned pink when Mrs. Pargiter, with Farley in tow, entered the store. She tried to maintain her usual disapproving expression, but couldn't manage it when Mr. Kim shyly kissed her. If I hadn't seen it for myself, I wouldn't have believed that stern Mrs. Pargiter and genial Mr. Kim had anything in common. Maybe it was their shared love of dogs that brought them together.

I left the bodega and headed down the block to Sami's. Although the restaurant was crowded, Antoine wasn't hard to find. His long, rangy body towered above people crouched over their drinks. He kissed me on both cheeks. I wasn't expecting so familiar a greeting. During rehearsals, he favored me with no more than a nod.

He signaled to a waiter, who brought us to a small table wedged between two other small tables. I ordered sparkling water while Antoine studied the menu. After many visits, I knew every dish they offered and decided on a Caesar salad. I'm not a big or adventurous eater and was pleased to be spared a fancy meal, filled with unrecognizable ingredients. Antoine ordered a burger and onion rings. After looking over the wine list, he grimaced and ordered a beer.

I downed most of my water and said, "Why did you want to meet me? Is this about your movie or something else?"

His eyes crinkled. "Does a man have to have a reason to invite a beautiful woman to dinner?"

Ugh. Not a good start. "Actually, yes, when the man and woman in question have a professional relationship."

Undisturbed, he leaned back and crossed his legs, which couldn't have been easy, given how tight his jeans were. "In that case, let us talk business. The film I planned has taken a different turn. It is now, most improbably, a murder mystery. And you seem to be at the heart of it. Start by telling me about Leland. Who were his friends? Who opposed him? What were his secret likes and dislikes? You were closer to him than Sierra or Hollis."

I was disappointed at his invitation to dish dirt. Leland and I often discussed ballet movies, from documentaries about the Ballet Russe to lurid Hollywood fantasies. Maybe it was too much to expect that a hotshot director would care what a ballerina thought about capturing dance on film.

I ignored his question about Leland and said, "How do you plan to make this a murder mystery if you're only filming the dancers?"

"You mistake me. I talk to everyone involved in the process. The exception is Arabella Vanderhof, who is, no doubt, too grieved to talk about her husband." He shot me a sharp look that didn't sync with his easy posture, and said, "Arabella's assistant, however, has agreed to an interview. He should provide interesting context."

It was a good call. Derrick Easton would indeed provide plenty of context if he were the killer.

The waiter arrived with our food. My dinner partner ate as if his last meal was last week, but I found myself without much appetite, for him or the salad. "Who besides Derrick and the dancers are you interviewing?"

Antoine tapped a few notes into his phone. "Terrence Benson, the designer. He is Arabella's lover, no?"

"That's the general opinion, but I don't depend on rumors for information, and their relationship may not have anything to do with the murders."

He took a long pull from his beer. "I hope my other subjects are not as clever as you at withholding information. It makes me wonder what secrets you're hiding." Antoine brushed aside my protest and said, "Perhaps it is Leland you're protecting? Your relationship with him was," he paused to give me a lascivious wink, "close."

So much for subtlety. In hoping he'd underestimate me, I'd underestimated him. "Leland and I were friends, nothing more. As for the rest, I can't tell you what I don't know. All I can do is help you sift through information you get from others. What have you learned so far?"

He ordered a second beer. "In other words, you want me to reveal all without giving me anything. *Bon.* Let's talk, then, about Sierra and Hollis. There appears to be…how do you say it? No love lost between you and them."

I wondered if this was his true purpose in questioning me. Maybe his talk about the murders was a ploy to distract me, and what he wanted was the kind of raucous conflict that was a staple of reality shows. I said, affecting indifference, "You've seen them in action. By now, I expect you've formed an opinion about us all."

"Once again, you haven't answered my question. And that, by itself, intrigues me." His unblinking stare and dry tone ceased to be amusing. It felt menacing.

"I don't know what you're after." This, more than anything else I told him, was the truth.

"Your colleagues are not so circumspect. They believe you got the Vanderhof Prize because you were having sex with Leland." He held his palms up like a sleazy magician showing the audience *See? Nothing up my sleeve.*

I didn't fall for his attempt at misdirection. "Sierra and Hollis think that by trashing me, they'll improve their chances of winning and getting featured in your movie." I reached across the table and drank his untouched water. "I'm surprised you fell for it. Is that what this dinner is all about? An audition for the starring role? If so, you're wasting your time."

Antoine's veneer of Gallic savoir-faire didn't alter, and his amused smile stayed fixed. But the pupils of his eyes dilated, and a muscle in his forearm tensed. His lovely French accent deepened, which was another tell. "As I said from the start, I need no excuse to dine with a beautiful woman. And if that woman is as photogenic as you, so much the better. As you say in America, the eye of the camera, it loves you. And that camera will continue to follow you, which I know you will appreciate."

The ice underneath those warm words chilled me. Antoine had the upper hand and knew it. I signaled for the check and said, "There's no point in dangling a starring role in front of me, thinking I'll bite, because I won't. If the fix is in, so be it."

Antoine insisted on picking up the tab, and I let him. As usual, I didn't have much cash in my purse, and I could see he was determined to have his way. I left before the waiter returned his credit card, but he caught up with me.

I refused his offer to walk me home and said, "How did you know where I live?"

"It is my business to know things." He flicked at his phone to reveal a picture of the mangled, red silk fan.

My choked questions elicited maddeningly vague answers. He denied texting me the image and said, "I was taking stills and did not know why this broken stage prop was backstage. Maybe now you will tell me what I want to know?"

"I haven't a clue."

Chapter Thirty-Five

Dancing and ballets would undoubtedly take on a new lease on life if the customs established by a spirit of fear and jealousy did not in some way close the path of glory...
—J.G. Noverre

I never wished for a different career, but, as the morning sun brightened a dark and restless night, I wished the one that chose me didn't consume every waking moment. An obsession with perfection, which was endemic among ballerinas, had become a burden I couldn't put down. When I wasn't physically dancing, I analyzed how I could do better, be better, look better. Choreographing a new ballet inflamed all those nervous habits. The music beat its familiar rhythm in my ears, and the sequence of steps waltzed around my brain in endless circles.

Ideally, I would keep my professional goals separate from the homicide investigation, but the confluence of people and events made that impossible. My notes on the murders were interspersed with tiny, penciled-in stick figures that pirouetted around the page, a nervous contrast to Jonah's neat columns and diagrams.

I was filled with doubt about the direction that the investigation and the ballet were taking. After my dinner with Antoine, the uncomfortable feeling that I'd made an embarrassing mess of both was a further torment. This emotion wasn't new. It followed me whenever I failed to do or say the right thing at the right time. Antoine and I hadn't argued, but I had the achy, unsatisfied feeling one gets after a fight, when all the punchy comebacks you should have said but didn't come back to haunt you.

His photo of my wrecked fan rattled me. I texted Jonah without thinking through how the spare explanation might affect him.

He called me back seconds later. "Why were you out on a date with Antoine? Yet another bad idea, Leah."

His reprimand, combined with the hot and sticky air inside my apartment, sent rivulets of sweat down my face and back. I mopped perspiration from my forehead and said, "I came to that conclusion five minutes after we met, but changed my mind after he showed me the picture. We now know Antoine has been shadowing all of us Vanderhof finalists, even when we don't know he's there. Will you requisition the rest of his photos? He might have captured something important without realizing it."

"We already have the videos and the stills."

I held tight to the phone despite an intense desire to throw something. "Are you holding out on me? I spent hours going through social media posts looking for clues, while you were looking at a complete record of what happened." I felt like shouting, but held my temper in check.

"Carina and I are cross-checking alibis using Antoine's footage. I'll share what I can with you, but this is evidence in a murder case. It doesn't leave the office." Louder, he said, "I'll get back to you to set up a meeting." And with that, he ended the call.

I didn't know if it was Jonah's new partner whose presence cut short our conversation. I did know the air-conditioner was unlikely to magically fix itself. The wheezing window unit, which was all I had to cool the apartment, was old, and with no time to wait for a repair person, I ordered a new one online. The store gave me a six-hour window for when they would deliver and install it. Before committing to the purchase, I ran downstairs to ask Mrs. Pargiter if she would let the delivery guy into my apartment.

She balked when she saw the size of the tip I left on her counter, but I made her take the money. "I can't get a banana delivered to the fifth floor without the promise of a big tip, and I'm getting cooked alive up there."

Mrs. Pargiter folded the bills and put them in an old coffee can. "Leave it to me. I'll get Squeaky to fix your broken air conditioner. He's studying electrical things. Or maybe plumbing? He'll do it cheap. And you better leave Farley with me until the apartment cools off. He doesn't like the heat."

Given her limited contact with the outside world, I was curious about this new friend and not thrilled with the thought of a stranger in my house. "Who's Squeaky? Is he one of the people you met at the dog park? You need to be careful of strangers, Mrs. Pargiter."

She rolled her eyes. "Don't tell me about being scared of strangers. That's my specialty. But Squeaky isn't a stranger. He's one of the kids who hangs out on the corner."

This morsel of biographical information didn't make me any happier about letting Squeaky into my house. "How did you get on a first-name basis with the juvies on the street?"

Mrs. Pargiter, who had six locks on her door and a baseball bat in an umbrella stand, said, "You know, Leah, you need to trust people more."

I walked back upstairs and assessed the value of my meager possessions. The only item worth stealing was my laptop, which I decided to take with me. Nothing else was likely to interest a thief. A stuffed bookcase with tattered paperbacks, a cheap set of pots and pans I never used, and an eclectic assortment of shoes wouldn't tempt the most desperate burglar.

With those pressing problems resolved, I called Terrence Benson, anxious to get to him before Antoine did.

An assistant answered the phone. When I told her I wanted to talk to Terrence directly, she put me on hold. After forcing me to listen to a prolonged stretch of canned music that belonged to no identifiable genre, she returned and said, "I'm happy to make an appointment for you, Ms. Siderova, but Mr. Benson doesn't need to see you until the costume fittings."

I was prepared for a brush-off and said, "I have several updates that he needs to know about immediately."

She hesitated and told me to hold again. After a second round of tuneless music, she said, more briskly, "How does next Wednesday at noon sound?"

"It sounds like an unnecessary delay for a matter that has to get resolved before then. Put him on the line, and we can get this done now."

Terrence practically barked into the phone. "What's the emergency, Leah?

I'm a busy man."

"And I'm a busy woman. If this wasn't important, I wouldn't waste my time, let alone yours." I wondered if he was avoiding me and if this avoidance had anything to do with Arabella. Could she be holing up with him?

He huffed into the phone and said, "Meet me at my office at eleven thirty. Don't be late."

I did a quick calculation and said, "It has to be at noon. I have an urgent appointment before I see you."

"It's a very dramatic life you lead. One urgent appointment after the other." He said it sarcastically, but it was an accurate appraisal. I thanked him, and with an annoyed *humph*, he hung up.

I was relieved he didn't press me to explain why I couldn't come earlier, because it was an ordinary ballet class that forced the delay. Outsiders almost never understood the crucial role that daily training played in dancers' lives. How many times had I heard, *What's the big deal if you skip one class?* But it was a big deal. Long after quadratic equations and the mysterious nature of pi vanished from my memory, the unforgiving math of ballet class remained: *Miss class one day, and you know. Miss class two days, and your teacher knows. Miss class three days, and the audience knows.*

* * *

I headed to Studio Dance, the best available substitute for Madame M's classes, racing to get there early. The school was popular, and competition for prized spots near the mirror was fierce. Ballet classes were grouped by skill level, from basic beginner to advanced professional, but all were open, and it was up to the students to decide where they belonged. You might find yourself next to a sixteen-year-old rising star, a sixty-year-old retiree, a Broadway hoofer, or someone who got lost on her way to Zumba.

The professional-level class was filled with people I knew well, including most of the dancers in the ballets Sierra, Hollis, and I were choreographing. My good friends, the Weird Sisters, occupied their usual corner. They jumped to their feet to greet me. The three women weren't weird, weren't sisters, and were nothing like the three witches in *Macbeth*, but they did exert unmistakable power.

The Weird Sisters also possessed a unique set of skills that had served me well in the past. Like all good friends, they didn't bother with small talk. Audrey moved aside to make room for me and said, "Mentioning no names, we're most interested in recent events, if you know what I mean."

I appreciated her discretion. "Unfortunately, I have to run right after class, but I promise to keep you posted, one way or another."

She nodded, and a few wisps of gray hair escaped her bun. "We've followed the story in the newspapers, though social media has been better at updates. Are you, er, involved in any way?"

They sat on the floor and stretched over straight legs. I did the same and pressed my face against my knees, which enabled me to talk without anyone else hearing. "It's complicated. And I have to be careful, in more ways than one. My position in the company isn't what it used to be."

Abigail pointed and flexed her feet. "That is most unwelcome news. But what of your choreography prize? That must count for something. We were thrilled when you were named a Vanderhof finalist and assumed your career was at an all-time high."

These ladies had helped me out of some tough spots in the past, and telling them the truth wouldn't alter our relationship, but a twinge of shame jabbed me, nonetheless. My self-worth remained tied to my work.

Audrey, who was a skilled chess player, said, "I can guess at the difficulties you must be facing, as an employee of ABC and as a Vanderhof finalist. Perhaps there's a perception of a conflict of interest?" Forgetting Abigail's promise not to name names, she said, "You have two queens, Arabella Vanderhof and Marty Sherrington. And two kings, in Leland and Jonathan."

"I don't know that a chess analogy will help in this case. Both kings are dead."

Isabel shared my doubts. "Leland Vanderhof qualifies as a king, but Jonathan Franklin? From what I saw of him, he was a pawn, despite his wealth."

Audrey gave Isabel an approving nod. "If that's the case, his death might be part of a much longer endgame. I'd love to know more about the other pieces. I mean, people. Because it sounds to me like someone is angling for control and position. Perhaps a lower-status person whose ambition turned deadly?"

Abigail rose to her feet, more lightly than most people half her age. "Leah, are you sure there's nothing we can do to help? Don't forget our superpower. Older women are invisible. It's a sad but sometimes useful fact of life."

The teacher entered the room, forcing an end to our talk. "If I could think of a way for you to get information, I would take you up on the offer. Unfortunately, this is one situation where I can't get you inside access."

Isabel took out her phone and flicked open the Studio Dance app. She pointed to a highlighted section and said, "We don't have an in with all those high society types, but Sierra Younger is starting a modern dance class for beginners. We'll go and report back to you."

Chapter Thirty-Six

When you do a difficult variation, the audience is aware that it is demanding and that you have the power and strength to do it. But in the end, when you take your bow, you should look as if you were saying, 'Oh, it was nothing. I could do it again.'
—Bruce Marks

The ballet class ended at eleven thirty-one, which gave me twenty-nine minutes to get from the Upper West Side to the Flatiron District. I tossed a cotton sundress over my leotard and tights and boarded the downtown 1 train. The frigid air inside the subway car, in contrast to the stifling fug on the platform, was ideal for an Emperor penguin. For a sweaty ballerina, it was agony. When the train pulled into the 23rd St. station, my joints were stiff and I was shivering.

I sprinted up the stairs and across three blocks to the address Terrence's assistant gave me. The first two floors of his design studio were devoted to retail. I entered a space that whispered its devotion to clothing with the hushed, airy feel of a temple. The ceilings were high, the décor an homage to all shades of white and gray, and the staff wore wrinkle-free clothing and expressions that elevated them above ordinary mortals.

With a practiced smile, one of the beautiful people stacking silk pajama pants approached me. If she was disappointed I wasn't in the market for a T-shirt that cost hundreds of dollars, she didn't let on. She directed me to Terrence's office, on the top floor of the building.

The elevator opened onto a hallway lined with photos of famous models wearing his clothes. A tall woman with dark skin so perfect it looked polished was waiting. I recognized her bored tones as belonging to the assistant who'd answered my phone call.

She ushered me into Terrence's office. He was dressed in a black shirt and black jeans, a dramatic counterpoint to the white sofas, chairs, and cabinets. I regretted the morning's decision to wear a faded blue sundress that incompletely covered up my leotard. Pink tights that had faded to an ashy gray peeked out from under the hem.

He snapped his fingers at his assistant, and she pulled back a pale linen curtain to reveal six faceless mannequins dressed in mockups of costumes for my ballet. I'd used my concern about the costumes as an excuse to meet him, but once I saw them, I almost forgot why I was there.

They were beautiful. Olivia's dress was a delicate pink, which would bring out the warmth in her olive skin. Tex's costume was sleek and dark, shot through with silver threads. Gabi's was a startling orange and black that would clash against Olivia's pink, a visual metaphor for their relationship. The remaining dresses, for the figures that would haunt the other three, were a flutter of loose, white panels.

Seeing them made the whole abstract effort of choreographing a ballet feel real and urgent, in a way that hadn't hit me before. As enchanted as I was with Terrence's creations, I didn't forget how it felt to dance in them. I examined the seams, the underarm sections, and the drape of the fabric. Each element was invisibly stitched to an elastic underpinning to allow for unfettered movement.

"You're a genius, Terrence. These are flawless." I'd planned to flatter him, no matter how the costumes came out, but he made it easy.

The downward curve of his mouth suggested he was used to being told he was fabulous and didn't much care if I added my voice to the rest. He said, "If that's all you need, my assistant will show you out."

I turned from the mannequins to face him. "There is one more thing. Where is Arabella? Is she staying with you?"

The temperature in the room plummeted to the same level as the subway car of the downtown 1 train. "I have no idea where Arabella is. As long as the bills get paid, I don't much care."

If Terrence was feigning indifference, he was a better actor than many I'd met on the Broadway stage. "Aren't you concerned that your client, who is also a good, er, a good friend, has gone missing?"

I wished I had my Aunt Rachel's *chutzpah*. That was the closest I could get to asking him if he and Arabella were hooking up.

A smile broke through his stiff upper lip. "I assume what you're really asking is if the performance and prize ceremony will proceed as planned. The answer to that question is yes. The players will change, but the game remains the same. A new panel of judges will be appointed shortly." He closed his eyes. When he opened them and I was still sitting in front of him, he said, "If there's nothing else, please go."

"There is one more thing. Were you at the Vee Arts Center last weekend?"

Terrence crossed his arms, a classic defensive pose. "Are you checking on my alibi or trying to establish one for yourself?"

"Neither. That's the job of the police. I'm worried about Arabella. The fact that you aren't suggests you know where she is."

He made a shooing motion with his hands, urging me toward the door. "I spent the weekend in the city. If you want information about Arabella, talk to Derrick. Not me."

I wasn't one of his models, who could be pushed and prodded. "You may not have been in Connecticut when Jonathan died, but you were front and center at Leland's murder. Who did it? Who killed him?"

His mouth hung open for three seconds before he filled it with words. "You got some nerve barging in here, asking me that question."

Terrence's hesitation and the way his jaw twitched made me see him differently, and I took a stab at guessing his guilty secret. "You suspect Arabella. And you could be right. If you hear from her, I suggest you call me or the cops."

I didn't need his sputtering denial to know I'd hit him where it hurt.

* * *

I had time to kill before my rehearsal and took a detour to Bryant Park to mull over my conversation with Terrence. He suspected Arabella was guilty, which didn't make it true, but did suggest a possible motive for her decision to run away. If my lover doubted me, maybe I, too, would be spooked enough to go dark until proved innocent.

The park was crowded, but I found a relatively quiet corner and made an overdue call to Madame. I'd hesitated to tell her about Marty's plot to force her into retirement, because I had no proof the gossip was true. Worrying Madame unnecessarily would do her no good, but leaving my beloved teacher vulnerable was worse.

I thought Madame was still at the Mayflower Hotel, but when I told her where I was, she said, "Am very close. Meet me at chess game. Will be with Olga."

I strolled over to the main branch of the New York Public Library and the usual lineup of chess players. Madame stood behind a seated Olga, who flashed a bright smile as her opponent resigned.

I congratulated Olga and, forgetting she'd met the Weird Sisters, said, "I have another friend who loves chess."

She gave up her chair to the next player in line. "Yes. It is Audrey of whom you speak. She is excellent, much better than me. But I am old-fashioned and love the real game. Audrey, she prefers the online bullet chess."

We went to a nearby diner, where Madame and I ordered coffee and green salads, and Olga requested a club sandwich with French fries. When I told them about the rumors circulating among the ABC dancers, neither was surprised.

Madame, after a scornful *pfui!*, said, "Marty has the business experience but does not understand ballet world. She will learn soon enough. This foolish plan to make me retire, if it is true, will never go through. As for Jonathan Franklin, may he rest in peace, that terrible man can no longer use his influence to work against me."

I took courage in her confidence. "You're right about Jonathan, but if your job is on the line, it won't help to discuss him in quite those terms."

Madame remained unruffled. "I speak nice about him to dancers and public. But we all know the truth. Surely, this very unpleasant person made many enemies."

She didn't mention my position with ABC when she speculated about hers, probably because there was nothing she could tell me I didn't already know. If I danced brilliantly, I would continue to perform. If I won the Vanderhof Prize, I'd star in Antoine's film and have a half dozen companies compete to hire me as a choreographer. I preferred not to think about a future where neither of those things happened.

Olga pushed some French fries onto Madame's plate. "Ballet very important, but we have two dead people. What is next?" She didn't add, but could have, *Who is next?*

I gave them the shortlist of suspects, which I'd reviewed dozens of times without getting close to a definitive answer. "The murders directly benefited Derrick Easton and Greta Bromley. They got promotions and fifty thousand dollars each. And then there's Arabella, who inherited a ton of money and can remarry without going through a divorce or wrangling over whatever prenup she might have signed before hooking up with Leland. They all had the opportunity to commit both murders."

Madame accepted Olga's French fries and said, "You are right, but I am not seeing how to prove guilt." She cocked her head to one side and said, "Many days have passed since I talked to your so very smart mother. I will invite Barbara to join us at dinner, and we can speak more of these matters."

I forked up a few greens from my salad. "Barbara said she's at a writers' retreat in upstate New York."

Although I added no editorial comments, Madame was quick to pick up on the phrasing of my answer. "Do you think she is telling an untruth? Why would your very kind mother say a lie?"

Olga's cheerful expression, which remained sunny in the face of our grim talk of murder, turned dark. "I will investigate. If two people disappear, this cannot be a coincidence."

Talking to these friends drove home the oddness of my mother's recent behavior. "Barbara is answering my phone calls, so it's not as if she's gone completely dark. She doesn't know Arabella, so there's no connection there.

It's more likely she's met a new guy, because if she were at a writers' retreat, she would have posted about it. Barbara never lets an opportunity pass to plug her books."

Olga said, "If you are worried, you can count on me. Olga will investigate."

Madame demurred. "Barbara is smart. If she does not want to be found, we should not pursue her." She picked up two French fries that were stuck together. "Perhaps the new man in her life is Jeremy. Is your father still married to that unpleasant woman? Truly, they have nothing in common."

I inhaled a sip of coffee instead of swallowing it and needed a thump on the back to recover my breath. "I should have thought of that! It explains why my father was so cagey the last time we spoke."

Madame was pleased with my reaction. "Let us wait to hear from her. It is better to use our time now to speak of other things besides murder and mysteries. Lelotchka, have you given thoughts to our last talk?"

I'd given more than a few thoughts to our last conversation, all of them grim. "Yes, Madame. I know I'm in a bad spot right now, and despite what you think, it may be that you are too."

For the first time in many days, I felt calm. Nothing outside me changed, but something within shifted. "The decision to end my career isn't Marty's. It's mine. She can cut me from ABC, but there are plenty of companies that will be happy to have me. I hope I'll know when it's time to go, but that time has not yet come."

Madame pressed her fingertips together. "The end comes for all of us. Is anyone ever ready for that farewell performance?"

"I can't speak for other people. For me, I'll take my final bow when I can still go out with a bang. And I won't need Marty, or anyone else, to tell me so."

Madame's eyes were damp. "That will not make it easier."

"I know."

Olga mopped up the ketchup with a fistful of French fries and said, "Again, with the ballet. It is lucky you have me to help with finding killer."

Chapter Thirty-Seven

My muse must come to me on union time.
—George Balanchine

When I arrived at the rehearsal studio, the door to the larger room was open, and Hollis was speaking loudly enough to make eavesdropping not only easy but unavoidable. To the sound of an electronic score that bleeped and buzzed, he yelled directives at his dancers. I looked inside and saw two men, at his urging, run backward. His shriek, telling them to change course, wasn't in time to prevent them from crashing into each other.

Hollis was the only one to find this unfunny. "Imagine how amusing that will be when you screw up in front of thousands of people." The dancers weren't fooled by his attempt to convey ironic bite, which came across as panicked weakness.

Antoine wasn't filming, which surprised me. I learned the reason for his absence when I opened the door to the second practice room. His camera was trained on Sierra, who was standing in front of a window that framed her orange hair in a flattering glow.

Annoyed at the interruption, she said, "Do you mind? We're in the middle of something."

I did mind. The room belonged to me as much as her, but I was wary of the camera's eye and the way Antoine might use our conversation. Conflict needs a villain and a victim. Antoine needed to stitch together a narrative with enough drama to propel his movie from documentary to blockbuster.

I smiled and said, "No problem, Sierra. I'll work in the hallway until you're done."

I'd been burned enough times to know how clever editing could turn innocuous episodes into viral gold. Although Sierra betrayed combativeness, and not me, this perception also had its dangers. Antoine could end up portraying her as a strong, creative woman and me as a weak-willed bunhead.

Like everyone else, I'd signed away my right to privacy and a whole lot more when I agreed to allow Antoine to film me, which was one of several rights I relinquished as a condition of the prize. Thinking of the indiscreet things I might have unwittingly revealed made my stomach curdle. What to do?

The answer to that question was easy. Nothing. There was nothing I could do if he recorded our conversation at dinner or caught me tripping over my own feet on the way to ballet class. But I could salvage what was unspooling now. Not with words, but with movement. With a graceful gesture, I ceded the field to Sierra, undulating my right arm as the Swan Queen would have, had she survived to live happily ever after.

Conscious that a second crew member's lens was trained on me, I unbuttoned my dress to reveal a leotard with spaghetti straps and black lace insets. It was the fanciest one I owned, and after getting caught looking like a bedraggled waif during the first rehearsal, I was determined to project a more polished look in subsequent filmings. I covered my worn tights with black stretchy pants that were nicer than my streetwear.

I slung my bag over my shoulder and walked out, smiling at the cameraman and thinking *Enjoy the show.*

* * *

My poise cracked as soon as I was away from those hungry gazes. I texted Gabi, **Can u meet me b4 rehearsal?**

The screen stayed blank for an obscene amount of time until it lit up with the unwelcome answer: **Can't make it today. Talk ltr?**

I retreated to the ancient bathroom. After checking underneath the doors of each stall, I called her. "Is everything okay?"

Gabi didn't sound like her confident, cheerful self. "I've got bad news and worse news."

"Let's deal with the bad stuff first." I had a sinking feeling about the worse news and wanted to put it off as long as possible, so maybe it wouldn't happen.

After a few muttered words in Spanish, she said, "Sierra is trashing you to anyone who will listen. The problem is that she doesn't come off as unhinged to anyone but me. She appears to have brainwashed Hollis, and I'm positive Antoine has captured a ton of what they said. And all of it is bad. It's one thing to post snide comments online, but it'll be quite another to have them in a movie that could be big. I don't know how you're going to fight that kind of battle."

I knew this, which didn't make hearing it any easier. "I'm more interested in anything Sierra or Hollis said that could have some bearing on the murders or Arabella's disappearance."

Over the sound of Lucie clamoring, she said, "On that topic, I don't have as much to tell you. Sierra made a point of saying she was at dinner with Antoine when Jonathan was killed, so I guess that's her alibi."

I cautioned myself against premature celebration, but the long wait for Sierra to bury herself seemed over. "Are you sure she said she was with Antoine and not with Hollis?"

Gabi soothed Lucie and said, "Yes. I didn't think about it at the time, but that leaves Hollis without an alibi. Check with Olivia, Tex, and a few of the other ABC dancers and find out if they saw him."

My best friend paused, and I braced myself for what she termed worse news. Gabi said, in a rush, "Please don't kill me, but I can't dance in your ballet. Something's come up."

I schooled my voice to a decibel level lower than the full-throated scream that wanted to tear itself out of my chest. I thought she was going to tell me she couldn't attend rehearsals for a week, which would have been bad but not catastrophic. "What do you mean? What's going on?"

She cleared her throat. Throat-clearing was never a good sign. "My husband saw the news reports about Jonathan's murder, and he's afraid for me. Sid, you have to understand where he's coming from. I've told him a million times there's no danger, but I've never seen him like this. And my parents are backing him up. I'm sorry, but you're going to have to find someone else."

"There is no one else. You're one of a kind, Gabi. It's not only that you're perfect in the role. You've already connected with Sierra, and I need you now more than ever. You're the only one I trust." My heart was pounding, and I felt as if my torso were gripped in a tightening vise.

Gabi didn't have to see me to know I was fending off a panic attack. "Take a breath, Sid. In, two, three. Out, two, three. You got this."

In a desperate, last-ditch effort to hold onto Gabi, I said, over Lucie's wails, "Your husband never minded any of the other times you helped me out. What's changed?"

Her voice dropped to a whisper. "Sid, you dummy. He didn't know. I'd long since retired from ABC. But after signing on to dance in your ballet, there's no hiding the fact that two people connected with the Vanderhof Prize are dead. Once he played the Mommy Card, I was done for. Lucie is more important to me than anything."

Yes. The Mommy Card was powerful. I had no counterargument that could eclipse it. Even if I had, I wouldn't try to change her mind, because what if her husband was right? What if I was endangering her? I wanted my best friend to spy on suspects in a double homicide. It was too much to ask.

Unwilling to lose Gabi's presence in the ballet, I said, "I'm going to send you videos with me dancing your role. Learn it and practice it, so when the killers are brought to justice you can still perform."

As if on cue, Lucie stopped crying. Gabi said, "You got it."

I bent over the sink to splash water on my face. A faint creak from behind set the hairs on the back of my neck quivering. I left the taps running and flung open the door. There was no one there, but an indefinable presence remained, a whiff of air, maybe. It reminded me of what Jonah said when I was snooping on his conversation with his mother. It was a feeling, not a matter of concrete evidence.

If today's eavesdropper was the same person who pursued me at the Vee Arts Center, I now had a closed circle of people as suspects: Sierra, Hollis, and Antoine. Sierra's weapons, as far as I knew, were the same as any mean girl. She might elbow me, trip me up, or rip apart a fan that I treasured. I'd assumed she was motivated by a desire to rattle me, not kill me. And yet, there was something off about her that I had not, perhaps, given the weight it deserved. Had Sierra's loathing turned to obsession?

Chapter Thirty-Eight

People come to see beauty, and I dance to give it to them.
—Judith Jamison

I was more conscious than ever of living under a microscope as Antoine and his crew filmed my rehearsal. Unlike previous sessions, when I occasionally forgot about them and let my enthusiasm take charge, I remained guarded in the words I used and the physical image I projected. It was impossible, however, to control a narrative with no script, and Antoine captured a collective gasp of dismay when I informed the dancers Gabi might have to bow out.

My friend's absence forced greater concentration. Although I danced the same steps she did, the difference in our height, the length of our arms, and the way we approached the music required constant adjustments for the others. We began with the last, dramatic scene, when Olivia confronts the ghostly images that have haunted her. The mood in the room shifted, from everyday workhorse mode to something more exciting. The steps for this new section poured out of me, and the dancers threw themselves into performing the complex sequence of moves.

When the alarm on my phone bleeped an end to the rehearsal, the dancers paid me the ultimate compliment. Startled at the swift passage of time, they groaned. Then, they clapped.

I joined in the applause and said, "That was extremely not bad." This inspired a round of fist bumps, which was the extent of any expressions of congratulations. It would be the height of foolishness to anger the dance gods by predicting success.

The dancers and crew left, and I fiddled around with a section of the ballet that needed a pop of energy to match the music. Gabi's technique was still strong, but her turns were rusty. If she wasn't going to perform, I could insert a more exciting series of pirouettes. I hummed the melody and tinkered, trying to hit the right balance.

After a few minutes, I realized Antoine had slipped back into the room. I stopped dancing, and he said, "Allow me to buy you a drink. No questions about the murder or Sierra or Hollis. Let us get to know each other."

My desire to know him better was equal to my desire for a cracked toenail. I asked him for a raincheck without offering an alternate day or time.

Antoine was famous for insightful portrayals of creative artists, but he failed to note the subtext in my refusal. This didn't surprise me. As a beautiful man with considerable status, he probably lacked experience with rejection. With a bemused look, he said, "What about tomorrow? Are you free then?"

"I'll see what I can do and let you know."

Before meeting him again, I wanted to verify from an outside source that he was with Sierra on the night Jonathan died. There was no mystery about where he was when Leland died. His social media posts had documented his presence throughout the party.

Antoine leaned in to give me a two-cheek kiss. I let him. If I didn't, it would be as great an insult as refusing to shake hands. He didn't immediately withdraw but looked at me with soulful eyes, which I met with an impassive stare. Those blue orbs masked a calculating heart.

When I stepped away, he placed his hand on my shoulder. His thumb circled my neck in a gesture that unnerved me with its intimacy. We were alone, and I was half his size. I swooped down to pick up my heavy dance bag and swung it a few inches in his direction.

Antoine laughed. "You are an original. Like me. We make our own rules."

Whatever. He was acting the part of a man pursuing a woman he desired, but he didn't do it well enough to convince me. Antoine was either hoping his flattery would trick me into confiding a tasty tidbit for his film, or, like a million other guys, he was projecting onto me some fantasy that had nothing to do with who I was.

Ambition masquerading as lust was the most likely explanation for his gesture and invitation. For players like Antoine, those motives were interchangeable. I didn't think he was guilty of murder, not because he was incapable of violence, but because he had no rational motive. I did believe, without the slightest trace of doubt, that he would use those tragic events to his advantage. And use me too if I let him.

* * *

I checked my silenced phone on the subway ride home, where I found messages from Aunt Rachel and my sister. Neither found anything odd about my mother's mysterious absence. They assumed, as I did at first, that she'd jetted off with a man she wasn't ready to introduce to the family. Under other circumstances, it was a rational deduction, but Barbara was in the middle of final edits for her new book. A battalion of attractive bachelors could come calling, and she would remain in her writing bubble.

I left a message on my mother's voicemail and texted an invitation to meet at Café Figaro. Three dots danced for a few tantalizing moments before disappearing. I sent her a **???** but got no response. On an impulse, I headed to her house instead of mine. I had to see for myself what was going on.

When I arrived, Gerald opened the door but didn't usher me to the elevator. He said, "Your mother isn't here."

My family moved into the building when I was in kindergarten, and Gerald was a new hire. Barbara knew the names and ages of his kids and grandkids, and he knew the titles of every one of her books. The bare statement, "Your mother isn't here," alarmed me.

I crossed my arms and said, "Where did she go? And when is she coming back?"

He stuck a finger in his starched collar and tugged at it. "She left when I wasn't on duty. I didn't see her leave."

"Gerald, what are you not telling me?" The flicker of worry got hotter.

He shifted from one foot to the other. "Nothing. But it's not like your ma to disappear like that. She always tells me when she's going to be away. Manny, the night guy, said she had two big suitcases with her. When he wanted to get her a cab, she said she wanted to take a walk first. But who takes a walk with two big suitcases?"

Two suitcases meant she planned an extended stay. "Did Manny say where she went?"

He scratched his head. "No. But that's not all. You gotta figure, if she wanted to walk, which is already kind of a weird thing to do at night and loaded down with luggage, you'd think she'd head toward Broadway. There's all kinds of construction going on the other way. But that's where she went."

"Thanks, Gerald. I'm going up to the apartment. Maybe she left me a note."

* * *

Barbara's apartment looked as it always did. The empty refrigerator told me nothing, as my mother subsisted on black coffee, red wine, diet soda, and takeout food. The garbage can had a clean liner inside. Her room was neat and empty of clues. The bed in the guest room, however, showed signs of use. It was carelessly made, the covers thrown over the pillows in a way that incurred my mother's wrath when my sister and I were kids. A foreign scent hung in the air. My mother used Joy perfume, but this smell was more like lemons than jasmine.

There were no signs of violence, no tossed cushions or drops of blood, no messages scratched out on the wall or floor. The simplest explanation was that my mother decided to go on a last-minute trip. Her apartment was as innocent-looking and devoid of clues as Arabella Vanderhof's house before she too disappeared.

Chapter Thirty-Nine

Bleeding feet will bond us.
—Liza Minelli

Over the years, my father insisted many times that he'd made a complete recovery from a heart attack that occurred after I told him I was going to skip college and join American Ballet Company. Despite these declarations absolving me of blame for his clogged arteries, I never quite got over the crush of guilt or the fear of precipitating another heart attack.

I didn't want to alarm him with the news that Barbara had set off for parts unknown, possibly with a new guy. Nor did I want to pry. If, as Madame suggested, my parents were secretly rekindling their romance, they'd tell me when they were ready.

After a few minutes of chatting with him about unimportant matters, I said, "Barbara appears to have gone on a spur-of-the-moment vacation. I was wondering if she decided to return to LA."

"If she's coming back, this is the first I've heard about it. I still don't get why she left."

Jeremy doesn't lie or obfuscate. It violates some philosophical ideal that never made much sense to my mother and was one of their irreconcilable differences.

"Dad, she came home because she thought I needed her. She also said all that sunshine and healthy food gave her hives. And, um, she's working on a new book."

I could feel the tension in his voice. "Do you think she's in trouble? I can be at JFK or LaGuardia tomorrow morning."

"No! That's not necessary. Everything is fine. I'll call you later. You know Barbara. Expect the unexpected."

My father was understandably suspicious. "You know what Kant said about lying. We have a moral imperative to—"

I loved him, but didn't have the mental bandwidth to get into a theoretical discussion of morality with a philosophy professor. "Yes. I know what Kant said about lying. Also Aristotle and John Stuart Mill. It's always a huge hit at parties."

Jeremy, thankfully, moved out of his abstract mode and back into the real world. "Talk to Jonah. Tell him your mother has gone AWOL."

"I'll call him as soon as we get off the phone."

Telling my father I would call Jonah as soon as we hung up was a slight exaggeration, as my attitude regarding truth-telling was closer to my mother's than my father's.

I tried Barbara's number one more time and left her a voicemail: "If I don't hear from you, I'm calling Jonah to have him put out an APB."

Don't fuss. Be back soon.

My mother added a smiley face to the end of her text, which was another first for her. She loathed nonverbal communication. I sent her another message, **Who are you and what have you done with my mother?**

Three dots appeared, vanished, and then resumed their dance. **Prof Romanova will explain soon. No need to panic. Or to call Jonah.**

The last thing I needed was another puzzle to solve. Did Barbara reference her fictional character as a joke? Or to prove she was the one on the other end of the line?

The answer came to me as I trudged home. Barbara mentioned her brainy protagonist because she—they—were on the case. I called the Mayflower Hotel and asked to be connected to Barbara Siderova's room, but they said she wasn't there. I left a message anyway.

* * *

I opened my apartment door and was greeted by a smug Mrs. Pargiter, a blissfully yapping Farley, and a cool blast of air. After many years of coming home to an empty home, finding my neighbor parked on my sofa, as comfortably as if she lived there, should have felt odd or intrusive, but it didn't. Until recently, the only roommates I had were plants that people who didn't know me well gave as gifts. They invariably died of dehydration and lack of sunlight. (The plants, not the gift-givers.)

I followed Mrs. Pargiter to the kitchen, where I found yet another surprise. On the stove, a pot of chicken soup bubbled. My neighbor added a pinch of salt and said, "You look tired. The soup will help."

I picked up Farley, who was extremely interested in the contents of the pot. "Mrs. Pargiter, that's the nicest thing you've ever said to me."

She handed me a twenty-dollar bill. "Here's your change. Squeaky said your air conditioner is fixed, but you should move to a lower floor, and he won't charge as much."

I didn't know which of the guys who hung out on my street corner was Squeaky. "You'll have to introduce me. I'd like to thank him." I mentally apologized to my new repairman and to Mrs. Pargiter for doubting them.

"You can thank him yourself. He's coming over." She ripped a page from the back of a yellow legal pad. In spidery handwriting was a list of ingredients.

After thanking her for the chicken soup recipe, which I was unlikely to ever use, I said, "Uh, well, I'd love to meet Squeaky, but Jonah will be here soon."

Unfazed, she said, "I know. That's why I invited him."

I had many reasons not to want to eat soup with Squeaky and Mrs. Pargiter. My mother was avoiding me, a famous film director was breathing down my neck, and I'd yet to find the person who dismembered my red silk fan. I needed to think, not chat, but I bowed to the inevitable and set the table for four.

Squeaky knocked on the door, having gained entrance to the building without me buzzing him in. He had short, bleached hair, an array of facial piercings, and, despite the heat, wore heavy boots and a steel-studded leather vest. He called into the kitchen, "Thanks for the invite, Mrs. P."

To me, he said, "Any friend of Mrs. P's is a friend of mine."

Jonah walked in through the open apartment door and took in the presence of a party he didn't know was happening. He kissed me and said, into my hair, "Who's the kid?"

"He's my new repairman. I'll explain later."

Mrs. Pargiter called us to the table, and we sat down to dinner. Jonah said, "So, uh, how do you guys know each other?"

Squeaky said, "We met at the dog park. I walk dogs in my spare time."

Jonah opened a bottle of wine and filled three glasses. After giving Squeaky the once-over, he poured a smaller amount for him. "What do you do when you're not walking dogs?"

Mrs. Pargiter said, "He's learning to be an electrician. But he's got a lot of talents. If you want your car hot-wired, he can do it. If you get locked out, he can get you in without having to call a locksmith. My place he couldn't do, but most people don't think ahead like me."

Squeaky bit into a matzo ball. "You got that right, Mrs. P. It's a regular Fort Knox."

She patted his hand and said, "Mr. Sobol here, he's a homicide detective, and I thought you two should know each other."

He recoiled. "I never did nothing like that, I swear."

Mrs. Pargiter consoled him with an extra matzo ball. "But it's nice to make new friends, don't you think?" She turned to me. "You need someone to watch out for you. Detective Sobol can't be babysitting you all the time. That's where Squeaky and his friends can help."

I put down my spoon. "Has something changed?"

Her eyes, behind thick glasses, were wide. "Yes. Someone has been watching you. Following you."

Part of me was relieved that I hadn't been suffering a paranoid delusion. The other part was scared sick to have been proved right.

A muscle in Jonah's jaw twitched. "Why didn't you call me? Or the local station? Why didn't you file a police report?"

She ladled more soup into his bowl. "The cops think I'm a paranoid old lady, always crying wolf."

Mrs. Pargiter was a paranoid old lady. Except this time, the wolf was real and coming for me. Jonah retrieved his notebook and a pen and said, "The details, please. Dates and times, if you have them. What did this stalker look like?"

She ripped the top sheet off the same pad that held her recipe for chicken soup. "It's all here."

Jonah examined the spiky letters, circled words, and maze of arrows. "It would be better if you read it to me."

Mrs. Pargiter adjusted her glasses and said, "He's been here three times. I wasn't sure if he was on the lookout for Leah until the second time, which was early in the morning on garbage pickup day. When Leah left in a cab, he drove off behind them. That got my attention. It was an alternate side of the street parking day. Why sit for an hour in your car, only to give up your spot?"

The first date and time occurred on the morning of Leland's funeral. The second was my cab ride to Grand Central Terminal. I couldn't recall anything particular about the third sighting.

My neighbor pulled out her phone and showed us the pictures she'd taken. "It's hard to tell, but he looks tall. See? His head is way over the steering wheel."

We passed the phone around. Jonah said, "Those are three different cars. Send the photos to me. We might be able to clean them up enough to identify who it is."

Mrs. Pargiter sent them and said, "I tried to zoom in on the license plate but couldn't manage it."

I enlarged one of the photos and pointed out the edge. "You did get a partial, but I'm not sure it matters. If he's in a different car each time, then it's probably a rental."

Jonah's expressionless face and voice were as dry as if we were talking about a random suspect and victim. "We can run this by a couple of agencies to see if they come up with a match. The most important thing is keeping Leah safe. Mrs. Pargiter, if you or Squeaky catch sight of this guy again, you call me directly. Do not engage with him."

Mrs. Pargiter, who for years was too scared of imaginary dangers to leave her apartment, said, "Don't worry, Detective. Me and Squeaky are on the case."

Chapter Forty

Although we do come from a silent profession, it is important for us to verbalize what we want to say...you could love someone all your life, but if you never say it how are they going to know?
—Suzanne Farrell

After the dishes were clean, and Mrs. Pargiter put the leftover soup in a plastic container for Squeaky to take home, Jonah and I talked long into the night. The original list of suspects in Leland's murder numbered four people: Jonathan Franklin Llewellyn III, Arabella Vanderhof, Marty Sherrington, and Terrence Benson. The first of those was dead. The second had vanished. The last two remained contenders, but others had joined their ranks.

I reclined on the sofa as Jonah kneaded my feet with long, strong fingers. "Arabella's disappearing act is doing her no favors. Carina is convinced she's guilty."

My feet were loving the massage. I didn't want to say anything that would cause him to stop and pick up his notebook, but ironing out the facts of the case was more important than my aching arches. "Leland wasn't a big man, but Arabella's arms are like sticks. No way she'd be strong enough to push him over the guardrail."

As I feared, Jonah removed my feet from his lap. "Don't eliminate Arabella based on her muscle mass. The tox screen came back for Leland. He had a huge dose of tramadol in his system. Mixed with alcohol, it would have disoriented and weakened him. She had the best opportunity to spike his drink, but she wasn't the only one. Any of the suspects could have done so."

"Leland was steady before the performance but was so shaky afterward, Tex had to help him off the stage. That should help determine when he was drugged."

He laced his fingers behind his neck and went into ceiling-gazing mode. "It narrows the time frame but not the list of suspects. They all had access to him in the hour before the ballet started."

I started pacing, which was my version of his ceiling-gazing. "I'm coming around to the idea that Sierra, perhaps aided by Hollis, is guilty. She's a lot colder and more calculating than I realized, and Hollis appears to be incapable of thinking for himself. She might have some hold on him that we don't yet know about. It doesn't have to get to the level of blackmail, but it could. Left to himself, I don't think Hollis would be quite so awful."

After a few minutes, Jonah sat up and said, "If Sierra is guilty, Antoine Moreau is a likelier partner in crime. He reminds me of Neil Sherrington. Like Marty's husband, he's always hovering around the edge."

I quit wearing a groove in the floor and said, "The more time I spend with Antoine, the less I feel I know him. He probably isn't guilty of murder, but it wouldn't surprise me to learn he's the one who's been on my tail. If so, there isn't much I can do about it without risking my bid to win the Vanderhof Prize. I signed away my right to privacy weeks ago, and I can't refuse to meet with him."

Jonah spoke in a strangled voice. "Antoine doesn't have the right to stalk you. And he doesn't have any claim on you outside of regular working hours."

"I agree that Antoine is borderline creepy, but it's not personal. I'll make sure we meet in a public place."

His voice cut like glass. "You can't meet that slimy, arrogant jackass without protection. Ask Olga to sit in. You got lucky the first time. Don't try it again."

Jonah's anger was out of proportion to the risk. "Having dinner at a local restaurant wasn't dangerous, especially with Mr. Kim and Mrs. Pargiter steps away at the bodega. Antoine is a filmmaker, not a trained assassin. Are you jealous?"

His face flushed, which almost never happens. "I am not jealous. But I've seen the way he looks at you. If I can't nail him for the murder, then I'll arrest him for stalking. Or for being an egotistical, pretentious, phony, loser."

"That loser, who won the top prize at Cannes, sees me as a means to an end. He's all ambition and zero romance."

Jonah's voice rose to exasperated heights. "Romance? Come on, Leah. Get real. The guy wants sex, and he wants it with you. I interviewed him after Leland died. You were on the other side of the terrace, but he couldn't take his eyes off you. You're blinded by his fame. I know his type."

"You know his type? Thanks so much for telling me how to deal with predatory men. Really appreciate it. In fact, I'll make a note of it."

In retrospect, sarcasm might not have been the best way to handle Jonah's anger. I stalked into the kitchen, which wasn't a long trek. Ten feet at most, but I didn't want to be in the same room with him, where I'd be tempted to make a few acid comments about his new partner. I stewed in the kitchen while he fumed in the living room.

The floorboards creaked with the sound of footsteps. I rushed to meet him halfway, in case he decided to leave instead of sticking around to finish the fight, but he was already past the door. He wrapped his arms around me and said, "I hate that guy, who gets to see a whole lot more of you than I do."

I breathed in his bitter and sweet smell. Blindfolded, I could pick him out of a roomful of people. "He doesn't get to see the best parts."

He laughed and held me tighter. "Good to know."

I slipped my hands under his shirt, and he responded with a sharp intake of air. "Don't tempt me. We have work to do."

I pushed him away. "How do you know this isn't a limited-time offer?"

Jonah's breath tickled my neck. "I'm a detective. I can tell when someone is bluffing."

I brewed a pot of coffee, and we got back to work. One of the many things I loved about Jonah was his willingness to drink coffee with me late at night. He laid out the case for and against each suspect.

I was familiar with Jonah's methodical mapping out of evidence and means, motivations and relationships, opportunity and psychology. After reading through his notes and mine, I got stuck in a loop of maybes and might-have-beens. "What if we're going about this the wrong way? You always say that most murders are committed by someone the victim knows, but what if the killer isn't close to the person who died?"

He pushed aside the curtain to look at a starless sky. "In some of those cases, the killer doesn't have a real-life relationship with the victim. He, and it's usually a guy, becomes obsessed with a woman who doesn't know he exists. But this killer doesn't strike me as someone with that kind of psychosis. It feels more calculated than that."

I copied the set of interlocking circles in Jonah's notes. He'd written one name in each: Marty Sherrington, Neil Sherrington, Arabella Vanderhof, Terrence Benson, and Antoine Moreau. A list on the side paired Derrick and Greta in one column and Sierra and Hollis in another.

In my notes, I put a check mark next to Arabella's assistant and her housekeeper. "We need someone who's not on the list to give us the inside scoop on Derrick and Greta. Their relationship with Arabella might be more complicated and a whole lot closer than that of employer-employee. We often spend more time with the people we work with than the people we love."

He cocked one dark eyebrow. "So, you are in love with me. I've suspected it for quite some time."

My cheeks got warm. Declarations of love didn't come easily to me. "Don't get distracted. Of course, I'm crazy about you."

"Or just crazy." He pulled me close, and his lips burned a path from my neck to my shoulder. "Time for me to see what you've left to Antoine's imagination."

My pulse beat in places that left me breathless. "I'm not finished."

He broke away to lead me into the bedroom, but we only made it as far as the sofa. "Me either."

Chapter Forty-One

When I first began choreographing, I never thought of it as choreography but as expressing feelings...that are difficult to put into words.
—Pina Bausch

The early-morning roar of sanitation trucks reminded me of Mrs. Pargiter's warning about a stalker. I slipped out of Jonah's grasp, pulled up the shade, and peeked outside the bedroom window. Mr. Kim, who was walking Betty, was the only person on the sidewalk until Mrs. Pargiter and Farley joined him. They proceeded to examine, without subtlety, drivers who were waiting out the time limits for alternate side of the street parking. None provoked suspicion from my cautious neighbors.

Jonah opened one sleepy eye. "What's on the agenda for today? Please tell me it's a ballet rehearsal and not a secret meeting in a concealed bunker."

"It's a ballet rehearsal. You don't have to worry about me. I'm booked."

He opened the other eye and sat up. "Are you also going to offer me a good price on the Brooklyn Bridge?" There was an irritated edge to his teasing tone. "Give me some credit, Leah, and don't hide your plans. We should be past all that now."

Jonah's talent for reading me was one of his best and worst qualities. "I'm not hiding anything from you. There's no need to arrange a secret meeting, because a bunch of our suspects will be at rehearsal today."

I flopped back on the bed and buried my face in the pillow. Jonah stroked my back. After a few minutes, he said, "If I kept going, how long would you stay in bed?"

"Until I passed out from dehydration and starvation. But I'd die happy."

"In that case, I'll stop now before you expire." He leaned over me to survey the street. "Don't take public transportation. Call a cab and wait inside until it arrives. Check if you're being followed. I'm almost hoping you are, because then we can nail this guy. Call me with the license plate number, and I'll get a panda to pull him over. Keep your car in motion until then. Don't stop if you get to the studio before we catch up with you."

In the space of a few minutes, my mood switched from dread to excitement. "Roger that. Any other instructions?" I climbed over him and wriggled into a T-shirt that had shrunk in the wash and a pair of saggy shorts that had lost their elastic.

"Only one comes to mind." He used the waistband of the shorts to pull me back to bed.

* * *

The Weird Sisters saved me a place at the barre at Studio Dance. They were full of theories about the murder. Abigail said, "Audrey thinks she's solved the mystery, but I'm not so sure."

I put a finger to my lips and glanced at the people closest to us to make sure no one was listening. The room was packed with dancers. Those who weren't chatting were wearing headphones of different sizes, from barely-there to the large, earmuff variety.

Isabel pooh-poohed my caution. "No one is interested in hearing what we have to say. Most people go out of their way to ignore us."

Abigail shushed her. "That may be true when it's the three of us, but being with Leah changes everything."

Audrey tilted her head toward the door. "Let's talk in the stairwell. No one uses the stairs unless the elevator is broken."

Before exiting the room, we left our dance bags on the floor and sweaters on the barre to prevent late arrivals from taking our spots. The dancers in the waiting area and behind the desk were too busy to note three elderly women and one ballerina leave. When the door closed, Abigail said, "Money is the obvious motive for Leland's death, but that doesn't mean you should focus solely on the major beneficiaries. Smaller bequests could be an equally powerful incentive. That could include charitable institutions. Audrey disagrees with me, but I suggest you follow the money."

Audrey blew air over her lower lip to emphasize her disagreement. "Your focus is too narrow. It's better to look at the big picture. The two deaths created a power vacuum."

Isabel was more hesitant than the other two. "Both ideas are worth pursuing, but there's a third possibility. Audrey, you suspect the queens. But what if the pawns hold the key?"

Everything my friends proposed was plausible. I nodded my appreciation of their analyses and said, "We might know more after you talk to Sierra. If anyone can get her to open up, it's you three. Concentrating on motive is a good idea, but in this situation, it's creating more questions than answers."

Audrey stuck a few bobby pins in her flyaway hair. "What do you suggest? Without forensic evidence, all you have to go on is psychology."

We were nearly out of time before the class began, which we'd now have to take without a proper warmup. I opened the door and said, "Isabel's idea to concentrate on those so-called pawns is a good one. Powerful people like Arabella don't have to resort to violence to get what they want. They use their money or influence to get ahead. Do your best to chat up Sierra, but don't underestimate her."

* * *

Applause at the end of ballet class brought me back to the world outside the studio. The mental discipline stayed with me, although I felt no further along in identifying the killer. Nor was I any closer to solving the mystery behind my mother's baffling behavior. Barbara continued to answer my voicemails with cryptic texts.

Determined to get through to her, I prepared a blistering message that went unsaid when she picked up the call.

"Leah! Darling! It's lovely to hear from you."

I recovered my equanimity and my voice. "Unless you've joined the Witness Protection Program, you've got a lot of explaining to do. Where are you? And what have you been up to?"

She played for time with a throaty and unconvincing chuckle. "You always did love to dramatize things, but that's what makes you such an extraordinary dancer. I assure you, there was no need to worry. I left town for a few days, and knowing how busy you are, didn't want to bother you."

I heard a door closing, the clatter of her heels, and a creak that sounded like the casement windows in her apartment opening. A muffled roar of traffic and the hiss of a vape pen followed. Barbara sighed and said, "Now, where were we?"

"We weren't anywhere. You were going to tell me where you've been hiding out, though it sounds as if you're back."

The silence lasted so long, I thought the call had dropped. Or, that she'd hung up on me. Finally, she said, "Professor Romanova would save that information for a big reveal."

I wanted to reach through the ether and shake her. "Are you investigating Leland's murder?"

The faint sound of a siren interrupted her tinkling *hahaha*. "Why on earth would you think that?" Barbara's real laugh was a full-throated roar that was almost shocking, coming as it did from her tiny frame. I was bursting with questions, but she claimed an incoming call and hung up.

* * *

After rehearsal, I called Melissa, my perfect and perfectly wonderful sister. If anyone could talk sense into Barbara, it was Melissa, because she was everything I wasn't. Brainy, accomplished, married, and with two adorable kids, she was the daughter my parents assumed they would have. I filled her in on as many of the details as I had in my possession, along with a few creative hypotheses, but I got the feeling she wasn't listening.

In the harried voice of a mom juggling work and kids, she said, "Don't jump to conclusions. I'm sure it'll all work out fine. Let's talk again soon."

Desperate, I called Aunt Rachel. There was nothing Rachel liked better than giving advice, often when it was neither requested nor desired. She gave me the same answer as Melissa.

And then, I finally got it. Even without my sister's genius brain cells, I realized the whole family was in on some secret. Except for me.

Chapter Forty-Two

No matter what you write or choreograph, you feel it is not enough.
—Alvin Ailey

Squeaky and his group of friends were at their usual spot, on the steps of Dependable Dry Cleaners, drinking from bottles inside paper bags. I usually walked on the opposite side of the street to avoid their stares and the haze of smoke. On this day, I stopped to thank Squeaky for keeping an eye out for me.

He puffed out his chest and said, "You got nothing to worry about. Nothing bad will happen to you with us around."

A tall kid with an aspirational beard stroked the sparse hairs on his chin. "Squeaky said you're some kind of dancer. Very cool."

Squeaky smacked his shoulder and said, "Back off, Bugger. Her hookup is a cop. Homicide."

Bugger took a long pull from his drink and said, as if to reassure me, "We won't hold it against you. Mrs. P said you're okay."

How Mrs. Pargiter became the trusted friend of this group was a mystery that begged further investigation, but more important than my neighbor's new social circle was her description of my stalker. Squeaky hadn't seen him, but maybe someone else in his group had. I scrolled through my camera roll and showed them pictures of Hollis, Derrick, and Horace. No one recognized them.

I saved the photo of Antoine Moreau for last. When Bugger saw the photo, he gave a low whistle and said, "Yeah. I seen him around. The guy with the camera."

Bugger confirmed what I'd suspected, which was that my stalker was someone who had access to the travel plans I filed with the Vanderhof Foundation. If it wasn't Derrick or Hollis, it had to be Antoine. Going forward, this would make eluding the filmmaker far easier.

I returned to my apartment and booked a ticket back to New Haven without updating the Vanderhof travel log. Farley kept me company while I repacked my suitcase. Unlike my critical mother, the dog approved of all my clothing choices.

Audrey, the chess-loving Weird Sister, called as I was sitting on the suitcase, a necessary step before zipping it closed. She sounded out of breath. "Leah, we have news. Can you meet us at the Lincoln Center Diner?"

"I have to be at Grand Central soon. Can this wait til Monday?"

A babble of voices from Isabel and Abigail drowned out Audrey's hesitant assent. While they argued, I checked the train schedule.

"If you can wait until I finish packing, I can take a later train and be there in twenty minutes."

I left Farley with Mrs. Pargiter, who refused to let me go until she talked to Squeaky. When he gave the all-clear sign, I got into a cab, lugging the suitcase behind me.

* * *

The Weird Sisters were sitting at a booth with cracked, red leatherette seats when I arrived at the Lincoln Center Diner. Rita, our favorite server, was on duty. She brought four cups of coffee and a quartet of tombstone-sized plastic menus. The Weird Sisters all chose corn muffins, the cheapest item on the menu. My friends spent most of their disposable income on ballet classes and tickets to performances, and it was near the end of the month. I ordered two sandwich platters that I would later claim I didn't have time to eat.

I was anxious to get them talking. "Ladies, I'm assuming you went to Sierra's class and have news for me. What happened?"

Audrey dropped several bobby pins that lost the battle with her flyaway hair. "Hardly anyone was in Sierra's class. Only five people, including us. It was embarrassing but turned out to be a good thing, because she stuck around afterward to encourage us to come back."

Abigail scooped up her friend's hairpins and said, "We told her we were big fans and couldn't wait to see her new ballet. Then, Isabel asked her, like it was the most natural question in the world, who she thought killed Leland Vanderhof and Jonathan Llewellyn Franklin III." She jiggled Isabel's arm. "Honestly, Izzy, how did you have the nerve?"

Isabel's cheeks were pink. "It popped out! I couldn't think of anything else to say. But here's why we had to talk to you tonight, Leah. You won't believe it when you hear it, but Sierra knows who the killer is. We couldn't get her to reveal the name, but she hinted that it was someone famous who would inherit a lot of money. We figured it has to be Arabella Vanderhof, and we wanted to put you on your guard."

This revelation didn't hit me with the same force as it did them. "You did great, Isabel, but you're right, I don't believe it. Sierra tells lies like other people breathe. And there's no better way to deflect attention from yourself than by blaming someone else."

Abigail regarded her muffin and me with equal doubt. "What if you're wrong? It could be a double fake, like the plot in your mother's last book. Sierra said she's working with Antoine Moreau. Do you suspect him as well?"

"Antoine wants a great story, with plenty of dramatic twists and turns. Sierra wants a starring role in his film and will do anything to make that happen. It's like a match made in PR heaven."

Isabel, the most worried of the three, said, "We assumed at first that Sierra was talking about Arabella, but she's not the only famous woman involved in this case. What if she's trying to pin the murders on you?"

Surprised by her question, I dropped a pickle into my coffee.

Audrey speared my coffee-soaked pickle with a fork. "Leah didn't inherit the Vanderhof fortune. Arabella did."

I couldn't lie to them, not even by omission. "It's true that Arabella will inherit a lot of money, but I'll also benefit. Leland left me a pair of earrings and, um, well, an apartment in the Vanderhof Building."

His bequest didn't feel real to me until I told the Weird Sisters about it. They didn't ask how much the Park Ave. apartment was worth. They didn't have to.

My talkative friends fell silent. Abigail recovered first and, with commendable delicacy, said, "This does change things. Does Sierra know about the inheritance?"

"I'm not sure. If she knows, then so does Antoine." I squirmed, thinking about Antoine's winking reference to my relationship with Leland. Not telling the filmmaker about the bequest made me look underhanded, like I had something to hide.

Isabel, the most impetuous of the three, said, "Why on earth didn't you tell us? Is there anything else you're holding back?"

I came clean and told them of Arabella's offer to pay me for investigating Leland's death. The Weird Sisters pondered this, each in her own way. Abigail rearranged everything on the table in precise lines and rows. Isabel crumbled bits of corn muffin. Audrey took out her phone and played a game of bullet chess.

Audrey emerged from her cogitations first. "You know Arabella, and we don't. If we assume she hasn't come to harm, and that the decision to flee the scene of Jonathan's murder was hers alone, that is a strong indication of guilt."

Her reasoning was good. But it was Abigail's glancing reference to my mother's books that caught my attention. I looked away from my friends and through the plate-glass window next to us, trying to figure out why. As a sudden breeze whipped bits of paper into the air, I remembered hearing the hiss of steam and the splash of water when I spoke to Barbara.

So many mysteries remained, but one tiny piece of the puzzle clicked into place. Barbara hadn't gone to a writers' retreat in the Adirondacks. You'd have to chloroform my mother before she'd agree to a cabin in the woods and marshmallows over a fire. Her natural habitat was a luxury spa with microgreens and massage on the menu.

On our last call, unlike the one before that, I'd heard sirens and honking horns, a good indication she was back in the city.

I tapped out one more text and sent it to her. **Put Arabella on the phone.**

Chapter Forty-Three

*A dancer should be able to raise an arm and make someone cry, in the way
Isadora Duncan did. It is a necessity for any art to move you.*
—Pauline Koner

I placed my phone in the center of the table and waited for Barbara to confirm that she was with Arabella. Isabel broke the hypnotic suspense that gripped me. "Leah, you're going to miss your train. What time do you have to leave?"

"Ten minutes ago, but it's an open ticket. I can take a later train or one in the morning." I looked up to find the Weird Sisters staring at me instead of my phone.

Abigail raised a scrap of muffin to her mouth before rethinking the move and returning it to her plate. "We didn't mean to upset you. We were trying to help."

"You helped more than you know. Your comment about Barbara's books jogged my memory and reminded me of a possible connection between her and Arabella. I'm positive they're together, and I'm not going anywhere until I hear back from one, the other, or both."

She pressed her fingers and palms together. "You should tell Jonah! What if Barbara is in danger? Arabella is, I mean, she could be…" Her voice trailed off, but the meaning was clear.

"I checked Barbara's apartment, and there was no sign of a struggle or that she left under duress. The doorman said she took two large suitcases, and I don't know of many kidnappers or killers who would wait around while

Barbara packed enough clothes for a luxury cruise. I'll call Jonah after I get confirmation that Arabella is with Barbara."

Isabel, a retired psychologist, said, "There's nothing your mother loves more than pretending she's a character in one of her books. It's a charming trait, but it makes her more vulnerable than someone who hasn't spent her whole life writing crime fiction."

Her analysis of Barbara's character strengthened my belief that my mother was a collaborator and not a victim of Arabella's machinations. "After Jonathan Franklin was murdered, Barbara said she was going to track down Arabella. I didn't take her seriously. That was on me, although it's still hard to believe that she succeeded where the rest of us failed."

Audrey paused her game of online chess. "If your mother succeeded, it's because Arabella answered Barbara's call and not yours, which didn't require a whole lot of skill. But I'll believe it when I see it. It strains credulity to think two middle-aged women would go all Bonnie and Clyde after knowing each other for such a short time."

When I told my friends about the display of my mother's books in the Vanderhof apartment, and that Arabella was a fan of Barbara's writing, Isabel's response reminded me of Jonah's. "Those imaginary connections between people can be very powerful. We see a public image and think we know the person."

Abigail's eyes, magnified behind thick glasses, were creased with worry. "Do you have any evidence that Barbara and Arabella are together?"

"I've got no direct proof. But when I talked to Barbara a few days ago, the background noises of splashing water and hissing steam reminded me of when we were at a spa. It also reminded me that, according to Derrick, Arabella hides out at a retreat in upstate New York when she needs a break. It makes sense that these two spa-loving women who dropped off the map might have done so together. It also explains why, when Jonah's partner called the spa, they had no record of Arabella making a reservation or checking in. But I bet they had one for Barbara."

Isabel was encouraging. "That's good. Is there any other link between them, other than Arabella's fondness for Barbara's books and hot stone massages?"

Though I didn't know it at the time, Gerald had given me another clue. "According to the doorman at Barbara's building, she turned left when she exited, toward the alleyway. If she wanted to hide the fact that Arabella was with her, an easy way to do it would be to have Arabella use the side door. Also, there were signs that someone spent the night in the guest room. Whoever did so left an unmade bed. Maybe that person was used to having servants clean up after her. Someone like Arabella."

Audrey approved. "That's very Sherlockian, Leah. I bet there's more where that came from."

There was, but it hung tantalizingly out of reach. It wasn't a bed that teased my memory. But I had the feeling it was a piece of furniture. Something…in Arabella's apartment? Office?

I lost the train of thought when Barbara texted. **Clever girl. Meet us at apt in 1 hr.**

The Weird Sisters indicated a polite desire to come with me. I didn't hesitate and replied, **Weird Sisters coming.**

Isabel giggled. "I love that name. Even though the witches in Macbeth weren't very nice, they were powerful."

Audrey twirled an imaginary mustache. "Yeah, like a lot of older women, they got a bad rap. All the same, it's time to make some trouble."

* * *

Abigail hung back when we arrived at Barbara's apartment building. "Leah, we don't have to tag along. Your mother might not want us there, and Ms. Vanderhof may feel awkward talking about personal stuff in front of three strangers."

I took her hand and pulled her inside. "If Arabella wants you to leave, she won't be shy about telling you. As for Barbara, when did she ever turn away an audience?"

My friends needn't have worried about my mother's reaction to their presence. Barbara enveloped us in a Joy-perfumed group hug. Behind her was my father, who met the Weird Sisters with equal kindness, though he embraced only me.

I poked him and said, *"Et tu, Brute?"*

He sat on the sofa and patted the space next to him. "I'm almost as late as you are to this party. Your mother took long enough, looping the rest of us in. Now that we're all on the same page, let's pool our resources and our knowledge. You know what Socrates says about—"

Barbara interrupted what promised to be a dense dive into the Socratic Method. "Jeremy, let's save the philosophizing until after we catch the killer."

Arabella, who was sitting in the most comfortable chair in the room, didn't greet or hug anyone. With a sour expression, she ignored my elderly friends and addressed me. "Well? What have you learned? I hope you and your boyfriend have made some progress in identifying my husband's killer."

Without answering her questions, which were transparently designed to put me on the defensive, I concentrated on the subjects that were important to me. "You thought you could buy my loyalty, if not with money then with influence. And you weren't completely wrong."

Arabella raised her shoulders and dropped them with an exasperated jerk. "Then what's the problem? Where is this even going?"

"You'll find out if you quit talking and listen."

With visible effort, she wallowed without speaking.

I took advantage of her silence to deliver a speech I didn't know I had in me. "Arabella, I know what it feels like to be tried and executed on social media, and I was sympathetic to what you were going through. I won't deny there was a big helping of self-interest mixed in, but I wouldn't have agreed to assist you if I didn't believe you were innocent. But you were only a part of it. I felt a bigger sense of obligation to Leland. He deserves to have the truth come out. I could never be loyal to you at his expense. It's why I wouldn't take your money."

Her lips, which had compressed into a tight circle, relaxed. "If you've changed your mind, I've got no problem paying you. But what have I gotten so far?" She held her index finger and thumb in a circle. "Nothing. Tell me something I can use, like evidence to convict the killer, or the status of the NYPD investigation, and we have a deal." She relaxed into the cushions behind her. "If you succeed, the Poppy Vanderhof Prize is as good as yours."

Abigail walked across the room and stood between Arabella and me, blocking our view of each other. The Weird Sister spoke with grave emphasis. "Leah, that's a *very* generous offer. You should *very* carefully think it over."

Isabel rose from her seat at the edge of the sofa to stand next to Abigail. Audrey joined her to form a triangle of solidarity and said, "It's late. You don't have to decide tonight." They waited a beat before retreating to the doorway.

I explained what they were too diplomatic to say directly. "Arabella, my friends think you're guilty, and they're worried that if I refuse to cooperate, I could be your next target."

Chapter Forty-Four

*So many dancers rely on some sort of magic happening on the stage. They never,
for various reasons, work full out in rehearsal. That's very uncreative.
They don't discover the kinds of things that add up to a remarkable performance.*
—Benjamin Harkarvy

Arabella glared at the Weird Sisters. "Leah, I hope you're not as stupid as your three friends. I didn't kill anyone, and I would never hurt you."

Her insult confirmed a decision I'd already made. "My friends don't know you, and they're right to be suspicious. You're banking on my relationship with Detective Sobol to help you out, but neither of us is for sale."

My father, who maintained his usual air of intellectual dispassion, said, "The endeavor to understand is the first and only basis of virtue."

My mother rapped the back of his hand with a rolled-up magazine. "Jeremy, that's not helpful."

"It's Spinoza. He's always helpful."

I didn't have my father's ability to analyze problems through the lens of great thinkers, but I knew a good argument when I heard one. "Dad is right. We need more facts and less emotion. Arabella can begin by telling us why she summoned me to the scene of Jonathan Franklin's murder and then explain why she roped my mother into helping her disappear."

Barbara bristled. "Arabella didn't rope me in. I called her."

I reiterated an amended version of my question. Arabella, acting like she was doing all of us a big favor, said, "Your mother is right, but it's a long story."

I wrested the half-empty wine bottle from her. "Take as much time as you need. I don't know if you're guilty of a double homicide, but there's no doubt you showed a reckless disregard for my safety by summoning me to the scene of Jonathan's murder and then running away. It's why I'll have nothing more to do with you."

Two patches of red penetrated Arabella's pale makeup. "I called you *before* I found Jonathan's body."

"Why didn't you call me afterwards? What if the killer went after me?" The more I thought about it, the angrier I got.

Arabella sounded less certain. "I wasn't, I didn't…how did you know the killer was still there?"

"I didn't. That's my point. And the only way you could know I wasn't in danger is if you killed Jonathan." I thought I had her, but there's never any point to writing a script when you can't control what anyone else says.

My accusation didn't elicit any sign of fear or guilt. I remembered that Arabella had been a professional actress, but if she were that good, she'd have had her name in lights.

She recovered her equanimity and said, "You're sadly mistaken if you think I deliberately put you in harm's way. How was I to know you'd go poking around a crime scene?"

Maybe I was wrong about her. Maybe Arabella wasn't a monster. She had more than her fair share of arrogance and selfishness, but her actions this evening, and on the night Jonathan died, weren't definitively those of a killer. They hinted instead that she suspected, and perhaps feared, who the killer was.

Terrence Benson thought Arabella was guilty. I wondered if Arabella thought the same about him, and if either was correct. If they had been lovers, it must have been one weird relationship.

My mother slid her feet out of four-inch heels and made herself comfortable. "Leah, you're complicating a very simple situation. After you told me of Jonathan's murder, I offered to come to the arts center. You refused, and so I contacted Arabella and offered my services. I was trying to help. She was in desperate straits."

Arabella took over the narrative, not an easy task when Barbara was the one doing the talking. "That is correct, and when you all hear what happened, you'll understand. On the night Jonathan died, but before I knew he was dead, I called Leah to discuss the investigation. I also wanted to talk about the apartment my husband left her and to offer to buy it. That offer still stands. I'll pay the fair market value. She doesn't have to worry about that."

New Yorkers. Was there ever a time when the price of real estate didn't suck the air out of the room? Without addressing her preemptive offer on the apartment Leland bequeathed me, I told her to get back to explaining her actions.

Arabella continued to talk about me in the third person. "Before Leah got to my house—and, by the way, she was late—the carbon monoxide detector went off. I switched off the alarm, opened the garage door, and found Jonathan. I was terrified and got out of there as fast as I could. No way I was going to stay in that house and wait for the cops to show up. The last time I called, it took a half hour for them to arrive."

Jeremy's scholarly, precise manner vanished. "Let me guess what happened next. After putting Leah's life in danger, you did the same to Barbara."

Arabella didn't meet his eye. "You can't blame me. I was in shock. I got in my car and headed back to the city, to my lawyer's house. It was late, but for what I pay him, I deserved special treatment. When I got there, I saw Barbara's email. Her message was like the answer to a prayer. You can't imagine how desperate and scared I was. So desperate, in fact, I came here. We knew Leah was safe, since she didn't contact Barbara until she was back at the arts center and the police had arrived."

She retook possession of the wine bottle and filled her glass. "We decided we needed to lay low for a while and left for a place with no distractions. There's no crime in that."

The more I knew this woman, the less I liked her. "Arabella, who killed Jonathan?"

For the first time, she seemed regretful. "I honestly don't know. I called Terrence, hoping he'd help me, but he said it would be better if we didn't see each other. He was worried about appearances. And once I left the house in Connecticut, I felt like I couldn't come back until the killer was arrested."

Barbara held up a copy of *The Tragedy of Errors*, her crime fiction riff on Shakespeare's *Comedy of Errors*. "In this book, Professor Romanova solves the mystery after following a trail of red herrings that are a lot like the ones that trapped Arabella. The first victim is drugged and pushed off a building. There are dozens of suspects and plenty of motives. Arabella and I cooked up a plan like the one in my book, and we're ready to trap the killer."

Audrey shook her head, which had the predictable effect of freeing a shower of bobby pins. "If you think you know who the killer is, call the police. Trying to recreate what happened on the page can be dangerous. Real life is unpredictable."

Isabel picked up a bobby pin that had landed on her foot. "Fictional situations can have emotional and psychological truth, but Audrey is right. That seems like a really risky proposition."

I'd read *The Tragedy of Errors* and understood why my mother and Arabella went undercover. The innocent suspect in the case gets arrested by the police and sits in jail for another one hundred pages, until Professor Romanova finds the missing clue and saves the day.

I focused on my mother. "We can talk about fictional plots after you tell us what you've learned."

She put the book on a table and folded her hands in her lap. "It was clear that someone was trying to pin the murders on Arabella. The only people who could do that were those who were close to her and Leland. If we eliminate friends and associates like Terrence Benson and Marty and Neil Sherrington, who have no motive, we're left with two people: her assistant, Derrick Easton, and her housekeeper, Greta Bromley."

Arabella said nothing about her failed marriage to Neil or her longstanding friendship with Marty. Nor did she discuss her relationship with Terrence. "Leland bequeathed fifty thousand dollars to Derrick and Greta. It doesn't sound like a lot of money, but I presume people have killed for less."

Audrey spoke with bitter precision. "To most people, fifty thousand dollars is quite a lot of money."

Barbara tapped her book. "Arabella left out the most important part. My mysteries are in her library at her home and office. Derrick and Greta must have read *The Tragedy of Errors* and followed the plot."

This struck me as the thinnest, least likely bit of evidence thus far. I read the back cover to refresh my memory and said, "There's nothing unique about committing one murder for financial gain and another to get rid of a potential witness."

Arabella reacted as if I'd agreed with her and Barbara, which wasn't my intent. "That's exactly right, which is why we're going to follow Professor Romanova's plan. Our next move is to entrap them. That's where you come in, Leah. Call Detective Sobol and tell him to stake out my place. I want him there when I confront Derrick and Greta with their crimes."

Chapter Forty-Five

*A toe shoe is as eccentric as the ballerina who wears it: their marriage is a
commitment.*
—Toni Bentley

Arabella and Barbara clinked glasses, toasting each other's brilliance. The rest of us refrained from celebratory gestures.

I put down my wine. With my mother and Arabella in fantasy land, I had to stay sharp. "Derrick and Greta are already persons of interest. Let the cops do their job. Arabella, you'll have to give a statement and explain why you left town. Tell your lawyer to meet you at the precinct in the morning."

Arabella's brow remained smooth and untroubled. "When I tell the detectives of my plan to entrap Derrick and Greta, I'm sure the police will back me up. I'll be a hero."

Jeremy, who rarely lost his temper, looked as if he wanted to go ten rounds against her. "Your best course of action is to follow my daughter's advice and give up this foolish plan."

He didn't understand her resistance to logic, but I did. Arabella was wrapped in privilege, from the tips of her bespoke shoes to the curve of her surgically sculpted jaw. Her wealth and status freed her from the constraints ordinary people respected, which meant appeals to common sense were doomed to failure.

I offered a compromise. "If you must go, get your private investigator to provide protection."

She answered with a perplexed frown, followed by an *ah-hah* sigh of comprehension. "I must have forgotten to tell you that I fired him. He was too nosy."

Audrey retracted her head, bringing her chin nearly to her neck. She looked like a turtle withdrawing into its shell. "He was a private investigator. That's what they do. How could you expect him to help if you weren't willing to give him the information he needed?"

Barbara intervened with a tactful cough. "Audrey, dear, that's all water under the bridge, if you'll forgive the cliché. Let's focus on the here and now."

This declaration was a further test of my patience. I told my mother to hold off until we could come up with an alternate plan, rose to my feet, and said goodbye. The Weird Sisters did the same.

Barbara walked us to the door. "You're not angry, are you? I wanted to protect you without involving you. Arabella had no business asking you to investigate. She's the head of the Vanderhof Foundation, and she put you in an untenable position."

I pecked her cheek and said, "We can discuss later your unselfish motives for ignoring my wishes, going behind my back, and lying about where you were and what you were doing. In the meantime, swear to me you won't go with Arabella when she confronts Derrick and Greta. If you're right, and they've killed twice, they won't hesitate to do so again. Professor Romanova won't save you. And, as we now know, neither will Arabella's PI."

Barbara glanced at the waiting Weird Sisters. "I thought this adventure would make a great true crime story. Arabella promised me exclusive access, which could remake my career. Sales of my last book were so low, my agent and publisher are going to drop me if I don't come up with something new."

A chill ran through me. My mother's worries about her career were much like mine, and I knew firsthand how those fears could lead to reckless behavior. "It's not too late to say no. Send Arabella packing and let the cops take over."

To my great surprise, Barbara agreed. Later, when I remembered how glib she was when she promised to stay away from the investigation in the first place, I became uneasy. My mother's flexible relationship with the truth, which always amused me, was a lot less charming when I was on the receiving end of her deceptive ways.

* * *

I talked the Weird Sisters into sharing my cab. "Attending Sierra's dance class cost you more than this ride will cost me. If you do the math, I still owe you." They were tired enough not to argue.

The trip home was quiet. Audrey's building was the last stop before home. As the driver pulled into an open spot, she said, "Derrick and Greta may fit Isabel's profile, but so does Arabella. She married into wealth and prestige but may have chafed at playing a secondary role to Leland and Jonathan."

I was thinking the same thing. "If Arabella is executing a truly epic con, then Derrick and Greta are the ones in danger. She could have set us up to later claim she acted against them in self-defense. But if she isn't the killer, then confronting them could have serious consequences, even if Derrick and Greta aren't guilty. They're loving their new power and positions and won't be happy to go back to being treated like low-level servants. I keep thinking about what you said a few days ago, about queens and pawns."

Audrey opened the car door but didn't get out. "Abigail, Izzy, and I will follow up with Sierra and get back to you. Leave that part of the investigation to us. I'll check the schedule at Studio Dance and we'll sign up for another of her classes."

"Sierra is due back at the Vee Arts Center tomorrow. I'll talk to her and let you know how it goes."

Audrey's eyes grew wide. "No. Keep away from her, Leah. Her face, when she talked about you, made me nervous."

Gabi had said the same thing. I assumed professional jealousy inspired Sierra's hatred, but maybe it was something else. There was one way to find out. I'd ask her. Not on a dark country road, of course. Someplace safe.

* * *

Jonah was waiting for me when I unlocked the door. After giving him a rundown of the evening's events, I told him about Arabella's plan and Barbara's promise to steer clear of further involvement.

I expected outrage at Arabella's juvenile tricks or frustration that she'd forced the NYPD to waste time looking for her, but Jonah was amused. He hadn't shared my fears about her safety, and Arabella proved him right.

He tapped out a text message. "Wait until Carina hears this. She was so sure Arabella did a runner."

My patience was further tested when he got a phone call that he took in the kitchen. After a brief conversation, his phone rang again. And then, a third time. When he joined me, I said, "You're a popular guy. Who was it? Carina or your mother?"

He sat on the bed. "The first call was from Carina and the second from Arabella. She kindly informed me that she and Barbara solved the case and asked me to station one officer at her townhouse and another at her apartment so we could catch Derrick and Greta in the act of trying to murder her."

"And what did you tell her?" His demeanor was too nonchalant for my liking.

Jonah said, "I instructed her to meet me at the precinct in the morning and that I'd charge her with obstruction if she failed to show up or got in the way of our investigation."

"Did she agree?"

"She did, although I don't think it matters much. I've got my eye on someone else."

Jonah and I had talked often about the broad strokes of the case but not about the granular details of his investigation. "Who is it? And why haven't you confided in me?"

"Leah, I'm not holding out on you. Two hundred people were at the Vanderhof penthouse. Tracking them down and cross-checking their stories takes time, especially when not everyone is telling the truth. Arabella was right to suspect Derrick and Greta, which is why I want you to stay in New York. Until we make an arrest, you're safer here."

I set my alarm. "You're that sure Derrick and Greta killed Leland and Jonathan?"

"I didn't say that. They're guilty, alright, but not necessarily of murder. Both are due at the precinct tomorrow morning at the same time as Arabella. I'm hoping to get the last piece of evidence from them. In the meantime, the safest place for you is my apartment. I can't guarantee your safety if you go to the Arts Center."

"And I can't resuscitate my career if I stay. Opening night for *Don Quixote* is tomorrow."

Chapter Forty-Six

The creative urge is the demon.
—Agnes DeMille

I boarded the 6:16 am train at Grand Central Terminal with a group of bleary-eyed commuters. We arrived at our destination two hours later, where I found the indefatigable Terry waiting in her taxi.

She was full of news about Jonathan Franklin's death, mostly as it related to an uptick in business. "I've been on the run day and night, ever since news about the murder hit the papers. And that's a good thing. We took a big hit at the beginning of the season, what with the bad weather and all." When we stopped at an intersection, she turned to me with wide eyes and a stricken expression. "Me and my big mouth. I'm sorry, Leah. I forgot that you knew the guy."

"No need to apologize, Terry. Mr. Franklin and I had a professional relationship, but we weren't close."

I refrained from further discussion of my connection to Jonathan. Like the hotel owners and taxi drivers, I benefited from his death. Without his opposition, I was in a stronger position to win the Vanderhof Prize. ABC also reaped a grim bonus. The opening night performance was now sold out.

News of the increased ticket sales was bittersweet. I'd have to watch from the sidelines while Kerry Blair danced the lead role in *Don Q* to a standing-room-only crowd. Despite this disappointment, I was determined to burn up the stage as Mercedes. It was a secondary role but a flashy one.

* * *

Antoine Moreau was in the lobby of the residence hall and did a double-take when he saw me. "Leah, how delightful to find you here! I thought you were coming on a later train."

He must have checked my Vanderhof travel log. At the last minute, I filled it out with fake information, listing a later train than the one I took. From the start, I'd had the uncomfortable feeling that Antoine was manipulating me, though this trait might have been an occupational hazard for filmmakers. Maybe, after spending your days telling people where to stand and how to speak, you can't stop yourself from stage managing them in real life.

We were in a public place, and I wasn't overly stressed or nervous. Nonetheless, I found myself leaning into a fictional ballet character for support. Swapping out Leah Siderova for a more powerful persona happened only when I felt threatened, which made no sense given where I was and who I was with, but I didn't fight the impulse. The character that captured my imagination was Swanhilda, the star of the ballet *Coppélia*. She's a trickster who pretends to be a doll that comes to life. It's a plot twist that flips the script on the Pygmalion story of a man fashioning the perfect image of a woman.

I'd often been described as doll-like. A small ballerina with big eyes can't easily escape that description, however much she might want to transcend it. In front of Antoine, however, I became a coquettish version of my true self. It seemed like a good match for his surface charm.

I looked up at him from under my lashes and said, "Let's do it."

After repeated rejections of his overtures, I expected him to be surprised by this easy acceptance, but he wasn't. Powerful men assume you'll be flattered by their attention. It's opposition that amazes them.

I suggested a conference room at the residence hall for our interview, but he demurred.

Grimacing at a deer's head mounted on the wall next to us, he said, "I do not want dead animals in my movie. Let us go to the Mayflower Hotel. They have a library with beautiful bookshelves and furniture that belongs in a museum. Very elegant."

Antoine's comment set off an uncomfortable feeling that had poked me before. I'd missed something important. Something to do with furniture, but what? Not a stage set, not a film set, not a studio.

I closed my eyes. *Library, books, bookcases.* And then, I got it. The glass shelf in Arabella's penthouse apartment, the one that held my mother's books, matched the glass desk in Marty's office. But what did that mean? Two wealthy women patronized the same luxury dealer. Nothing to see there.

And yet. It was one more connection between Arabella Vanderhof and Marty Sherrington. The two women shared more than an affinity for elegant furniture. They both married Neil Sherrington. They both held prominent positions in the art world. What else did they have in common?

The answer, when it finally came to me, was maddening and amusing, obvious and obscure. My mother, or, more specifically, my mother's books, was the link. Though Barbara's Professor Romanova mysteries occupied a prominent position in Arabella's penthouse and a neglected corner of Marty's office at ABC, this felt like one coincidence too many. If my mother's far-fetched theory was correct, and the killer copied the plot in her book to commit two real-life murders, I now knew of at least one more person who could have been inspired by it. Unfortunately, like every other clue, this information did little to whittle down the list of suspects. In addition to Marty, any of the dancers at ABC could have gotten their hands on *The Tragedy of Errors.* Antoine, Sierra, Hollis, and Terrence could plausibly have done so as well.

Antoine took my elbow with a proprietary gesture and steered me toward the parking lot. "I have a car. No need to call a taxi."

I detached my arm from his. "Is it the same car you used to stake out my apartment?"

He stopped short, stared, and then laughed. "I said before that you are too clever. You have found me out. But you see, it is the only way to catch my subjects *au naturel.* No makeup, no artifice. No barriers to the real self."

For the first time, I saw the passionate filmmaker lurking beneath the façade of a nonchalant playboy. He shrugged and said, "If I openly follow you with a camera, people will look at me. This, I do not want. Hidden, I catch them looking at you. Do not—how do you say?—do not hold this against me. Though you hide behind dark glasses, you will be pleased at what you see."

My anger receded. I resented his manipulation but respected his commitment. "Antoine, I won't hold it against you if you let me see your videos."

"This is still raw. Not for others to watch." He hesitated before adding, "Except the police. I give it to them."

I already knew this. "I want to see the unedited version. How about if we limit the viewing to footage from Leland's party?"

"This I can do. I have watched it many times, but it revealed nothing to me." He guided me down a dirt path. "Interview first. Viewing after."

I had only a blurred memory of what transpired after the performance at Leland's birthday party. Tex had escorted Leland down the steps of the stage. Marty Sherrington and Arabella Vanderhof were at the bottom of the stairs. They'd walked off with him.

That moment had been captured on numerous social media posts. Only one, however, revealed Antoine in the frame, his lens directed at two indistinct figures in the background. Maybe Jonathan and Terrence? Or someone else?

I was on fire to see the filmmaker's record of what happened in real time. The clue wouldn't be obvious. If it were, Jonah would have picked up on it.

We were halfway to the parking lot when Marty Sherrington's call stopped me. I showed the screen to Antoine, who scowled as I stepped away.

The interim director of American Ballet Company said, "I'm at the Mayflower Hotel. When your train arrives, come directly here."

I wasn't in the habit of refusing my boss's demands, but didn't want to delay seeing Antoine's video. "Marty, I'm already at the residence hall but have other plans. Let's meet after rehearsal."

"This can't wait. Reschedule those plans and leave now. When you get to the hotel, take the stairs to room 307. The elevators here are horrible, and I don't want you to get stuck. Rehearsals have been delayed until noon." More kindly, she said, "This won't take long. We'll have brunch together."

She hung up without saying goodbye. I returned to Antoine and said, "I need another raincheck. Marty wants me to meet her. It sounds urgent."

He scowled. "You remain my most elusive subject. Let's meet tonight. I'll buy you a free drink at the after-party, and we can find a suitable spot for the interview." He brightened and said, "On second thought, don't change out of your costume. We'll talk backstage. It will make for a dramatic background."

"That sounds perfect. But first, maybe you can tell me something about this piece of furniture." I clicked on a photo of Arabella's bookshelf, the one I'd sent to my mother the night Leland was murdered.

Antoine enlarged the picture and showed me the initials *MLF* etched in one corner. "I knew who the artist was the moment I saw it. Melville Franklin is better known as an architect, but he designed this piece as part of a larger installation for the Museum of Modern Art. Very few are in private hands."

This was interesting, but was it relevant? When I told Antoine that Marty had a similar piece in her office, he laughed so hard he could barely speak. "The Vanderhofs and the Franklins go way back. It is how Jonathan got a seat on the Vanderhof board. Nothing new there. Who among us doesn't trade favors?"

It seemed as if I'd come to another dead end. "Telling me the Vanderhofs and Franklins go way back doesn't explain how Marty Sherrington got her hands on that desk or why you find this so funny."

He winked at me. "You were friends with Leland. Don't you know?"

His mocking smile annoyed me. "I don't, or I wouldn't have asked."

"Leland was a generous man to the ladies. That, you surely know. He gave jewelry to his favorites. When he tired of them, he gave something more substantial. A gift they couldn't refuse. Very civilized, always. Leland chose women who were most discreet. Like you. No lawsuits or tell-all books."

Although I knew my protest would simply confirm Antoine's perception of me as one of Leland's discreet women, the temptation to defend myself was too strong to resist. "I didn't accept gifts from Leland. We were friends and nothing more." I turned to go, but at the last minute remembered one more question I had for him. "Did you have dinner with Sierra on the night

CHAPTER FORTY-SIX

Jonathan was murdered?"

He stepped back and, most annoyingly, snapped a picture of me. "I did not. Why do you ask? Are you jealous?"

I was suspicious, not jealous. Sierra's alibi was in shreds. Or maybe Antoine's was.

When I told Antoine I wasn't jealous and that I had a boyfriend he said, "As you should. But why only one?" With more grace and less moisture than Neil Sherrington, he kissed my hand.

I declined his offer to drive me to the Mayflower Hotel, and by the time Terry's taxi arrived, the filmmaker had cornered Tex. My partner looked delighted at the attention, but he was too modest. Tex's star was rising, faster than he realized. Antoine, of course, was quite aware of his growing fame.

I was as happy as Tex about the chance encounter. I didn't trust Antoine, and if he was hoping to dig up dirt against me as part of his interview, he was barking up the wrong company member. Tex would provide a positive counterbalance against Sierra's hatchet job. Having endured my rival's comments that maligned my intelligence, choreography, ballet bun, and age, I shuddered to think what she said about me when I wasn't there.

* * *

The double staircase that was a focal point in the lobby of the Mayflower Hotel ended in a second-floor balcony. I avoided the elevator, as Marty instructed, and took concrete back stairs to the third floor. Compared to the five flights I faced at home, it was an easy climb. She opened the door while I was mid-knock.

Marty's room was charming, with white wicker furniture and bright blue pillows. Although it was sunny and warm, the curtains were drawn, and the door to a terrace outside the sitting area was closed.

She ordered me to sit opposite her at a table set with a coffee pot and a plate of croissants. I had a cross-body bag with a can of pepper spray inside, and I kept it on. Although I was expecting an attack on my career and not my person, I trusted no one. Directors of ballet companies, unlike my former boyfriends, preferred to sever relationships in person rather than via email or text.

Marty took her hands out of the pockets of a loose jacket, poured me a cup of coffee, and told me to fetch a folder from the bedroom. I peeked inside it before returning to the sitting room. The top page had a roster of dancers for the coming season. My name wasn't on the list. I swallowed hard and, for the second time in less than an hour, assumed a ballerina-inspired role that was better suited to the occasion than my real self.

Nothing in my repertoire matched the rage that burned inside me. I was always cast as the sweet Sleeping Beauty and never as Carabosse, the wicked fairy who puts a spell on the princess. But Carabosse was now a better fit.

I walked back to Marty but didn't sit down. I tossed her the folder and stood opposite her, my arms crossed to prevent them from trembling.

She gestured to the chair. "Please, Leah, have a seat. We have to talk."

I remained standing. "Unless your plan is to cut me from tonight's ballet, in addition to not renewing my contract, I have a rehearsal to get to."

She pushed the coffee closer to me. "It's not what you think. This roster is a work in progress. Before I make a final decision, I need a commitment from you."

A hard laugh hurt my throat. "You've been the interim director of American Ballet Company for less than a year. It's insulting for you to talk about my commitment when I've dedicated my life to this organization."

A brick-red flush climbed up her neck. "I'm not questioning your past commitment. I'm talking about going forward." Her fingers shook as she drank from her cup.

Her eagerness to have me join her for a meal while my career was in ruins further enraged me. Why would Marty want to prolong the conversation? Why not drop the guillotine and get it over with? *Unless,* the evil Carabosse whispered in my ear, *she wanted to stop me more permanently.*

The Weird Sisters' profile of the killer was of someone resentful of those with more power and influence. Someone insecure, who chafed against a second-class status. Someone like Derrick or Greta, who lacked autonomy. Not a wealthy woman who'd attained a high position.

It occurred to me, looking at Marty's rock-hard expression, that maybe the rumors about her romance with Leland were as false as the ones about me. If they weren't lovers, then perhaps the glass-paneled desk Leland gave her didn't mark the end of a personal relationship. It could have softened the close of a professional one. Marty was the interim director of American Ballet Company. Without Leland's support, she was unlikely to secure a more permanent position.

The clues I'd missed for so long revealed themselves to me, in one long procession of squandered chances. A powerful woman wouldn't have curried favor with anxious climbers like Sierra and Hollis. A powerful woman wouldn't have threatened to fire Madame Maksimova. Or me.

With a flash of horror, I realized it wasn't I who was Carabosse, but Marty Sherrington. With a certainty born of instinct, I knew if I drank the coffee in front of me, I'd fall asleep, not for one hundred years, like Sleeping Beauty, but forever.

Chapter Forty-Seven

It isn't hard to be good from time to time...
What is tough, is being good every day.
—Willie Mays

Experience had taught me that while intuition could lead the way, it was useless without proof. I didn't know if Marty's hard eyes and twitching fingers were a reaction to my jab about her short tenure or evidence of her guilt. A sliver of doubt made me hesitate. Made me linger, longer than I should have.

I dropped the evil fairy persona and again took on the mantle of Swanhilda, the clever ballerina who pretends she's a brainless doll. With a Barbie-worthy smile, I said, "Marty, tell me what I need to do to stay on the roster. You can count on me."

She moved the silver milk jug, spilling a few drops. "The first thing you can do is sit down. Drink some of this delicious coffee, and we'll talk."

I pushed my chair farther from the table before sitting and pretending to take a sip. "Now it's your turn."

"You need to decide your priorities and your loyalties. Arabella Vanderhof called me this morning. She wants you to continue to investigate Leland's murder. She also said, without mincing words, that if you were successful, as she believed you would be, you were favored to win the Vanderhof Prize." Marty's lips curled, cracking her stiff face. I was relieved to see that her loathing of Arabella outstripped her anger with me.

With the expressionless face of my doll-self, I said, "Arabella left out one important point. I refused her offer. Make me a better one."

Her hands curled into fists. "One of you is lying. For the moment, I'll assume it's Arabella, since I'm positive she killed her husband. Don't ask me how I know. I just do. I'll help you come up with evidence to prove it, which you will pass along to your detective friend. Next, you will support my bid to be named the permanent director of ABC, and you will get Madame to do the same. Do that, and both of you remain at ABC."

I pretended to think it over. "I also want a commitment to stage my ballet, regardless of whether or not it wins the Vanderhof Prize."

Marty's smile didn't reach those marble eyes. "We have a deal."

In retrospect, that would have been a good time to leave. What stopped me was my conviction that if I didn't do something right there, right then, Marty Sherrington would get away with murder. I felt the same way as when I was a kid and standing on a high diving board, afraid to back down and afraid to jump.

This time, I jumped.

"I agree to your terms. But between you and me, let's be honest. We both know Arabella didn't kill Leland. You did."

My accusation seemed to send her into a trance, which felt safer than anger. "Leland opposed my bid to be named director of ABC. And he convinced Jonathan to side with him. So I took them both out. You should thank me. Jonathan was dead set against you winning the Vanderhof Prize. It was a win for both of us."

The Weird Sisters didn't have supernatural powers, but their insights were potent. Marty was a would-be queen whose ambition fatally weakened her. "Did Leland have someone else in mind besides you?"

She gave a short laugh. "He wanted his saintly niece to take over ABC. Poppy Vanderhof's death put a quick end to that."

If I hadn't cemented Swanhilda's expression to my face, I couldn't have masked my shock. Had Marty just admitted to killing Poppy Vanderhof?

I said, as if admitting to a hard truth, "You're right about me. I do owe you. Because although I liked Leland and was willing to use him, I'm equally willing to cut a deal with you."

Marty pushed those clenched fists into the pockets of her jacket. "You're a smart woman. Do right by me and I'll do right by you. You can't dance forever, and someday you could be sitting in my chair."

I suppressed my brain's sarcastic response: *Yeah, that's tempting,* and listened to my heart, which was pounding a warning. "Absolutely. That would be something. I could, uh, I could learn a lot from you."

I inched backward toward the door. Marty's quick confession and agreement was too easy, and I didn't trust her not to conk me over the head with the coffee pot. I stuck one hand inside my bag and grasped the pepper spray. With the other, I felt for the doorknob. In that instant, she pulled a metallic device from her pocket. I recognized a Taser and wasted two precious seconds unlocking the safety catch on the pepper spray, thinking if she couldn't touch me, I'd be safe.

I was wrong. She blasted me from a distance. The shock that rammed through my body sent me into a shuddering heap on the floor.

My muscles, for several frozen minutes, refused to work, which gave Marty time to pull me to the center of the room, kick the pepper spray under the table, and zap me again. With a business-like air, she withdrew a syringe from a drawer in the desk and said, "This won't hurt a bit."

Though weak and sore, I wasn't completely incapacitated and used my body, the only weapon at hand, to defend myself. When she bent over me, I kicked her arm and then swung my head up against her chin. The resulting crack was most satisfying, not for me, but as payback for my murdered friend.

This is for you, Leland.

She recoiled, tears streaming from her eyes. Despite painful tremors, my legs were stronger than hers, and I beat her to the syringe. Years of practicing *grand battements* will do that for you, not to mention mastering those thirty-two *fouetté* turns for *Swan Lake*.

Marty's mouth struggled to form words, and a thin line of drool dripped down her chin. "You're insane. You broke my jaw."

Though it seemed beside the point, I said, "I'm not the crazy one. You killed three people, and you tried to kill me."

She gasped for breath. "It's your own fault. Why couldn't you leave well enough alone? I would have *made* you." She threw herself at me in an effort to get the syringe. I kicked her hand hard enough to bruise, if not break, a few of the more fragile bones. This bought me enough time to retrieve the pepper spray from under the table and thoroughly dose her.

I took no pleasure in her pain. Over her howls, I dialed nine-one-one right before Jonah, his partner, and police chief Perryman crashed through the door.

Chapter Forty-Eight

I can die now. I've lived twice.
—Edith Piaf

A series of embarrassing questions dogged me for many days after the police arrested Marty Sherrington for the murders of Leland Vanderhof and Jonathan Llewellyn Franklin III. I got my first crack at answering those awkward queries during an interview with Police Chief Perryman. Jonah and Carina Russo sat in on the meeting, which took place while I was still feeling weak and bruised from tangling with the former director of ABC.

Perryman's first question was the emotional equivalent of Marty's Taser. "Why did you confront the person you suspected was a killer? Why didn't you report your suspicions to the police?"

"Until we started talking, I didn't know for sure that Marty was guilty. As for why I agreed to meet her, that's easy. She was my boss. What would you do if your boss summoned you to a meeting? Turn her down?"

In a dry tone edged in sarcasm, he said, "If I thought she was going to kill me, then yes. But since you chose differently, let's take it from there."

Jonah intervened. "Ms. Siderova has access to a closed world that most people, let alone cops, know nothing about. Ballet has its own set of rules that don't translate well to outsiders. I suggest we let her tell her story her way."

I needed my best doll-like impassivity to resume the narrative without throwing my arms around him. "I didn't have much to go on, other than what we all knew. Like a ton of other people, Marty was at Leland Vanderhof's birthday party on the night he fell to his death. Like almost everyone in American Ballet Company, she was in Connecticut when Jonathan died. Unlike the rest, she also was at the scene of the crime when Poppy Vanderhof died."

Perryman stiffened. "Poppy Vanderhof's death was an accidental drowning. She loaded up on booze and drugs and, while the rest of the household was sleeping, fell into the pool. There were no defensive marks, no signs of a struggle, and no one who benefited from her death."

My goal wasn't to antagonize him, and I kept my tone as dry as his. "Leland had tapped his niece as the next director of American Ballet Company. Marty desperately wanted the job, but Poppy Vanderhof was much better qualified. Marty didn't stand a chance against her, so she eliminated the competition."

"Are you suggesting Ms. Sherrington killed three people to get a job directing a dance troupe?"

Clearly, the police chief wasn't a fan of ballet. "Attaining that position was the height of Marty's ambitions. She'd finally prove she belonged in the Vanderhof circle, which values achievement as much as money. Maybe more. The problem for Marty was that the Vanderhofs stood in her way. She was determined to overcome them and take over. And she very nearly succeeded."

He scratched his head. "What set her against you? What did you do to threaten her?"

This was another of those uncomfortable questions that would shadow me for many weeks. Instead of telling him how I'd accused Marty, I offered a less self-incriminating reason. "Arabella Vanderhof told Marty I was investigating Leland's death. Maybe Marty thought I was getting too close for comfort."

Perryman's tone was patronizing. "Why would Ms. Vanderhof ask a ballerina to investigate her husband's murder? She could have had her pick of PIs."

Carina delivered unexpected support. "Don't underestimate Ms. Siderova. She's had some experience in investigating crime. Hear her out."

I turned my head to give Jonah's partner an appreciative smile. I suspected Perryman's interruptions were infuriating her as much as they were me.

I recounted my first conversation with Arabella in an attempt to get Perryman to understand the admittedly weak logic behind my decisions. "There was a lot of circumstantial evidence, involving both love and money, that made Arabella a prime suspect. She was having an affair with Terrence Benson, and Leland's death meant a huge chunk of the Vanderhof fortune would be hers. On top of all that, there were rumors her husband was in the market for wife number four."

Perryman looked at me with a triumphant, *gotcha* smile. "Multiple sources have told us you were the person Mr. Vanderhof wanted to marry."

I should have been prepared for his accusation. Sierra had flogged that story every chance she got. Overcome with emotion, the smooth, doll-like exterior I'd depended on to that point disintegrated. I searched for a more authoritative role model, but with three pairs of eyes on me couldn't think of one. The unvarnished Leah Siderova would have to suffice.

"The rumors weren't true, and Arabella knew that. Although I was willing to help at first, after she returned from her disappearing act, I quit. I can't work with someone who doesn't trust me, and because she didn't trust me, I stopped trusting her."

Perryman barreled past most of what I said to repeat the question I didn't want to answer. "What did you do to tip off Marty Sherrington? How did she know you were onto her?"

"She didn't know. I didn't know myself until I got here this morning. You have to understand that Marty was as insecure as she was ambitious. American Ballet Company has gone through multiple directors in the last few years, and the board made her appointment temporary. As Leland's protégée, she saw me as a threat."

Jonah let me finish before filling in a central missing piece. "I interviewed Arabella earlier today. She told Marty you'd solved the case, not knowing that she was talking to the actual killer. That's why Marty summoned you and tried to murder you. Marty thought you'd uncovered evidence that proved her guilt."

Arabella's treachery hit me hard. "She swore me to secrecy. The last thing I thought she'd do is tip off the killer."

Jonah's eyebrows met in an angry, unbroken line. "She didn't know Marty was the killer, but that doesn't excuse her reckless behavior. In retrospect, I think the biggest clue we missed was Marty's plan to fire Madame Maksimova. Getting rid of Madame deflected attention away from her primary goal, which was getting rid of you and stopping your investigation."

Jonah was right. I, of all people, should have been suspicious of Marty's motives. I was so insecure about my future, it didn't occur to me to question other people's doubts.

Carina said, "I can't wrap my brain around the fact that a rich lady would kill to get a job. It's not like she'd go hungry."

I'd shared her prejudice. "Same here, Carina. But for Marty, it was about status and not money."

Perryman was uninterested in that line of reasoning. He said to the detectives, "I doubt we'll get enough to charge her in Poppy Vanderhof's death, but the DA will have no trouble nailing her for the other two homicides."

Carina looked as if she'd bitten into a lemon. "It won't be easy. Ten minutes after we took her into custody, Ms. Sherrington lawyered up with the same attorney who got a mistrial for two guilty-as-hell bankers charged with sexual assault."

Jonah was more sanguine. "When the jury hears Leah's testimony, it'll be game over."

Chapter Forty-Nine

Ballet never gets old. We might, but it doesn't.
—Rosemary Sabovitch Blech

Marty Sherrington's arrest didn't delay or prevent the evening performance of *Don Quixote*. I recovered sufficiently to watch the ballet from the wings, though it hurt to miss out. The best part of the night was seeing Olivia steal the show as Mercedes. Her triumph made me so happy I almost didn't mind seeing Kerry in the starring role.

The weeks that followed our stint at the Vee Arts Center passed in a fast-moving blur of activity. American Ballet Company was temporarily without a director, but that was no great loss, insofar as the dancers were concerned. Madame M, though she hated the business side of running a company, filled in while the board searched for Marty's replacement. When ABC released the roster for the fall season, I was on it. So was Olivia, who finally got the promotion she'd earned.

* * *

The biggest surprise came at the opening night showcase for the Poppy Vanderhof Prize. Though I pleaded with Gabi to perform, she refused. "You don't need me, Sid. You got this. It's yours."

I was the first to arrive at the theater, although my ballet was last on the program. Sierra and Hollis got thunderous applause at their curtain calls. They deserved it. Both were so happy, they accepted my congratulations.

Hollis hugged me, which I did not see coming.

When the curtain rose for my ballet, I was more nervous than when I auditioned for ABC. More nervous than for my debut in *Swan Lake*. Stage fright gripped me with such force, I could scarcely breathe.

The moment I stepped onstage, the dance took over, as it always did. But this time, it was my ballet, my steps, my vision. For me, that mystical connection between the performers and the audience had never been more intense. At the end, when I skimmed across the stage and exited into the wings, there was a silence that grew deafening. Unsure of the reception we'd get, I walked back onstage with my fellow dancers, regretting that my program notes were so short. Should I have explained, as Sierra and Hollis did, more about what I was trying to accomplish? Why was the audience so quiet?

And then, the clapping started. And it didn't stop. The curtain came down. The lights came on. And still, it continued.

Critics called it a historic performance. I don't know about that. Ballet is ephemeral. You have to be there. But thanks to Antoine Moreau, it would live on film, long after our collective memories faded.

Quite a lot of controversy followed the Vanderhof board's decision to split the prize between me and Hollis. I was as stunned as Sierra when she was excluded.

At a midnight snack at the Lincoln Center Diner with Gabi, Tex, and Olivia, I got the inside scoop after swearing to take the secret to my grave.

Tex said, "Gabi got the ball rolling. She told Hollis, not knowing if it was true, that she had proof Sierra vandalized Leah's prop for *Don Q.* Turns out, Hollis knew all about it. He freaked."

Gabi squeezed my hand. "I felt so bad about quitting your ballet and punking out on the investigation, but then I realized I could help you more as a true outsider. I had nothing to lose by being wrong."

Olivia kissed Tex, which seemed to herald a new chapter in their relationship. She said, "Tex followed up and told Hollis if he didn't report Sierra, and the judges found out he knew about it, that he'd get disqualified."

Tex doubled over in laughter. "I also told him that without Sierra, he had a better chance of winning. I may have also mentioned that if he didn't do the right thing, that I'd report both of them."

* * *

Marty Sherrington's lawyer won her multiple delays in the court date, despite a mounting pile of evidence against her. The police found an empty bottle of tramadol in her hotel room and a high dose of the drug in the coffee she tried to foist on me. It was the same narcotic found in Leland's blood, as well as his niece's, and the DA reopened her case in Poppy Vanderhof's death. The defense suffered another blow when Derrick and Greta, who'd confirmed Marty's alibi on the night Leland died, "realized they made a mistake" and recanted.

Jonah's work schedule didn't ease up, but I persuaded him to take a midday break to meet me at a deli near the precinct. I wasn't thrilled to see Carina Russo walk in with him, but he made up for it by sliding into my side of the booth and holding me close.

After the detectives ordered the lunch special of corned beef on rye, Jonah said, "Arabella was right to suspect her assistant and housekeeper, although Derrick and Greta were mostly guilty of being stupid. Marty really played them for fools. Both were inside the Vanderhof apartment when Leland died and were nervous about the fact that a few days earlier, Leland had added them as beneficiaries to his will.

"It wasn't a good look. Marty told them she would cover for them if anyone questioned their innocence. If Derrick or Greta suspected she was using them to cover for her, instead of the other way around, they kept quiet about it."

I remembered how Greta emphasized knowing about her inheritance "for ages" and wished I'd picked up on that clue and so many others. After filching a slice of corned beef from Jonah's sandwich, I said, "Derrick and Greta got a major upgrade in the Vanderhof organization after the murders. That increased salary and prestige was probably another hold Marty had over them. It's human nature to want to believe in the people who help you out."

Carina, whose appetite belied her slenderness, poured an ocean of ketchup on her French fries. "Once Derrick and Greta confirmed Marty's alibi, they became complicit and maybe would have stayed silent if Jonah hadn't put the screws on." She picked up her sandwich and told Jonah to talk while she ate.

He seemed happy to oblige. "When I explained the charges that were on the table for them, they got a lot more cooperative, but to be honest, we got lucky. Derrick and Greta also got lucky. They were standing by a window in the kitchen and showed up in the background of Antoine's time-stamped video. When they realized a murder charge was off the table, but that they'd be on the hook for aiding, abetting, and perjury, they coughed to everything else. If it weren't for Antoine, I'm not sure we could have broken them or gotten the proof we needed."

I had yet to see this evidence and had to rely on Jonah's descriptions. "Will Antoine's footage be enough to exonerate them and convict Marty?"

He squirted more mustard on his sandwich. "That's the plan, though it isn't a slam dunk. After hours of frame-by-frame examinations of the video footage, the techies captured Marty giving Leland the spiked drink and pulling him inside the apartment. Two people went in, but only one came out. Derrick and Greta never left the kitchen."

I took out my notes and checked off most of the questions, but not all. "What about Neil Sherrington? He alibied Marty the night she killed Jonathan."

Jonah threw back his head and laughed. "You were more right about him than you know. Neil Sherrington, ever the ladies' man, resisted my pressure but fell hard for Carina's charm. He admitted he hadn't been with his wife on the night Jonathan died and instead had been entertaining Sierra Younger in a separate hotel room. She claimed she was with Antoine, who threw her under the bus."

Carina used air quotes to tell me that because Neil "wanted to be a gentleman," he didn't out Sierra, or, more importantly, himself or his wife.

Jonah's partner, whose detached approach had grated on me, showed a more sympathetic side. "Poor Jonathan. He literally never knew what hit him when he tangled with Marty. I have to admit, she had me fooled. I was so sure Arabella was guilty, it didn't cross my mind that there was another woman out there with her kind of privilege, who would kill to get what she wanted.

"We think that when Marty walked from the Vee Arts Center to the Vanderhof estate, she planned to kill Arabella. Jonathan must have intercepted her on the way, and she ended up going after him. Maybe she intended all along to frame Arabella for his death, but either way, Arabella was right to do a runner, even if it was for all the wrong reasons. I would have locked that—I would have locked her up."

Jonah pressed his leg against mine. "Your instincts were good. Someone was in the forest at the same time you were. And now, you're our star witness. I hope you're up for another turn in the spotlight."

* * *

My mother's novel, *The Tragedy of Errors*, figured largely in reports about the case, although Marty steadfastly denied ever reading it. The resulting sales from that book, and the subsequent release of *The Gaming of the Clue*, earned Barbara a sizable advance for three more Professor Romanova mysteries. She also got a nice bump when the @litpicker account was revealed as hers.

I was looking forward to a few vacation days before again subjecting myself to Antoine's camera crew, though I found myself under an even more searching scrutiny on the day I met Jonah's family. I was more nervous than when I was standing in the wings and waiting to leap onto the stage for the opening of my ballet, though not as scared as when Marty tased me.

I changed my clothes seven times before leaving the apartment. After blow-drying my hair, I pinned it into a bun, unpinned it, gathered it into a ponytail, and, on the way down the stairs, let it hang loose. The diamond and sapphire earrings Leland bequeathed me I left in my jewelry box.

They weren't me. Neither was the apartment at the Vanderhof Building, which, on paper, was mine. Barbara thought I was crazy not to move in, but the place held too many sad memories. More practically, I couldn't afford the maintenance fees and most definitely could use the cash from a quick sale to Arabella.

I didn't talk much on the ride to Queens. Jonah sensed my mood and said, "Stop worrying. My family is going to love you. For sure, they'll like you a lot more than your mother likes me. I think Barbara is still hoping you'll marry that doctor."

"My crazy family conspired to hide Barbara's involvement with a murder suspect, so I wouldn't worry too much about what they think."

Despite Jonah's encouraging words, I feared Leah Siderova, on her own, wouldn't make a good impression on the Sobol family. The real me was insecure, ambitious, and competitive. She didn't cook, didn't know how to drive, and hadn't gone to college.

Unfortunately, no other character seemed appropriate to the occasion. The Firebird was too exotic. Juliet too tragic. The Swan Queen too fragile. I was still undecided when Jonah's mother opened the door of a small, aluminum-sided, split-level house. I put out my hand to shake hers, but Miriam Sobol pulled me in for a hug. Her warmth melted my fears, and I decided to risk meeting her as me.

She said to Jonah, "It's about time."

And it was.

Acknowledgments

For creative inspiration, I look no further than my kids and their partners. And there are a lot of them! Luke, Jacob, Geoffrey, Gregory, Jesse, and Becky, plus Emily, Linh, Natalia, Meris, and Kris. I'm equally indebted to the newest generation: Oren, Aleksy, Henry, Alice, Ella, Ava, Viola, and Skylar. Like me, they love a good story.

If I had my choice of sisters, I couldn't do better than the one I grew up with and those I got through marriage: Karyn Boyar, and Barbara, Lisa, Jane, Gail, and Lolly Robbins. I also want to thank my talented Sisters in Crime.

To my brother Richard: I wish you were here to see the publication of this book.

Much gratitude is due to the many people who provided their expert advice. Chief among these is Brian Sher, whose generosity disproves every lawyer joke out there. Many thanks as well to editor Shawn Reilly Simmons and Deb Well.

My longtime critique partner, Corey LaBranche, made this a better book than it ever could have been without him. Any lapses are mine, not his.

Of the many ballerinas who went on to become brilliant teachers and coaches, two stand out for their dedication and talent: Rosemary Sabovitch Blech and Olivia Galgano. Your kindness and talent know no bounds. Thank you, from the bottom of my heart.

To Vladimir (The Duke) Dokoudovsky (1919-1998), His star still shines, for those of us lucky enough to have earned a place in his class.

This book is dedicated to Glenn, who still thinks—after all these years—that he's the one who got lucky.

About the Author

Lori Robbins is the Amazon bestselling author of the On Pointe and Master Class mystery series and a contributor to *The Secret Ingredient: A Mystery Writers Cookbook*. She is the recipient of three Silver Falchion Awards, the Indie Award for Best Mystery, and a silver medal in the Daphne du Maurier Award for Mystery and Suspense. Short stories include "Leading Ladies," which received Honorable Mention in the 2022 Best American Mystery and Suspense anthology.

A former dancer, Lori performed with a number of modern dance and classical ballet companies, including Ballet Hispanico and the St. Louis Ballet, but it was her commercial work, for Pavlova Perfume and Macy's, that paid the bills. After ten very lean years onstage she became an English teacher and now writes full-time. Her experiences as a dancer, teacher, and mother of six have made her an expert in the homicidal tendencies everyday life inspires.

You can find her at lorirobbins.com

AUTHOR WEBSITE:
https://www.lorirobbins.com/

SOCIAL MEDIA HANDLES :

https://www.instagram.com/lorirobbinsmysteries/
https://www.facebook.com/lorirobbinsauthor/
https://www.bookbub.com/profile/lori-robbins
https://www.goodreads.com/author/show/16007362.Lori_Robbins

Also by Lori Robbins

Murder in First Position

Murder in Second Position

Murder in Third Position

Murder in Fourth Position

Lesson Plan for Murder

Study Guide for Murder

Short Stories:
  "Leading Ladies," *Justice for All*
  "Recipe for Revenge," *New York State of Crime*
  "Mirror Image," *Thicker Than Water*
  "Killing It In the Catskills," *Mystery Most Traditional*
  "French Fried," *Mystery Most International*

www.ingramcontent.com/pod-product-compliance
Lightning Source LLC
Chambersburg PA
CBHW030131010826
48973CB00002B/510